GRINNY

GRINNY

NICHOLAS FISK

Published in Great Britain in 2013 by Hot Key Books
Northburgh House, 10 Northburgh Street, London EC1V 0AT

Grinny first published by William Heinemann Ltd in 1973
You Remember Me! first published by Viking Kestrel in 1984

A CIP catalogue record for this book is available from the British Library.

ISBN: 978-1-4714-0145-9

1

Typeset in Sabon by Palimpsest Book Production Ltd, Falkirk, Stirlingshire

Printed and bound by Nørhaven, Denmark

www.hotkeybooks.com

Hot Key Books is part of the Bonnier Publishing Group
www.bonnierpublishing.com

Foreword by Malorie Blackman

I love science fiction! The best science fiction deals with, amongst other things, possible futures, alternate realities, the uses and abuses of technology, aliens, the paranormal and futuristic science. Science fiction deals with not just the probable but the possible.

The very first sci-fi novel I remember reading as a child was *Chocky* by John Wyndham at the age of ten or eleven. After that I was hooked. I loved TV programmes like *Star Trek* and *Lost in Space* but that novel was instrumental in getting me hooked on science fiction literature.

Science fiction is one of the most imaginative and provocative of all the literary genres. The best sci-fi makes you gasp in wonder and surprise as you read. These stories may present worlds and ideas that you have maybe never even imagined before.

We, the readers, may be presented with enemies from within this world and beyond who will require all of our courage and intelligence to defeat, but they also present us with the enemies inside ourselves – intolerance, stupidity and fear.

And that's what Nicholas Fisk gives us with both *Grinny* and its sequel *You Remember Me!*

Both books feature a boy called Tim, his friend Mac and Tim's younger sister, Beth. *Grinny* starts, rather ingeniously, when Tim is fifteen – four years after the incident with Great Aunt Emma, otherwise known as Grinny. In the introduction to *Grinny*, Tim has written the story from his diary, his memory and other writings, and has shown it to Nicholas Fisk (the author), who then encouraged him to get the story published as a warning to others as to what happened in the past and what may happen again.

Grinny and its sequel *You Remember Me!* were actually written a number of years apart but in the sequel Tim is now a young reporter still in his teens working for a local newspaper.

In the novel *Grinny*, Tim's attitude to his younger sister is incredibly patronising and dismissive until he begins to realise that maybe, just maybe, his sister is right about their so-called Great Aunt. Grinny turns up on their doorstep unannounced and uninvited and convinces Tim and Beth's parents that she *is* their Great Aunt Emma with the words – *You remember me* . . . Words that take on a very sinister turn in both stories. It takes Grinny's horrific accident to confirm Beth's suspicions and the final confrontation where Tim, Mac and Beth have to outsmart Grinny is nothing less than thrilling.

You Remember Me! has Tim reporting back to his friend

Nicholas Fisk. It 'stars' the TV personality Lisa Treadgold, spokesperson for a sinister group called Rule of Law. In an early look at the cult of 'celebrity', the whole country seems to adore Lisa – everyone, that is, except Tim's sister, Beth. In *You Remember Me!* the stakes are higher and the consequences of the failure to stop Lisa even greater.

Science fiction stories like these from Nicholas Fisk present us with a thrilling, compelling view of the possible. And like all good stories, whatever the genre, they provide life lessons such as believing in yourself, even when everyone else around you is telling you otherwise.

Enjoy!

GRINNY

Timothy Carpenter's Introduction

I was only eleven when Great Aunt Emma came to stay with us. My sister Beth was seven and my friend Mac (real name Steven) Rainier was eleven too. Now I am fifteen. I was too young to have done anything about Aunt Emma when she was with us because I was never sure what it all meant and even when everything got frightening and sinister I could neither have proved anything nor gone to someone for help.

This book is based on my diary and other writings of the Aunt Emma period. My diary was a Christmas present, a big bound book in blue Morocco leather with gold-edged leaves. I remember how excited and pleased I was when I first started writing in it and thinking how handy it was that Aunt Emma had come just at the right time, to give me something exciting to write about.

And then, later on, it all turned sour and I used to be

almost frightened of the diary and writing the next page. Everything I had written seemed to add up to something horrible. The more I wrote, the more certain it seemed that the horror was true and would get worse. I did not keep a diary any more.

I showed the diary to Mr Nicholas Fisk, the writer, as a result of talking to him about my wanting to adopt journalism as my future career. Of course, I can never talk to my father and mother about Aunt Emma – they quite literally *would not hear me*. You will understand why when you have read this book.

Mr Fisk said that I should get the Aunt Emma story published if I want to make people aware of the possibilities facing them and to prepare them for the next time – if there is a next time. It is Mr Fisk's opinion that the danger is most probably over – the thing happened, the experiment failed and there would be no point in trying it again.

I wish I could feel sure he is right.

Diary

Book One

Jan. 14

Astonishing news! I had come back from Mac's house and had just been shouted at as usual by Mum (TAKE YOUR BOOTS OFF) when I heard the station taxi grinding up the drive and soon after, our bell being rung. I was still in the porch so I opened the door and there she was, all five feet one of her, with two gi-normous trunks. I did not know what to say, but she said, 'I am your Great Aunt Emma. You must be Tim,' and I mumbled something about calling Mother, but Mum had heard the bell go and came hurtling along the corridor shouting, 'If it's the Guides, it must wait till Tuesday and if it's Mac, tell him to TAKE HIS BOOTS OFF.' When she goes to heaven, she will say this to all the archangels.

I said, 'It's Great Aunt Emma, Mum, were you expecting –?' but she simply said, 'Most amusing, you *witty* lad!'

in her Wednesday matinée voice and went belting past on her way to the kitchen. Then she caught a glimpse of Aunt Emma and stopped in her tracks and came to the doorway. '*Who?*' she said. 'Great Aunt who?' I could see she was completely foxed and had never heard of GAE, as I will henceforth refer to Great Aunt Emma, as she is bound to figure largely in these pages from now on.

GAE said, 'You remember me, Millie!' but Mum could only see a vague shape and replied, 'Oh dear, I am afraid I don't quite remember –' Then I switched on the porch light and Mum could see GAE properly. GAE leaned forward and said again, 'You remember me, Millie!' and this time the penny dropped and Mum cried out, 'Great Aunt Emma! Oh do come in, you must be freezing. Tim, help with the luggage!'

So we got her inside and she is rather a queer old party. Very short, with a hat with a veil, and gloves, and a way of smiling vaguely. Her teeth are very good (false?) and she is very neat. Her shoes hardly have creases in them over the instep, as if she never walked, yet she is quite spry considering her age and soon she and Mum were chattering away about the journey and so on. At first Mum didn't seem quite with the situation, I could tell she was faking a lot, but she is such a good faker (unlike Father) that only an outsider could have told that she was a bit baffled by GAE. Anyhow, this soon passed, I saw her (Mum) wipe the back of her hand across her brow which is always a sign that her mind is now made up and Into

Action! After another few minutes you could have sworn that Mum had been expecting GAE for the last fortnight, that the bed was aired and so on. She is very good at that sort of thing.

Then Father and Beth came in from feeding the rabbits. He made a complete bosh of it as usual, saying all the wrong things and making it quite clear that he hadn't a clue about the very existence of Great Aunts. But she fixed him with her beady eye, and grinned, and said, 'You remember me, Edward!' and he re-entered the Twentieth Century in great style, pouring everyone sherry. He gave Beth (who is seven) as much sherry as me (eleven) which is typical. Beth was as ever the Outstanding Social Success and shook hands and said, 'Oh what a lovely surprise,' and looked more like a telly ad than ever. I suppose it's a graceful accomplishment, but it's also the mark of a little cow. She swallowed the sherry pretty fast and went across to pour herself some more but Mum caught her eye and said, 'Beth . . . !' and that was the end of that. I got another half-glass later. It is quite good sherry, a Manzanilla.

Mum drew me aside and of course it was me that had to go and put hot water bottles in the spare bed and turn on the heaters and so on to get the room ready for GAE. When I got back to the living-room they were all talking away.

GAE obviously has a knack for social chitchat, she just asks questions that set people talking again. When I came in, she said, 'Tim, are you old enough to smoke?' I said no, of course, although I have smoked (what a ridiculous habit). She said, 'I am so glad, now I won't have to be polite and offer you one of these horrid things. I have only four left.' She pulled out a packet of Gauloises and lit one – she had already had one, the stub was in an ashtray – and said, 'Let me see, are you fourteen or fifteen, Tim?'

I felt myself turning pink at this ridiculous question and mumbled, 'Eleven. Nearly twelve.' Sure enough, Beth said, 'But he's old enough to shave, Aunt Emma!' in her Sweet Little Girl voice and everyone began to say, 'What shave When shave Why shave Who shave How shave', just as Beth intended. What makes it all worse is that I tried Father's shaving things that time simply out of curiosity, not to prove myself a great hairy man or anything stupid like that. But of course as Father is always reminding me, WAW, Women Always Win.

Anyhow, what an absurd thing to ask me if I am fourteen or fifteen, quite obviously I am not. If GAE thought she was flattering me, wrong guess. I tried to cover up by asking her how old she was. Beth murmured, 'How rude' – another point to her – but GAE said, 'I have been sixty-nine now for more years than I care to remember,' and everyone laughed politely.

So it went on like that and she eventually went off to bed in high style. Thank heaven she is not a kisser, just a peck-on-the-cheeker. When Aunt Lilian was here, saying goodnight was like those old movies with sobbing violins.

Will get Beth somehow.

Jan. 15

Got Beth over hogging black cherry jam – none left for breakfast. Kid stuff, but A Man Must Do What A Man Must Do. Father packing Land Rover with cameras and gear for undercroft photos, wish he would take me; it's the best part of the cathedral, terrific spooky smell. He was in a panic because he'd messed up the lighting gear as usual and GAE kept asking questions. Antiquated old gear he bought in the fifties, weighing a ton.

Memo – push catalogues of Jap electronics under his nose again.

GAE no fool. I wonder how old she really is? Very alert and always asking questions, most of them good. Asked Father WHY he wanted to know about Roman settlement below undercroft and he lost another three minutes telling her. Most women merely think his work Quaint, like that woman who kept saying, 'So *historical*!' but GAE wants to know what it's all for. Kept asking even when Father gone, so not just faking.

GAE asked where she could get more French ciggies, saw Mum flinch (though she does not mind them as much as ordinary fags). Told her only one place, Tillots in the village, and even then she would be lucky (she was – they did stock them). She said would I take her, had to say yes. So we walked there, me dreading slow tottering steps and having to hang back. But she kept going at a fair old pace. Very cold, nose dripping (mine not hers – she didn't even mention cold). Funny really, she wore a black long coat, black boots, black hat with fur and veil again. Said it kept her face warm. I said something about the early days of motoring and women wearing veils then but she said she didn't remember and started asking me about cars. What is a sports car for, she asked, and I said, to go faster. How much faster? I said not really much faster, in fact some saloons were faster than some sports cars. Then why did people buy sports cars? Etc., etc. Lots more of this sort. Questions that made *me* think. I told her about electric cars but (as we found out later) GAE hates anything electric, which is one of the odd, old-ladyish things about her. She seems to think that anything electrical could *leak* electricity . . . she flinches away from electric fires, irons, anything.

Funny that she asks all these questions at her age, I suppose old people get a second wind when they start looking at life all over again and asking all the questions they didn't ask when they were young. She never talks about the past.

All in all, rather enjoyed the walk and certainly she's a good goer – quite unpuffed on return, lit a Gauloise and read paper right through without a further word.

Father back early in temper, lighting gear failed as I

predicted. Gave him Jap catalogues. This time he may actually look at them.

Jan. 20

Muscle Beach* this morning, Father a bit hearty, saying 'Swimming in January! There's luxury!' Beth as usual moaning and ending up by crying 'It's NOT luxury! It's NOT luxury!' which made Father and me laugh. We stripped and dived in, horrible anticipation but very nice once done. Water 67°. Father ploughing up and down doing his 30 lengths, very stern and dutiful, but must admit he looks better than most men of his age. E.g. cannot imagine Dr Parry (six years younger than Father) stripped to the buff, must be obscene. Physician, heal thyself.

Beth doing her amazing breaststroke, head and bottom sticking out of water, mouth going 'Pouf! Pouf!', eyes closed most of the time.

---

* Muscle Beach – the Carpenters' swimming pool, built by Mr Carpenter. It has a removable glass roof and is heated for winter use. The pool is Mr Carpenter's greatest luxury, the only item, he says, on which he has ever spent more than he can afford – and the only thing, his work apart, about which he is somewhat fanatical and insistent. He uses the pool daily and makes it plain that he expects the family to follow his example at week-ends, even in darkest winter.

The Author

I did length underwater, then two lengths = 50 feet. Nearly burst lungs.

Mother as usual found excuse, did not come. Yet she is far best swimmer. My theory – she never really approves of the naked bit. Is it her appendicitis scar? Probably. She is quite vain and I don't blame her as very pretty considering age (34). She moans about the scar – surgeon was a butcher, etc., etc. – but not seriously. But she does mention it. I read an article in the paper the other day that said all this modem thing about families romping around naked and unashamed was a snare and a delusion. I must say I never thought about it at all, the swimming-pool was just a thing we had and it's always been there – since I was four anyhow – and you don't wear clothes in your own swimming pool, although you do in someone else's or on the beach. No one in our house goes around naked indoors or leaves loo door open. But since the Permissive Scene came on, you can't even brush your teeth without feeling that you've got to prove something. I wish I was Father, who simply doesn't comment – just does what he wants to do. But of course, even that's all changed now because of GAE.

There we are splashing in the pool when – ker-doing! – door opens, icy blast ruffles water, and lo! GAE has come among us, wearing gumboots and mild grin! All is instantly confusion! The great traditions hallowed by the Carpenter family are shaken to the corblimey! – particularly the tradition whereby Muscle Beach = unembarrassed starkers. Beth is least affected – she merely says, 'Eeek!', then recovers herself and goes on with her rotten breaststroke, this time with her eyes open to see how dear Papa and dear Brother take the situation.

I zoom out of the pool at the far end and slide like a seal into a towel in one easy movement. So I am now unnaked and therefore unashamed. Not trendy, but true.

But Father is visibly taken aback. He stops swimming, stands in the middle of the pool and says, 'Oh.' Then he adds, 'Aunt Emma. Oh. Good morning.' And, trying to look unconcerned, completes his thirty lengths. But he's concerned all right, because instead of doing racing turns at either end, which he learned with great labour from the swimmers on TV, he now turns in the modest amateur hand-push manner: the difference being that the amateur manner just causes a swirl of water round his shoulder while the racing turn shows his *bottom*.

At last he can swim no longer and once again he stands in the middle of the pool and says, in an abnormally normal voice, 'Oh, good morning, Aunt Emma. You're up bright and early.'

She looks out through the glass overhead as if to check the truth of his statement and replies, 'Yes indeed,' – then calmly sits down and stares at Father, waiting for him to say something else.

Taking the bull by the horns, he says, 'Well, cough cough, that's enough swimming for me, hum hum, I think I will get out now.'

Aunt Emma says, 'Yes indeed.'

Father's eyes flick first to Beth, who deliberately turns her back to him and duck-dives; then to me – but I pretend to have my arms caught in a sweater. Seeing that he will get no support from his nearest and dearest, Father says, loud and clear, 'You must leave now, Aunt Emma, I'm getting out.'

'Oh,' says Aunt Emma, the grin fading. 'Why?'

'Because I'm not wearing anything !' Father grates.

'I should hope not,' says Aunt Emma. '*It would only get wet!*'

I was going to go on to examine this situation in depth, but it's too good to spoil and I am sleepy. So I will leave him in the water, facing Aunt Emma (still seated) and laugh myself to sleep.

Jan. 21

Will continue with the events of Saturday (yesterday) as not much doing today. (Incidentally, GAE's footprints in the snow are interesting. Our footprints lead straight to and from the pool. Hers make a long detour round the filtration unit – with its *electric* pump and *electric* humming noise!)

Father in very good form about the Aunt Emma 'get wet' story, and made Mum laugh a lot when GAE had gone for her afternoon rest. We were still sitting around the lunch table. Mum said something about it showing what a good sense of humour GAE has, but Beth interrupted her and said, 'Oh no! She was quite serious, she really meant it.'

I saw Father look puzzled, then Mum said, 'Beth, you don't live to the age of seventy-something without knowing the existence of bathing costumes.' But Beth said, 'She meant it, she was quite embarrassed when Father told her to go.'

So Father explained to Beth what was meant by a dry sense of humour and said GAE was being drily funny, which caused Beth to make the obvious joke about everyone being wet at the time, etc., etc., etc. The subject was dropped.

Thinking about it later, I believe Beth was right – that GAE really was serious when she made her 'joke'. But of course that's impossible. Not that it matters one way or the other.

Jan. 22

Yet another 'Emmanation', as we now wittily describe strange remarks made about GAE. Mac's mother called to ask where was Mac (he was with me, backwashing the pool filter). So Mum called us into the house and GAE came in and we had to introduce GAE to Mrs Rainier. Mum said, 'Great Aunt Emma, let me introduce Mrs Rainier, our nicest neighbour,' etc., etc., and Mrs Rainier said, 'Oh, how interesting, you never told me you had a Great Aunt, Millie!' and GAE said, 'Oh, you remember me, Mrs Rainier, you remember me' (which seems to be GAE's formula when being introduced) and then Beth came in and said, 'I don't remember you, Aunt Emma, not properly. Only Grandma, I knew her, but Mum never told us about you!'

There was an awkward pause, then Mum wiped her hand across her forehead and started talking about cakes and a failure she had had and would we all please eat the good bits. The cake was brought in. It looked OK but burnt. Beth was being the perfect TV kiddie and saying, 'Oh how perfectly scrumptious,' etc., etc. Then she said, 'I love the smoky taste of the burn. All cakes should be smoked, shouldn't they?'

Mrs Rainier, sucking up to the brat, said, 'I so agree, ha ha, cakes should be smoked, they really should, ha ha, like kippers!'

At which GAE said, 'Oh, Mrs Rainier, you must think me so rude!' – and offered her a box of matches!

Reading this over, I suppose it's not so funny after all and I must stop using 'and' all the time to link sentences. But it was the way GAE said it – deadly serious. Perhaps she has got the famous dry sense of humour.

Beth has a point. I wonder why we were never told about GAE by Grandma when she was alive, or by Mum? Perhaps we were told and I did not listen. Mrs Rainier seemed to know all about her once they'd got talking.

Feb. 2

Father has actually bought Tasaki lighting gear! As usual, is very chuffed with himself and prone to explain it to me as if I wasn't the one that made him buy it in the first place. But suddenly caught himself doing this and very graciously said, 'Well, it was your idea really, Tim, I tell you what, come to the undercroft tomorrow and be Lighting Technician. Mind you, you'll have to carry it, I don't see why I should have to hump it about, etc., etc.'

I said, 'But it only weighs fifteen pounds, that's one of the selling points I was telling you about!'

He said, 'Then why moan about carrying it?'

I fell into the trap and said, 'I wasn't moaning –' and he chuckled and said, 'That's how women argue, you can't beat it!' and laughed some more.

I quite agree with him, that's women. Even Beth at the age of seven can do it. So can GAE. Told Father about GAE and Competitive Spirit: I had scored second goal and we won 4–2 so naturally I was highly chuffed and maybe went on a bit about how we had massacred the other side, etc., etc., and GAE started asking questions about why winning mattered so much. I said the whole point of a game was to establish a winner, it was like a sort of friendly war. That got us on to wars and all the obvious arguments – if *they* do this, then *you* have no alternative but to do that, etc., etc. She said that perhaps history would have come out much the same if all the great battles had been settled by the toss of a coin. I said, you mean you would just accept invasion, not fight back? She said yes. So I leaned forward and took her packet of ciggies and placed them on top of the grandfather clock where she could never reach them and sat down again and grinned at her.

Instead of taking it as a joke, she exhibited the old aggro. She got really cross. 'It's only an invasion, Aunt Emma,' I said, 'only an invasion. Why fight it?'

At that moment Mum came in and Aunt Emma said, 'Tim is being rude and unkind,' etc., etc. I said, 'Oh! An appeal to the United Nations!' Aunt Emma said, '*I insist that you give me back those cigarettes!*' 'Then it's war?' I replied. Anyhow, Mum gave her the ciggies and all was peace and light. Just as well because GAE was looking upset and I was feeling a bit stupid. Later I said sorry.

Father said, 'There you are. Never argue theories with a woman. They can't see further than personalities and in any case, WAW.'

I find I am writing very slangily. Various uses of 'chuffed' in this entry and lazy use of 'and'. *Memo: if you are going to write this much, even in a diary, you might as well write it right.*

Feb. 3

Now Beth is at it, doing what Father and I agreed to call Weathercocking – i.e., you just disregard the facts and main lines of an argument, and come in from any point of the compass that suits you. If you were north one minute you can be south the next and still expect to win. All part of the WAW phenomenon.

Beth has taken an aversion from (Memo – not to: you cannot avert yourself to something, only from) GAE. There was a slight scene last night about kissing GAE goodnight: Beth just smiled and waved instead of kissing. Mum said something, Beth kissed GAE and then left the room, giving me a Look as she passed. Later I asked what she had been pulling faces for and she said, 'Ugh! I hate kissing her, kissing Aunt Emma makes me want to puke!' etc., etc. I said, was it the feeling of her skin (which is a bit odd, I must admit – much too smooth and soft – but that's old age for you, one cannot help getting pouchy). Beth said Poo, ugh, no it wasn't that, it was because GAE *does not smell*!!! I sat back and prepared for some weathercocking, viz –

'You say she does not smell?'

'Yes, that's right, it's all wrong. Ugh, poo,' etc., etc.

'But she smokes all the time so she must smell.'

'Oh yes, but that's only her ciggies, that's not what I mean.'

'But French ciggies have a very strong smell.'

'Oh yes, I quite like the smell of French ciggies. It's *her* smell I can't stand.'

'But you just said she *doesn't* smell.'

'Yes, it's disgusting, ugh, poo, that's why I can't stand kissing her goodnight, stupid!'

'But you didn't like that babysitter, Winnie What's-her-name, because she *did* smell.'

'Well, that's not as bad as *not* smelling, how could it be?' . . .

Beat that for weathercocking. And Beth is only seven. By the time she is grown-up she will be fifty times as hopeless.

Feb. 6

Beth barmy, weather freezing, soccer latest, GAE disaster!

This winter worst in several years, snow again yesterday, about an inch, and frost is apparently here forever. Even Father looking a bit bluefaced on way to and from pool.

GAE Disaster! Poor old thing slipped on ice and fell down heavily when walking to bird feeder with bacon scraps. I was at school, did not see, but apparently lay there for a little time until Beth rushed out and started to get her up.

Then for no reason whatsoever, Beth let her fall again and pelted indoors white-faced and shaking and would not say a word – not that there was much time for words, as GAE still lying there. So Mum went out and got her to her feet and indoors. GAE now has right wrist wrapped in bandages and sits in wing chair smoking French ciggies and trying to do the crossword, which she is very bad at, particularly the obvious clues. Good at spotting anagrams, though.

'Right wrist wrapped' a tongue-twister? 'Nicely white lightly wrapped wrist' . . . 'Lily's right wrist wrapped lightly.'

Beth has now gone into the opposite of her TV Sweetie act and refuses to say anything to anyone about anything – palely pudding-faced with eyes like peeholes in the snow. Tried to be nice to her this evening (mending her fountain pen) and carefully broached the subject of GAE – but Beth screamed, 'Shut up! Shut up! Shut up!' and ran to her room. Seemed quite all right later but noticed how cunningly she avoided kissing GAE goodnight. Beth went over to her, placed her hand on GAE's wrist and exerted slight 'accidental' pressure (hoping GAE would say Ouch and thus Beth could make speedy exit). But GAE took no notice. said, 'Goodnight, Bethy!' and Beth had to kiss her after all. Beth looked very sick as she walked out and serve her right for being too clever and complicated about everything. Last time we had pale pudding-face act, long-term, was when Mac frightened her with fireworks, Nov. 5.

Am deputy skipper for Saturday's away match, not that it matters.

Cannot think what Beth has against GAE. Also cannot be bothered to think about it. GAE a bit boring, this questions thing of hers goes on too much. She is always asking questions and some of the questions are so stupid or mock-stupid or whatever. I think she puts on a Dear Little Old Lady performance (1) to gain attention (although she is not a limelight hogger like, say, Aunt Lilian), (2) to prove she is still young and sprightly, (3) because her mind is getting a little perforated, like a gruyère cheese.

She went on this evening about Sleep, of all things. How strange, she said, that we have to sleep each night. What is sleep? How did trees sleep? And oceans? And continents? As there are obvious answers to the first two questions, it was boring to have to listen to Father giving them. And as there are no real answers to the last two questions, I wish she hadn't asked them because it got Mum and Father talking about balances of power, the decline of the West, the rise of the East and all the rest of it.

Like the time there were two dogs at the end of our garden. One was Mrs Folger's bitch and the dog (unknown) was trying to mount her. GAE immediately burst out with, 'Oh! How strange! What is that dog trying to do to the other dog?' at the top of her voice – this in front of all the family and Mac – and for that matter Beth, but she is a hardened rabbit and guinea-pig breeder. Anyhow, someone told her what the dogs were doing and you'd have thought she would have shut up and left it alone. But no, she had to go on and on asking more and more questions covering the whole animal kingdom and the human race as well. Perhaps she has some antiquated notion about Bringing Things Out Into The Open For The Sake Of The Children or perhaps she has rotten eyesight and wanted to cover up what she thought to be a gaffe. But it would have been far better if she had just shut up and smoked another ciggie.

Feb. 8

Beth being stupid and embarrassing again today with GAE. Asking GAE questions about Granny – were they very fond of each other when they were children, what games did they play, etc., etc., etc. GAE was trying to answer by turning the questions – 'Oh, it was a long time ago, dear . . . What is your favourite game?' But Beth very persistent. At last Mum must have overheard because she called us into kitchen and told us not to pester GAE. Mum said GAE might be very upset by even least mention of Granny, for sisters can be very close and when Granny died, who knows what the effect was on GAE, etc.

So Beth did the right thing and went up to GAE saying (in her best TV-commercial way), 'Oh, Aunt Emma, I'm sorry if I ask too many questions, I hope I didn't upset you,' etc., etc. GAE replying 'No not at all, smile smile.' Beth proceeded to overcook the whole thing by saying, 'Oh, I am glad you are smiling, that proves you are not cross, *I must call you my Grinny Granny*!'

This so sickening that I nearly brought up my lunch on the best carpet – Beth only needs a lisp to make herself quite unbearable ('I mutht call you my Gwinny Gwanny'). But GAE (presumably I must now write of her as GG – joke about the Old Grey Mare coming up, Ho Ho) highly chuffed, grinning more than ever, and Beth liked the TV Kute Kid who gets the chocolate biscuit with the yummy-yummy-O-my-tummy marshmallow filling.

If I say anything of this to Mac, he gets all gruff and gormless – he fancies Beth like mad although she is only seven, and wants to come the Big Brother act. If he actually had a kid sister he'd know different as I keep telling him but he only goes Strong and Silent.

GAE got working on Mac today and said, 'So you and Tim are friends? Really friends, you really are friends? Great friends?' etc., etc. What can you do except look stupid and mumble. But she went on and on asking about friends – would a friend do this if such and such happened, how could you be sure if a Great Friend, etc., etc. ad nauseam. The Quaint Old Lady bit.

We lost 3–1 to Millhouse, thanks almost entirely to Cutler's useless centre-half play. I got six out of ten for English Comp. and (as usual) the comment TOO SLANGY. The bike's dynamo is wonky.

Altogether a grotty day.

Feb. 9

This is not easy to write. I know I send up Beth all the time and make jokes about WAW and so on and she is after all only a seven-year-old (but soon to be eight) – but she is nothing like such a fool as I like to make her out to be and if she is a liar, she is doing it very well – even crying with the lying. I don't know what to make of it.

She was sitting in her room and refusing to come down. Eventually Mum sent me up to tell Beth that dinner was nearly on the table and that she really must come down. I crashed into Beth's room and said, 'Oh, come on, Beth, it's dinner time and I've had to come all the way upstairs,' etc., etc. She just burst into tears and said she wasn't coming down, she refused to come down, leave me alone and so on.

She looked so awful that I didn't start on her in the usual way but tried to be nice – what's wrong, did something happen at school, aren't you well. She said, 'No, no, it's her – Grinny! It's Grinny!' Anyhow, Mum was standing at the foot of the stairs yelling for us to come down so I pulled her (Beth) to her feet and said, 'Will you tell me after?' and she replied, 'Yes, but only if you promise!' Which means of course promise not to tell anyone else.

She was quiet and white at dinner but I don't think anyone took much notice as there were two men from the site, a stonemason and a photographer, having a meal with us and they and Father kept talking shop at the top of their voices all the time. Beth ate as much as usual. But as soon as the meal was over and we had cleared the dishes, she tugged at my arm and made me go back with her to her room.

She said, 'I've been longing to tell someone, but they'll only laugh. Will you laugh?' I said no. She said, 'Do you think I am just a stupid little girl or don't you? Because I'm not!' She started crying again so I gave her the old hug and kiss treatment, which I don't often do, so when I do do it it works all the better (*do do it it* is like a word puzzle). It worked now – she stopped crying, stared me straight in the face and said –

'*Grinny's not real.*'

I said, 'Oh!' I was disappointed in her for being so childish, actually.

She said, 'Yes, I knew you would take it like that, you just think I'm stupid, but I am not. *Grinny is not real*, she's not a real person at all!'

It went on like this for a little while, then I said, 'Tell me exactly and precisely what you are talking about and no messing about and above all do not cry!'

She said, 'You remember the day she fell down on the ice and hurt herself?' I said yes. 'Well, I was the first one there, I was there just about a second after she did it, she was still lying on the ground and I was there beside her. And I saw something you will never believe, never!'

I said what was it and I would try to believe her.

She said, 'Something horrible, it was *horrible*! I saw her wrist actually broken and the bone sticking out!'

I replied, 'That's impossible. Do be reasonable, she was perfectly all right quite soon after. If you break your wrist it is very serious, it takes weeks or months to mend. Particularly if you are old. And it is very painful, agony, in fact. So you just couldn't have seen it, Beth, you only thought you saw it because you have a good imagination.'

Beth said, 'I haven't got a good imagination, Penny writes much better essays than I do and so does Sue. I saw it, I saw it, I saw it!'

So I made her tell me just what it was she saw. She started off by repeating that I would never believe her and so on, but in the end it came down to this – I am choosing my words very carefully so as not to distort what she said –

'She was lying on the ground in a heap. She was not groaning or moaning, just lying there and kicking her legs, trying to get up. I went close to her and got hold of her elbow so that I could help pull her up. She did not say anything to me, like "Help me" or "My wrist hurts" – she just tried to get up. When I seized her elbow, I saw her wrist. The hand was dangling. The wrist was so badly broken that the skin was all cut open in a gash and the bones were showing.'

I told Beth I understood all this, but she seemed unwilling to go on. She looked at me and wailed, 'Oh, it's no good, you'll never believe me!' but I made her go on. She said:

'The skin was gashed open but there was no blood. The bones stuck out but they were not made of real bone – they were made of shiny steel!'

I have these words right. Beth did say what I have written. I am quite certain about asking her what sort of bones, what sort of steel and so on. Her answers were, that the steel was silvery shiny and that the bones looked smaller than proper bones – more like umbrella ribs. When I asked her what umbrella ribs look like, she answered (correctly) that they are made of channels of steel, not solid rods like knitting needles. She said that GAE's bones were in 'little collections' of these steel ribs and that the skin had been torn by a few of the ribs breaking away from a main cluster and coming through the skin.

So I asked her again about the absence of blood and she was positive. She said there was no blood, no blood at all, the skin was just split open. I asked her what colour the skin was and she said the same colour outside as in. I said, well, there must have been meaty stuff where the bones were, but she said no. There was nothing but the steel ribs and that the skin was just a thick layer 'like the fat on a mutton chop before it is cooked', but with a tear in it.

I thought of all kinds of reasons for her telling this story, ranging from my linocut set, which has very sharp

(= frightening) gouges, some of them the same section as umbrella ribs; right down to playing in the garden when we were much younger with an old tattered umbrella, all spokes and no cover (it was pelting with rain and we were making a joke of the useless umbrella, etc., etc.).

As I was thinking of all the things that might have caused Beth to think she saw what she said she saw, she began again. 'I saw her wrist mend! I saw it heal itself!' she said.

I must say, this gave me goose pimples. I said, 'What do you mean?' and Beth told me that as she watched, *the skin came together over the broken bones leaving a bump covering the breaks*. That was when Beth became really frightened and ran inside.

I said to her, 'You know that people actually can have metal bones?' She said, 'Oh yes, I've always known that and so have you. Father nearly had one, you remember.' I did remember – he broke a bone and the hospital thought that he might have to have a steel rod inserted to pin the bone. In the end he didn't. Some people do, however, and it may be permanent. A man in the village has a metal plate in his skull.

So it is no good me trying to pretend that Beth has some fixation or other about bones and umbrella ribs because she simply hasn't. Cream, coffee, chocolates, chicken and stuffing – she's certainly got fixations about them. But not people's bones.

By now she was saying, 'I told you! I knew all along

you wouldn't believe me!' and preparing to have a good cry again. I managed to avoid this by more kiss and hug treatment and in the end I said, 'All right, so Grinny has an artificial arm, let's say, made by some super surgeon. For all we know, she's got false teeth, wears a wig, has a cork leg and a glass eye. Fine! But what difference does it make? Why get upset and refuse to kiss her goodnight and all the rest of it?'

Beth set up a great howl and shouted, 'Oh, how can you be so stupid! It's nothing to do with false legs and glass eyes – IT'S BECAUSE SHE'S NOT REAL, that's why I can't stand her. NONE OF HER IS REAL!'

She was making such a row that I said, 'All right, all right, I understand now. And then of course you don't like the way she smells and it all adds up in your mind –'

Beth went very white and said, 'Yes, and she doesn't smell of anything, that's another thing! And she asks those stupid questions! And she's frightened of electricity! It all proves it, she's not real!'

I quietened her down eventually (she had started crying again in a very big way) and let her come into my room while I did my homework. She was fairly happy by her bedtime. But I must admit she has put the frighteners on me. I am writing this rather late and I keep expecting a crack to appear in the wall, then a hole, then a metal hand come through the plaster. That sort of thing. A good story might be written about a metal hand.

I just do not know what to make of it all. Beth's only a little girl but she is *not* an idiot.

Feb. 10

Big family row today, BAM, POWIE, ECHHHH! Beth the cause. Would not eat her breakfast, doing her White-faced Orphan act, 'Oh no, Mama, I am not unwell, I am quite all right, it is just that I am not hungry.' Mum slamming buttered toast down in front of her and saying, 'Look, you little viper, eat this toast or I will hang you from a hook over a slow fire,' etc., etc. Lurid imagery. Father moaning, 'For heaven's sake shut UP, where are those Canadian boots of mine, blast Beth, I must have dry feet.' I felt rather sorry for Beth in a way because for once in a million years she could actually have slept badly because of Grinny and the metal bones. Eventually she nibbled at the toast and made a disgusting sick noise and deposited what she had chewed on the plate. Mum instantly all sympathy and tenderness but Father unexpectedly went ape and shouted, 'Disgusting! What the hell do you mean by,' etc., etc.

At this moment, Mac entered looking wholesome and fresh-faced. He had come to pick me up. He instantly sized up the situation and went to work on it with his usual nasty skill. That is what I like about Mac, he is very quick on the uptake. Even though he fancies Beth, he couldn't resist pushing things a little further. He kept being Cheerful and Nice, a true British Boy, while Mum fumed and Father erupted in grunts and snarls and Beth looked puke-y, Puky? Pukey? Mac said, 'Gosh! What a super marmalade, Beth! We never have the chunky stuff at home! Gosh you are lucky!' and so on and Beth looked sicker and sicker. Eventually she fled from the room, wailing. I thought he was overdoing it with the 'Goshes' and Father suspected him too, but Father likes Mac because Mac genuinely enjoys swimming even when the water is cold, unlike us, who do it from a sense of duty towards something or other.

Anyhow, Mum offered Mac a cup of coffee and deliberately put only one spoonful of sugar in it to let him know that she was on to him and Father read the paper very busily, not looking up. Beth then came back looking rabbit-eyed from a quick weep-in and Mac said, 'Here's your toast and marmalade, Beth, it's still OK. Eat hearty!'

This was pushing his luck. Beth scooped up the toast and flung it at him shouting, 'Pig ! Beast! Swine!' etc., etc. The toast missed Mac and hit the wall, where it slowly slid down because of the stickiness of the marmalade. It was a marvellous sight, I could not help laughing, but Father was really angry and yelled, 'Get out, the whole bloody lot of you!' and went to get a dishcloth to wipe the wall. He made it too wet and now the wallpaper is coming up in a big blister.

I cannot think why I bother to write all this down, it is so childish and futile. Or perhaps I can think why after all. The point is that GAE was ABOUT TO COME DOWN FOR BREAKFAST. (Astounding, my dear Holmes! But I confess, I remain baffled. Pray be more explicit . . .) What I mean is this. Grinny has got us all on the run. The mere fact of EXPECTING her to enter the dining room is enough to put everyone on edge. Beth was already on edge of course and who can blame her. But Mum and Father are feeling it too, they do not like the continued presence of Grinny in the house. Before she came, we used to have our breakfasts in a surly but comfortable silence, with Father chomping away and reading the papers, Mum vaguely instructing us in how to be better Citizens of the Future ('Well, if you think I am going to clean your shoes for you, think again, you will not leave this house until those shoes are cleaned,' etc., etc.), Beth practising her feminine wiles and me trying to eat as much as possible without exposing my fingernails ('You are *not* leaving this house with cabbages growing from your filthy fingers. Edward, *say* something, he is *your* son,' etc.).

In short, we were quite comfortable and ordinary. But now at breakfast and at many other times of the day, we are all in some funny way awaiting the arrival of Grinny. Father will make to rise from his chair but Grinny will say, 'Oh, Edward dear, don't get up,' – so Father will grin at Grinny and Grinny will grin at Mum and Mum will smirk at me and I will kick Beth under the table, etc., etc.

At first I thought this uneasiness was something to do with age. Grinny is a very old lady and we, the family, are used to each other and don't think about each other's ages, we just accept it (except Mum, who is prone to smile as if she had false teeth when it's her birthday. I would hate to be a woman but would not mind being a girl – they get it all their own way for the first twenty years or so).

As I was saying before I so rudely interrupted me, at

first I thought it was just the presence of an old lady, a foreigner, in our midst. Now I have caught Beth's bug – 'Grinny is not real' – and find myself brooding about her a lot. But the broken wrist story is a bit too much. When Mac and I were on our way to school I said, 'Mac, what do you think of Grinny?' He said, 'Queer old party. Rather you than me.'

I said, 'What do you mean, queer?'

He replied, 'Her Mona Lisa smile. She looks like the cat that swallowed the canary. As if she knew it all.'

I said, 'But she doesn't know anything much, that's what's so annoying about her. She's always asking daft questions, you must have noticed.'

He said, 'Yes, she fixes you with her eye and asks all those questions . . . What does she live on?' 'Food,' I replied. Mac said, 'You're so *cute*. I mean, has she any money? Does she pay you rent or something? Has she an income?'

I had never thought of this, but am thinking about it now. I am also thinking about how long she will stay, why it is that Mum and Father never talk about her going (they certainly talk about certain of our guests going, and the sooner the better!) and why it is that even now, after all this time, nobody ever talks about Grinny's early days with our Granny.

I have been nice to Beth this evening, but she is still in a silent and won't-play mood. How strange if Beth were right and Grinny is not real! And if she isn't a real GAE, what the hell is she instead?

Feb. 12

Beth now in a very different mood. She has gone all defiant and We Shall Not Be Moved. Strike Action. She now refuses to kiss Grinny goodnight and barely talks to her. Big scenes with Mum, who says, 'You must,' but Beth just says, 'I won't.' And she doesn't, I must hand it to her for that.

I talked to her (Beth) about it this evening and you gotta hand it to the little lady, she's convinced herself. Do not confuse me with the facts, my mind is made up, etc., etc. She says, 'Grinny is *not* real, she is horrible. I won't have anything to do with her. And that is that.'

Grinny takes it very well, just smiles vaguely and lets it pass. She does not attempt to be nice to Beth and strike up conversations. Father hardly notices.

Feb. 18

Re Beth's Operation Grinny (see Feb. 12). Report from all Fronts. Beth still on strike, Mum still saying, 'Oh do see reason', Father still silent, Grinny still grinning, Mac now more curious than anyone but me.

At teatime (Mac with us after soccer) Mac asked her point-blank about earlier days. He did it all very well, the uninstructed youth bowing before the wisdom of old age, etc., etc. Where did she spend her childhood, he asked, and wouldn't let go.

Mum tried to interrupt by saying something or other, I forget what, but Mac kept asking. At last Grinny said, 'Oh, the past is over and done with, I never think of the past.'

Mac still pressed on and said, 'Oh, but surely you must think about your sister, Tim's granny?'

Mum sort of gasped and made a face to shut Mac up but Grinny replied, 'Well, you see, my sister and I were so very different. Quite different. Very close, of course, but quite different.' Then she gave a sort of little laugh which could have been embarrassment but which Beth said later was *sinister* (Beth's new word).

Mac said, 'But –' and Mum came in very strong saying, 'Mac, I would rather you didn't pester Aunt Emma with questions.'

Mac said, 'But –' again, and Mum said, 'More tea, Aunt Emma? More tea, anyone?' and that was that.

Now comes the significant part. An hour or more later, I found Mum in the kitchen and said to her, 'Oh, I do wish you had let Mac go on, I was hoping we'd find out.' She said, 'Go on about what?' I said, 'About Aunt Emma's past and about Granny and everything.'

She looked me straight in the eye and said, 'What are you talking about? Mac said *what*?' She did this as if she really meant it – as if she really had forgotten the conversation. But she doesn't forget things, she has the usual terrifying WAW memory about anything to do with *people* – what they wore, what they said, etc., etc. Anyhow, I kept on at her a bit more and even said, 'Don't you remember telling us not to pester Aunt Emma with questions about Granny?' but either Mum wasn't really hearing me or she was making everything slide out of her mind.

Unless, of course, someone else – Grinny herself! – was making her forget.

Then suddenly Mum looked ill. She put her hand to her head and said, 'I'm so tired. My head aches.'

I have just reread all this and have realized what a complete fool I am making of myself. Going on like a girl about what *this* one said and what *that* one said and if you want *my* opinion . . . worse than a girl. And all about a perfectly ordinary old lady.

I HEREBY RESOLVE TO SHUT UP ABOUT GRINNY and concentrate on things that matter. I WOULD BE ASHAMED IF THIS DIARY WERE FOUND because it is full of drivel and has nothing that matters. IT IS ALSO APPALLINGLY WRITTEN.

TIMOTHY CARPENTER, TURN OVER A NEW LEAF. TIMOTHY CARPENTER, TURN . . .

Feb. 19

I resolved yesterday to stop writing about Grinny and start writing about something important.

I must break the first promise if only to keep the second.

Something extraordinary happened last night and it concerns Grinny.

I must make sure to get everything in the right order and into plain English.

First the UFO (Unidentified Flying Object). There have been various UFO scares in this district, and I never believed in such nonsense. Now I have changed my mind. I saw a UFO myself. So did Beth and my father.

It happened like this. I prepared to go to bed after writing up my diary at about 12.30, which is late for me. I suppose I was the last person awake in the house except for one – but more about that later.

I looked out of the window because it was a cold night and I like the look of the moon on frost. The moon was very bright indeed, almost full. Unusually bright – the frost made the whole scene super-real, like a stage set with special pale blue lighting.

In spite of the brilliance of the light, I saw *it* perfectly distinctly.

When I first saw it, it was fairly near the moon's position in the sky. It was far brighter than the moon and had a yellowish brilliance. I remember thinking how it clashed with the steely blue of the moon. I also remember seeing the yellowish reflections of its light on the frosted grass of the lawn – the sort of effect you get when you look at a boat with a light on it, far out at sea. Only very different of course, because it made warm, yellowish reflections on the blueish grass.

I had plenty of time to look and all the time I stared at it, my heart was going faster and faster. So I was excited, but only physically, not mentally. I remember thinking, 'If it stays there much longer, I will be able to get Father and he can agree with me about what I am seeing.'

It *did* stay in position – or rather, it travelled so slowly that I had to keep checking the gap between It and the moon's position. It went very slowly *and not steadily*. Sometimes it paused. When it started to move again, it made *an oval luminous halo or nimbus*. I think (and so does Father) that it was flying within our atmosphere and this nimbus was the result of very cold air being disturbed by the thrust and/or movement of It. Rather like the contrails (condensation trails) you get from ordinary aircraft.

Without taking my eyes off it, I moved away from the window and felt behind me for my telescope, which is hung on two hooks on the wall. It is not a high-power instrument, just a World War Two military telescope used for artillery spotting and so on. But it does give a very sharp image, as good as the best modem field glasses, Father says. I felt for and found the telescope and, constantly keeping my eyes on It, pulled the telescope into rough focus. Then I lowered the window and rested the telescope on the frame to steady it and the UFO just *jumped* into focus!

I could see nearly everything about it. I could even see that it was revolving slowly, in a clockwise direction, and had several 'windows' or vents. I could very easily see its halo or nimbus, which looked like cirrus cloud (the very high, veil-like cloud).

At this moment, I heard my parents' bedroom door open quietly and Father's footsteps padding along. He was going to the loo. I ran backwards to my door, still keeping my eyes on It, and called him. He said, 'Oh, aren't you asleep? *Now* what's the trouble?' and came rather grumpily into my room.

He said, 'What are you doing in the dark?' and turned the light on. (I forgot to mention that I had turned the light out the better to see the moonlit frost.) I said, 'Turn it off! Quickly! Come over here!'

He was still saying things rather crossly and sleepily but I said, 'Look! Up there, in the sky! Look through the telescope!'

He looked for a long time and said, 'My God!' Then he said, 'Pinch my arm, Tim.' I thought he was joking but he was not, so I pinched him fairly hard. He said, 'All right, all right. My God!'

A little later he said, 'I must get my camera, it should be a cinch to get a picture with the long lens. It can't be far away, you can see it so well, so clearly . . .'

I said, 'What about the police? Shouldn't I telephone them, no one will ever believe us!'

He replied, 'I would rather you got the camera – no, I've a better idea, wake your mother and Beth, the more witnesses the better.' Then he changed his mind again and said, 'No, don't wake your mother, she was so tired . . . get Beth, then the camera. Quick as you can.'

I said I would and asked if anything was happening (my father was looking through the telescope, not me). He said, 'No, it's just moving in occasional lazy spurts, always in the same direction. And each time it moves it makes a mist –'

'Like a nimbus?' I interrupted.

'Yes, I think it's simply condensation, frozen vapour!'

Which is exactly what I had thought. Father and I agreed this point later. Presumably it must have been well within our atmosphere for there is no moisture to condense in true space.

I got Beth. She wakes very fast and I could hear her exclaiming while I prodded about behind the desk in Father's study (it is next to their bedroom) looking for his camera case. I found it and took it to him. He was just taking the telescope from Beth, who was murmuring, 'A space ship! It *is* a space ship!' in an astounded sort of way. Father said, 'Can you put the longest lens on, Tim?' but I replied (rather craftily, because I wanted to get back to the telescope), 'No, I'd rather you did it, Father, it's safer!' So I got the telescope from him while he opened the camera bag and got the body and long lens out. Then he started swearing mildly, saying, 'It's got a blasted colour film in, it will be too slow, I'll have to change to black and white – is the thing still there, Tim?'

I said yes and Beth kept tugging at my arm so I let her have another turn at the telescope.

Suddenly she shouted, 'Oh!' and I said, 'What's happened?'

She said, 'It's gone! Oh no, it hasn't, it's moved. But it went so fast . . . ! It just *flashed* away! It's all right, I've got it now . . .'

Father was still fiddling with the film and trying to keep his eye on It at the same time. I felt sorry for him. Beth announced, 'I'm going to get Mummy!' and Father said, 'No, don't.' I said, 'She wasn't well, she had a bad headache –' Beth said, 'Can I get Grinny, then?' I said, 'Why?'

She said, just as Father and I had done. 'The more people see it the better.' Then she thought for a moment, shuddered, and said to me, 'I'd rather you went to fetch her if you don't mind,' in the sort of polite voice girls use when they intend to pull their femininity on you and make it impossible for you to argue.

Drawing by Mr Carpenter. He and his children each made a drawing of the UFO. They then compared their three drawings. Finally, they agreed on the sketch reproduced here.

Many readers may find this drawing shows something familiar. If so, the reason is simple enough: UFO sightings most commonly relate to cigar-shaped, cross-shaped and saucer-shaped craft. The Carpenters say they saw what thousands of others claim to have seen – a 'flying saucer'.

The Author.

I said, 'Oh, all right,' and went to wake Grinny.

She sleeps in the spare bedroom up another flight of stairs. As I went up these stairs I remember looking out of the little window just at the moment when it suddenly darted off again. It seemed to accelerate instantly – one minute it was going slowly, the next very fast indeed, with no warm-up. It travelled some 30° through the sky and stopped in its new position just as immediately as it had started. A sheet of nimbus enveloped it so that for a moment you could only just see it through the veil. Then the yellowish lights were there again just as before.

I then went on again up the stairs, walking very quietly so as not to disturb Mum, who was below me. I opened the door of Grinny's room . . .

At first I just couldn't take it in. I couldn't believe it. So I was not frightened, only shocked.

Grinny was lying flat on her back on the bed, with her arms by her side above the covers. She was rigid and still, like a corpse or an Egyptian mummy. *But she was luminous*. There was even a faint glow through the bedclothes. I remember thinking in a matter-of-fact sort of way, 'She doesn't seem to need much covering. Just one blanket . . .' Because of course the light couldn't have passed through several blankets.

I went closer – I wasn't frightened yet – and saw another thing: *her eyes were wide open*. She was staring at the ceiling, staring at nothing. And her eyes were lit up from inside. Like water when you put the lens of a lit torch in it. Her mouth was open. She was grinning. I don't mean she was making the movement of smiling, I mean her mouth was set in a grin. And from her open mouth I thought I heard a slight fluttering, twittering sound. But it might have been my own pulses.

I think it was the reflection of her luminosity on her teeth that made me give a sort of scream.

Then things happened very quickly. She woke when I made the scream or whatever noise it was. As she woke, her luminosity faded, just like *that*. At the same instant, I heard Father shouting and heard his footsteps and Beth's in the passage. I think he said, 'It's gone!' In fact, he must have said this, because at the very moment that Grinny woke up the spaceship just whipped off into invisibility. I heard Beth answer him and they must have been making excited comments while Grinny came to.

If anyone ever reads all this, they will ask, 'But surely you must know exactly what happened within those two or three seconds?'

The answer is, No. It is still a bit vague and this is why. Grinny sat up in bed – I remember that she just sat straight up as if her body was hinged at the base of the spine – and gripped me by the wrist. It was like a claw, her hand. It fastened on me like a parrot's claw, very strong and funny-feeling. Like a clamp.

Anyhow, she clamped me with her hand and then looked me straight in the eye. I remember that her eyes still had a trace of the luminous, lit-from-within look about them. And she was still grinning. And I remember her mouth opening to say something. I remember that quite distinctly. What I cannot remember, however hard I try, is what she said. Everything seemed to go . . . furry. She was there, the room was there, she was speaking, Father and Beth were outside and about to enter – I had a furry impression of all this and still have. Yet I cannot remember what she said.

It wasn't fright that makes me forget. I don't know what it is. I can even remember another thing – when she caught hold of me with her clamp-like hand, I remember my wrist trembling in her grip, and thinking to myself how solid and strong her grip was. I was vibrating against something solid, so to speak.

But what she *said* to me – what really *did* happen during the few seconds before Father and Beth came in – well, I just cannot bring it back. I keep searching my memory but it is no good.

Father and Beth came in very excited, both talking at once. They said that the UFO had just whisked away and gone without a trace, etc., etc. Grinny was full of old ladyish excitement – she kept saying, 'Oh, I *wish* I could have seen it!' and things like that.

I was still feeling a bit furry or fuzzy and didn't say much. A week ago I had to fight Stannard, who is a very good boxer. He doesn't hit all that hard but he just seems to get through to you and you can't get through to him. Anyhow, we fought the usual three rounds and he of course was announced the winner and I went back to the centre of the ring to shake hands and so on and so on. What I am getting at is this: after being hit so many times by him,

I was quite cheerful and normal and all the rest of it but I did feel a bit cloudy; as if I was watching myself going through the actions.

And that is just how I felt now. As if I was watching myself being Timothy Carpenter.

In the end, everyone went to bed and the house became quiet. I lay awake for a long time. I was trying to work it all out. I could remember seeing Grinny in that horrible luminous state, with her eyes lit up and her teeth glinting. Remember it? – I couldn't forget it! But then what? Had she wiped me out – my memory, I mean? And if she had, why hadn't she done it better? Why leave me remembering the luminous bit?

Here is another funny thing. When I try and write about my thoughts, as in the preceding paragraph, I get a sort of mental itch. I just cannot get going. To sort it all out. And I keep getting different ideas about what happened and didn't happen. Mind you, it is very late and I didn't sleep properly last night of course. Yet I don't feel sleepy. I wish I could get it going. Unscramble it.

Feb. 25

Talked to Beth about Grinny, but didn't tell her very much as she is already hysterical enough about the subject. I just said, 'It was very odd that night before you came into the room.' She kept saying, 'I told you so, there's something awful about her, I told you so,' etc., etc. I kept the pot boiling without letting it boil over – in other words, I kept picking at her, trying to find out her opinions about Grinny. I got her to the point where she ticked off all the things she doesn't like about Grinny. She was ticking them off on her fingers, mouth pursed and her eyes completely circular. Her list amounts to this:

1. G isn't real. Metal bones, etc. She doesn't smell right (or doesn't smell at all).
2. She is frightened of electricity. I really cannot see this one at all. Many perfectly reasonable people are frightened of electricity, gas, losing their keys, going out without their spectacles, etc., etc., etc., etc. Beth, however, says it is *sinister*.
3. She asks stupid questions or makes stupid comments, yet –
4. She is not stupid at all. In fact she is very lively minded.
5. She keeps *looking* at you, especially when you have no clothes on.
6. She never *says* anything, she only talks.

Points 5 and 6 are fairly new to me. Point 5 – she keeps looking at you . . . I asked Beth what she meant. She was very embarrassed (so was I) but she got it out in pieces in the end. She said that Grinny looked at her all over when she was in the swimming pool and looked at me too. I said Nonsense, but Beth said, 'No, it's true.

She had a good old *look*. And she asks questions about Sex!'

I couldn't help laughing at this, but Beth flew into a temper and said, 'It's all very well for you to laugh, but it's *true*. I know it's ridiculous, but she *does*. She wants to know about me and your dim friend Mac – oh, go on, laugh, but he is fond of me because he hasn't got a sister of his own and his mother isn't all that nice to him and he wants someone pretty *just to smile at him* –'

(I interrupt this flood of Bethism to point out that I think she is absolutely and 100 per cent RIGHT. If Mac could, he would live here and be a Carpenter. His mother is a cold fish and his father is worse and he does fancy Beth because he sees in her something he hasn't got at home. So WAW, as usual.)

Beth went on to say (this time I won't try and write her own words as they were so rambling) that Grinny looks at Beth and me and anyone else as if they were foreign bodies. She wants to see how they are made, why they are made like that, what effect it has on them and their behaviour and so on and so on.

It sounds like nonsense to me but that is what she says. And the puzzling thing is this: though I disagree with Beth simply on logic, I *feel* Beth is right. And then, what about the dogs? – the ones mating on the lawn?

Beth's point 6 was that Grinny never says anything, she only talks. This is absolutely true and quite obvious. She is like the wise old owl who lived in an oak, the more it saw the less it spoke. But I cannot see that it matters much, there are many people who go through life 'not committing themselves'. You hear two women in a bus, one does the talking and the other one just says, 'She never!', 'He didn't!', 'Well, it goes to show!', 'Fancy that, then!' This woman is the Receiver and the other one is the Sender. If Grinny chooses to play the part of Receiver, that's her affair.

Yet, once again, I can see what Beth means. Grinny never tells you anything about herself, about Granny, about the old days (most old people love talking about the old days) or about anything at all.

In the end, I got into an argument with Beth, which is always fatal because she cannot argue. She just gets passionate or stubborn. This time she became both at once and shouted, 'You don't take any notice of me, you think I'm just stupid. Well, if I'm stupid, so's Grinny, only worse! What about Grinny and the cast-iron conker?'

I admit I had quite forgotten it. It happened only last night and did not seem important at the time. But Beth thought it important.

We were having dinner and Mac was with us. Mac and I were talking about the crazes at school – the crazes that sweep the whole place for anything from a week to a term, it might be anything at all with the juniors. I said to Mac, 'I've still got All-time Champion, the cast-iron conker!' He said, 'You haven't? What, Old Cast-Iron himself? I don't believe you!' etc., etc. Grinny said, 'I don't quite understand . . . What is a conker?'

I was a bit surprised, but told her. She said, 'Oh, of course, conkers!'

I went upstairs and got it. Mac said, 'It's not quite the conker it was, it looks clapped out. But its soul goes marching on.'

Grinny was peering at it so I said, 'It's unique, Aunt Emma, it came from the only cast-iron conker tree in the world – just over there, by the bottom of our garden! Every conker warranted gen-u-ine solid cast iron!'

She reached out her hand and I gave her Old Cast-Iron. She looked at it for some time, turning it over and over, and then, quite shyly, said, 'I don't think it really *is* cast iron, Tim . . . it seems to me to be made of vegetable matter, not cast iron at all!'

Then, poker-faced, she handed it back to me.

Was she serious or wasn't she? Beth swears she was. We (Beth, Mac and I) have formed the GCG Council to explore Grinny's Credibility Gaps. We are going to do it conscientiously, systematically and artistically, so that we can find out who's fooling who (whom).

The object is to discover (a) Is she suffering from lapses of memory – or (b) has she just a very dry sense of humour, so that she pretends to believe impossible things, or not know things she ought to know? (c) Just how far can we push her ignorance, innocence, cunning, dry humour or whatever it is? (d) And if it turns out that there is something odd about her, how can we learn what particular oddity it is?

To fulfil these objectives, we are going deliberately to stage impossibilities between the three of us. That is, we are going to contrive situations that she must react to.

When she reacts, we can judge her reactions. When we judge her reactions, we can also come to some sort of conclusion about her 'realness' or the opposite.

Feb. 27

The first exposure of Grinny's Credibility Gap came this evening. It was quite unplanned. It happened after dinner. Mac was not with us which is a pity, but he can take our word for what happened – it was all very simple.

We were talking about last Christmas – what a panic it had been, our presents, etc., etc. Beth was talking about her school nativity play and she was getting very enthusiastic about it in a rather showing-off sort of way (she had been chosen to play the Virgin Mary and didn't intend us to forget about her starring role). She was being all little-girlish and starry eyed, rambling on and on, until she came to the point where she said these words –

'– And then they put the Baby in my arms and of course I cuddled it and the funny thing was that that was the first time I'd ever really and truly felt like a real, proper mother!'

This was the only part of Beth's sickening speech that Grinny heard – she had been upstairs and was now down with us. Anyhow, Grinny leaned forward and said, 'A baby, Beth . . . ? But I never knew! Where is it?'

Beth was thrown for a moment by the sheer idiocy of this question. Then I saw that cunning look come on her face. She said, 'Oh, Aunt Emma, you can't expect me to start having babies yet. I mean, it's physically impossible *for at least another year or so*.'

To which Grinny replied, perfectly seriously, 'Yes, of course.'

Beth said, hammering it home, and glancing at me to make sure I was getting the point, '*When I am nine. Or even ten*.'

Grinny made no answer in particular. She just made some sort of noise of agreement and fumbled with her cigarettes.

Let us recap.

Here we have Beth saying, in effect, 'I have had a baby' (at the age of eight) and Grinny saying, 'Let me see it.' Beth then says, 'No, you are mistaken, girls cannot have babies until they are nine or even ten.' Grinny does not quarrel with this. In fact, Grinny does not do anything except look lost and confused.

What are we supposed to make of that?

March 10

News from GCG.

The next test situation we put Grinny to came about of its own accord. We (the whole family) were talking about the UFO we had seen and Grinny was saying she wished she had seen it, how terrible to have missed such an extraordinary event, etc. Beth looked at the clock and said, ‘Oh dear, you’ve just missed some beauties.’ Now, I knew what she meant, so did everyone but Grinny. Beth meant that half an hour previously, the TV programme LONESPACE had been on the air – and if Grinny had been watching that, she would have seen all kinds of superdeluxe spacecraft, UFOs, etc., because that is what the programme is all about. She would also have known that the spacecraft are carefully made models and the actors are puppets, etc., etc.

But Grinny did not know this, she took Beth’s remark at face value. Grinny said – very sharply – ‘Where? When? What spacecraft? What did you see?’

By luck, I managed to catch Beth’s eye for a split second and she played it straight when she answered. She said to Grinny, ‘Oh, the sky is absolutely full of them, Grinny –’

‘At certain times of year –’ I put in. I meant, of course, when the LONESPACE series is running.

‘That’s right, at certain times of year,’ Beth went on. ‘Tim and I love watching them, don’t we, Tim?’

She said this without a blink, which was clever of her. But then she is always quick to catch on. Grinny was by now taking it still more seriously. I have never seen her look more alert and determined. She said, ‘How long have you two been seeing them? What did they look like?’

‘Two or three years,’ Beth replied. ‘That’s right, isn’t it, Tim?’

I said, ‘No, even longer than that.’

Grinny rapped out, ‘But that is impossible! I mean, it

is most unlikely . . . What were they like?' She seemed really upset.

I let Beth answer, because I could see she was in the mood. She did it perfectly, picking at a tuft of wool in the carpet and not looking at all interested – just matter-of-fact. 'Well, some of them have a lot of jet things at the back, whole clusters of them,' she began. 'Those ones are often pointed, rather like a dart, and then there's the jets at the back with smoky stuff coming out –'

'Have you seen spaceships like that?' Grinny asked me, leaning forward in her chair.

'Oh yes. I think they must be the interstellar ones – the really big craft, carrying lots of people – if they *are* people . . . But then there are several other sorts, aren't there, Beth?'

'Sometimes you get the flattish ones, rather like rays – you know, manta rays, the fish – they go much slower. And they don't leave jet trails, they just *go*.'

'And then there are the container-shaped ones,' I cut in. 'Very elaborate sort of tin cans, some of them linked together with a sort of lattice of steelwork. And you might see ones like huge rings with the living quarters in the middle –'

Grinny was drinking all this in. Once or twice her lips moved as if she were about to say 'But –'. She asked several more questions about When, Where, How Long, but we managed to answer them without giving the game away. She was getting more and more tensed up.

In the end, Mum shouted for Beth to lay the table so

she got up and I said, 'Oh, I suppose I'd better help,' and went with her. This was just as well, because Grinny would soon have forced us to say we saw all these wonderful spacecraft in a TV programme called LONESPACE. As it was, we left her looking very worried indeed.

I am worried too. It is the same old problem. Here is an old woman who can be told by two children that they have often seen things in the sky – elaborate spacecraft of various sorts – and take it all seriously. Very seriously. She was *worried*. I remember that she was particularly worried when we said we had been seeing them *for years* – that was when she said, 'But that is impossible!' She looked really worked up then.

Continued tomorrow, too tired tonight.

March 11

The other trick we played on Grinny worked so well that it means the end of GCG. It worked too well.

This one did not happen by itself, Mac, Beth and I arranged it to test Grinny's reaction to electricity. You will remember that she has always been peculiar about electricity and we wanted to find out more.

So Mac brought a Wimshurst machine to our house. This is the antediluvian device with two big contra-rotating wheels and sticks with knobs on the end of them sticking out. You wind the handle, the two wheels turn, static electricity is generated – and you get exciting blue sparks zipping about between the two knobs. My father was delighted when he saw it, he said they had one at his school when he was a boy, it was supposed to teach the lads about electricity. He chuckled a lot and wound the handle faster and faster trying to get bigger and better sparks. He said he was amazed to know that such a load of old nonsense still existed, where did we find it, etc. Mac told him that it was mouldering away in a storeroom in the school, which is quite true.

Anyhow, we waited until Father and Mum were somewhere else and carted the ridiculous contraption into the drawing room, where Grinny was. Then we started turning the handle slowly and chattering to each other, hoping to attract Grinny's attention.

Sure enough she started asking all the right questions and we gave her some rather wrong answers. Mac said it was a bacon-slicer. I said, 'It's not, don't be such a fool. Have you ever seen a bacon-slicer like this, Grinny? Really . . . !' She said no she never had. Beth then said, as arranged, 'What *does* a bacon-slicer look like, Grinny?' and Grinny gave an evasive answer. I don't think she has ever noticed a bacon-slicer in her life, which is odd, because big shiny slicers used to be a focal point of grocery shops – we still have a beauty in our shop.

I then piped up and said, 'Don't be such morons, it's a Wimshurst machine. It generates electricity.'

Grinny looked uneasy. I added, 'The voltages are very high – thousands of volts.'

Grinny looked still worse.

I said, 'Wind her up and see if we can't get a spark or something.'

Grinny said, 'Please, children, I would prefer that you took that machine elsewhere.'

We pretended not to hear and wound away like mad. Soon we had long snaky sparks going and Grinny was trying to look blank. The sparks were reflecting in the wainscoting, the whole corner of the room was flickering blue.

As arranged, Mac said, 'There must be some power behind all that! I mean, just look at the sparks!'

I said, 'Nonsense, no power, just volts.'

He said, 'Well, I bet you wouldn't put your hand through the spark!'

I pretended to be half afraid but boastful. In the end, after a lot of 'I will!' and 'You won't', I did put my hand in the spark and got the tickling I expected. I then made a great song and dance about it – jumped up in 'agony' but said, 'Told you so, didn't hurt a bit, couldn't hurt a flea,' etc. – and eventually made Mac and even Beth be as 'brave' as I had been. Grinny was getting very uneasy all this time. I saw her put her hand to her face in an uncertain dabbing sort of way, get half up in the chair, open her mouth without saying anything, etc. She never changed colour, however. She never does.

We pretended to become boisterous and over-excited. We pulled the machine about on the floor so it got closer to her, I then lifted it on to a table in the middle of the room and started twirling the handle again. Then we began whispering and at last Beth said, 'I bet she would! You would, wouldn't you, Grinny?'

Grinny said, rather jerkily, 'I would what?'

'Put your hand in the spark! It feels super! All tingly and funny!'

Grinny said, 'Certainly not, no, no. Certainly not.'

But Beth was well into her enthusiastic TV Kiddie routine and was saying, 'Oh, but it's marvellous, it's fantastic, we all did it, oh do be a sport, I told them you would! –' and Mac and I lifted the machine off the table and brought it to a table next to Grinny's chair. She stood up and made a sort of noise but Mac pretended not to notice and wound the handle to make the sparks come and Grinny backed away and fell back in her chair again.

At this moment, Father came in.

What happened next is obvious enough without being. written out in full. The words Yob, Brat, Yahoo, Bloody Impertinence, etc., etc., resounded freely through the ancestral halls. Mum came in. She sized up the situation in an instant by forcefully mentioning the word teasing, which is precisely what we had been doing. We had been teasing Grinny in an attempt to get an indicative response.

When Mum had quite finished with us (Father standing behind her, jetting in the occasional expletives) we were feeling not only thwarted – for we had never finished our experiment – but also humiliated. It was Grinny who came to the rescue.

She said, 'I don't think they were teasing so much as testing! Don't you think that possible, my dear? An old lady like me . . . No, I'm sure they meant no harm. And no harm is done, none at all.'

'There are a few tests I can think of myself,' said Father. 'How strong is a walking stick? How flexible is a slipper? How sensitive is a backside?' This sort of talk means that he is beginning to enjoy a situation: it is when he is too choked to do anything but utter monosyllables that you run risk of lasting physical damage.

Beth now rounded things off neatly and with excruciating bad taste by saying, in effect, 'Oh! We are truly repentant! And all too conscious of shortcomings! We are but little children weak, not born to any high degree, forgive us our trespasses and never again shall we stray from the path of rectitude,' etc., etc., etc. ad nauseam. Not that she spoke these words, all she needs is her eyelashes and a voluntary compression of the tear glands. What she did say was something about us not teasing, just testing (weally and twuly) and if Grinny wanted to test us right back, that was only fair.

To our surprise, Grinny took this up. She said that would be fun, she would like to test us, was there a game called Memory or something?

From then on, the evening became a sort of Mental Agility Olympic Games. We played that stupid game with a tray – someone goes out and loads the tray with mixed things, all listed, then the tray is brought in and everyone tries to remember as many things as possible. Father always wins at this.

Grinny won.

Next we played the card game in which the cards are put on the table any old how, face up – then turned face down – and each person tries to name, from memory, the card he chooses to pick up. If you're right you just keep going, and the person with most cards wins.

Grinny won.

When I write 'Grinny won', I don't merely mean that she won. She decimated – obliterated – smashed us. Her performance was not merely outstanding but phenomenal. Her memory wasn't just retentive, it was Total Recall.

March 12

When you think back on it, these memory games we played – in fact everything that happened that evening – proved yet again that Beth was right. The trick with the electricity is no longer important; we expected her to be frightened, she was frightened, QED.

But the memory games are another matter. What I-think happened is that she simply was not aware of her extraordinariness when she infallibly got the right card or remembered each and every item on the tray. To her, it was just normal practice, just as it is normal for a cat to leap from floor to mantelpiece and land up there without disturbing a single object. Humans can't jump five or six times their own height and land like a computer-programmed feather: very few humans could compete with Grinny when it comes to remembering things.

But now look at Grinny's contradictions! Here is a person who cannot remember conkers – but can remember every card in the pack.

You can go on like this forever – contradiction after contradiction in the things she *can* do and *can't* do.

Add all the rest of the extraordinary things about Grinny (including my parents' relationship with her – why do they never question her about leaving, about our grandmother, about anything?) and you come to this:

Beth is right – Grinny isn't real.

But you also come to another thing or two.

IF SHE IS NOT HUMAN, WHAT IS SHE?

WHY IS SHE HERE?

WHAT IS SHE FOR?

Diary

Book Two

April 10

It's late at night and perhaps that has something to do with it. But I've been re-reading my diaries, looking back to those days in late Feb and early March and thinking – well, what *have* I been thinking? 'Cor!' just about sums it up. Cor, fancy being so nice-minded about Grinny. Cor, fancy not seeing more clearly just how right Beth has been all along with her WAW sort of reasoning. Cor, fancy sitting down and solemnly writing out all the things that make Grinny different from us – and still avoiding coming to the point, coming out with it by saying, 'Grinny! You're a freak and I forgive you for that. But you're a dangerous freak. You're a threat, a menace, a monster with a capital M, like Movie Monster, Murdering Monster, Man-eating Monster.'

No, it's worse than that. You're here for something. At the moment, you're just a sort of suitcase and nobody notices the ticking noise. Later – WHOOMPF! – and people screaming and bleeding, broken glass and blood on the pavement. 'Oh yes, Officer, I saw this feller with the suitcase sure enough, I saw him plain so I did, but how was *I* to know . . . !'

But I can't say that, I can't pretend any more. I have-seen Grinny plain. I've seen her for a long time. I've seen my own parents not see her, so to speak. I've listened to Beth, but not listening properly because she's just my kid sister. I've been going around pretending to myself that it's all perfectly OK, mustn't make a fuss, doncherknow, not British. Like that story Father tells about the war, during the Blitz. When the raid started they could actually hear the bombers overhead so they all went into the hotel shelter – the story happened in a London hotel. But even in the shelter they could hear the bombers overhead going VOOM-er VOOM-er, VO O M-er, and then they heard bombs falling. Everyone in the shelter was very quiet. Then there was the most colossal bang and plaster fell. Then there was another bang, even worse, the lights went out, they could hear the building falling down above them. Still nobody said anything. At last an American woman's voice, thoroughly bad-tempered and disgusted, yelled out, 'For chrissake, WHY DOESN'T SOMEBODY SCREAM?'

As Father says, it was funny at the time, but the really funny thing was that the woman was right. It's not natural not to react.

And it's the same with Grinny. It's not natural for us just to sit here and say, 'Oh, isn't it strange, here's this sinister freak come to stay with us for ever and ever, she lights up at night and seems to have something to do with unidentified flying objects, please pass the muffins.' We've got to get at her, find out more, look for her weak spots, discover what she's all about.

Talking about muffins, that song keeps going through my mind. I can't remember it properly. It's on an old record of Father's, it starts off something like

> The King of the Cannibal Islands
> Invited me to tea.
> And there at the top of the menu
> Was ME!

That's the position we're in here. At the top of the menu, waiting to be eaten. But whether we're going to be served boiled, fried or just docile, I don't know. We must find out, we must.

I suppose I'm writing all this strong-arm stuff just to nerve myself for what's ahead. It's so still and cold and calm tonight. You look out into the garden and there it is, quite still and bleached by the moonlight. Nothing moves. Everything seems to be waiting, waiting, waiting. Waiting for what? For lights in the sky and a thundering noise and lots of little green men getting out of a spaceship, then walking up the garden, very fast and determined? I'd believe that, I'd believe anything at this moment. But, there's nothing out there, nothing at all, not even a cat or two. Not a thing moves.

It's the same in my room. I mean, I'm here, I can move. I stood in front of the mirror a minute ago and pulled faces at myself. I winked one eye, then put out my tongue, then raised an imaginary hat to my reflection. They used to do a gag on that in the old silent movies, you'd have the villain feeling very suspicious – he thinks he's being watched and of course he is; the chief comic, made up to look just like the villain, is in the room with him – so the villain goes up to an open space, a connecting door for instance. He takes it for a mirror. He starts going through all sorts of ridiculous motions. And the comic, pretending to be his reflection in the 'mirror', imitates everything he does. It gets funnier and funnier because you're sure the comic can't keep it up. And in the end he doesn't, he makes a wrong move. It really is very funny, terrific.

And yet when I was doing it just now – making faces at my reflection – it didn't seem funny at all, just sort of frozen and waiting. The whole room feels like that. The whole house does. As if something was going to happen, not now, not just yet, but soon enough. The house has felt like that ever since Grinny came. No, that's not true – ever since Beth started her hate act. If Beth hadn't come out and said it, wouldn't anyone else have done so?

I wonder what Grinny's doing now? I wonder if she really does sleep in some way, like we do? Or is she just lying there on the bed, ticking over like my clock? It makes a hell of a racket, no wonder I can't sleep. If you can't sleep, it's better to get up and do something, lying in bed listening to your pulses doesn't do any good. So

I got up and wrote in my diary. In the morning, of course, everything will be the same as ever – Mum yelling the time at me and sending Beth up to get me out of bed and Father losing things and the trees moving again in the garden.

But even in the morning, there'll still be Grinny.

We've got to do something about her or *to* her. It isn't just the night and the quietness, I've got this feeling that there isn't much time. We must think of something to *do*.

April 13

Tried 'Eyes Right' on Grinny. It worked. Could be the breakthrough . . . ?

April 14

We tried it again today – Eyes Right – and it worked just as well as before. It works on Grinny just the same way it works on anyone normal, only more so. I remember Mac and I once made Beth almost hysterical when we kept Eyes Right up for a whole afternoon. The effect on Grinny is even more dramatic: it doesn't just upset her, it seems to throw her right off her tracks. Even I would call the effect sinister.

The beauty of Eyes Right is that no outsider can really be positive you're doing it. So you cannot be accused of anything. Not that I would mind much if someone did accuse me. I am sick and tired of the whole Grinny situation and the sooner we can bring it out into the open the better. Beth was right all along. It only remains to find out just what she was right about.

Mac wanted to make what he called an Elegant Variation and do it to the left instead of the right, but I said no, we'll stick to Eyes Right. It must always be done the same way so that the effect builds up.

So after dinner, when we were alone with her, we gave her the treatment. We all stared at a point just one foot to the right of Grinny's head whenever we spoke to her, instead of looking her in the eye in the usual way.

We opened the proceedings by a minute or so of silent Eyes Right. Then Beth said, 'I did like the pudding, didn't you, Grinny?'

As before, Grinny was shifting in her seat, trying to get into our line of sight. She was twitching towards the place where our eyes were all focused. She said, 'I have a slight headache. I am not well tonight.'

Mac said, 'Can I get you an aspirin?' She tried to catch his eye, but couldn't of course. She bobbed to the right and said, 'Oh no, it is nothing serious.'

'Let me get you one,' said I. She tried to focus me but couldn't.

Beth said, 'Is it very bad, Grinny?' and Grinny was obliged to look at Beth . . . who was looking where Grinny wasn't. Anyhow, it went on and on until she started dabbing her hand towards her face as if trying to reassure herself that she was there.

Then the next stage set in. She began to lose her temper. She became waspish, just like the last time. She said something about 'behaving oddly' which was a mistake – Beth got to her feet and went nearer Grinny, still looking one foot to the right of her eyes, and said, 'O Grinny, do let me get you an aspirin, you must have such a bad headache.' Of course, the nearer you get to the person, the worse the effect is. Grinny started to twitch her mouth and shift her head. But as usual she never changed colour. Nor did she breathe faster.

In the end, the same amazing thing happened as before.

She seemed to go into a funny state where she was only half with us. She started speaking in 'Grinnish' – the very fast twittering sound, much faster than a real person, could talk, all mixed up with ordinary English. Her eyes were not focusing, they were flittering about very slightly. I am going to try and write down what she says in this condition:

I do not know why they you impolite so very rude inconsiderate mean no harm (Grinnish, for some seconds) *perfectly calm such charming children not at all could not possibly guess* (Grinnish) *look here here* (very fast) *look at me me me the girl knows nothing everything* (Grinnish) *it was a mistake oh dear me quite a serious mistake a mistake but none of us is perfect not a vital mistake but a mistake* (Grinnish) *too late to remedy now knowledge is power look at me LOOK AT ME* (Grinnish) . . .

These are not her exact words, they could not be. She was gabbling, sometimes very fast. She accelerated until she lapsed into the twittering of Grinnish, then came out of it back into our language.

The things I have got right, however, are important. The feeling is right, I am sure. She seemed to be practising clichés, set phrases – 'none of us is perfect' is obviously a phrase she had picked up and saved for future use in ordinary conversation.

It is important that she said, 'Look at me, look at me.' She must have had at least a suspicion of what we were doing to her with our Eyes Right trick – but she did not know the countermove; she didn't know how ordinary people would behave (Father, for instance, would just have said, 'All right, joke over!').

There is another possibility, though. Perhaps she never knew that we were playing a trick at all. Perhaps she thought that something was wrong with her own body – that it had slipped in space.

This could be the answer. I can easily imagine myself, wearing the skin and bones of an alien being, finding things just a little difficult now and then. You have been briefed on every possible thing – your bosses instruct you that you show you are pleased by bending up your mouth so . . . the word for that is 'smile' . . . that when you sit down, your legs must not straddle apart if you are a lady . . . that you do not touch people or let them touch you very much – though sometimes a human may come up to you, take hold of *this* hand, the *right* hand, and shake it up and down. Or even press his or her food-hole against your face! – a kiss.

Right. Fine. You learn all these millions of crazy rules – you have a fantastic memory – but you still make mistakes. For instance, you *reveal* your fantastic memory, which is itself an error. You appear to believe impossibilities. And when the Eyes Right game is played on you, you know something is wrong, *but you don't know what*! You think, 'It could be me, I've slipped sideways in my alien skeleton and skin!' Or you think, 'This must be one of the things these foreigners sometimes do . . . I dare not make any comment.' You could react in any of a dozen ways, all of them wrong.

I will write down what I think happens to Grinny when we give her the Eyes Right treatment. It is this:

She feels the same uneasiness, even fear, that humans feel – that a dog can feel. The fear turns to a sort of panic. Then the panic, in Grinny's case, turns to a hypnotic condition of some sort. She is not only feeling – literally – out of place: she feels out of character, out of mind. Again literally, she does not know where she is.

And that is why she lapses into Grinnish – *which I assume to be her own language.*

And serve the old hag right. It's only justice. She says, '*You remember me*,' to adult humans, and puts them into some sort of coma. We do an Eyes Right on her, and accidentally discover that we can do much the same thing to her – put her in a coma.

Serve her right.

April 18

Got Grinny in the garden, on her own. We manoeuvred her nearer and nearer the swimming-pool motor to soften her up (fear of electricity) then started the Eyes Right, all three of us. It was faster this time, she tranced v. quickly without much resistance. Strange feeling in open air watching 'old lady' gibbering and squeaking then talking polite old-lady English.

(Am writing this fast because something is going to happen, soon, and I want to leave a record – but everything is in a mess because of Mac's hand and the big row so must scribble.)

Beth looking very mean and purse-mouthed, obviously determined to have a go but not knowing how. Grinny babbling. Mac accidentally started Grinny off by trying to get through the trance to her. He said, 'Tell us about spaceships, or something but no reply so he said, 'You can tell me, Grinny, it's Mac, *you remember me.*' (!!!)

This is Grinny's own trigger phrase and it made a bang all right – she suddenly came right out of her trance, snap! and looked about her for a split second then fastened on Mac and said, 'I beg your pardon?'

Then she reached out her hand and took Mac's hand.

He jerked. She seized it. He went white straight away, she must have hurt him. She looked at him with her mouth working but not saying anything then at last she said, 'It is not polite . . . It is not polite to . . . Not polite . . .' While she was saying this, I saw Mac's hand go dead white. The pressure from her horrible little steel claws. He jerked. She let it go for an instant, but then grabbed again and caught his thumb and he let out a yelp. She was still trying to find something to say, she said, 'Most upset, cannot understand . . .' and Mac had tears coming out of his eyes from the pain. I don't think she knew she was putting on so much pressure. He made a sort of snatch trying to get thumb away but she snatched too and there was a dull click and Mac screamed and went down on his knees.

Then she did let go, she looked puzzled and uncertain. Beth went tearing in hitting G. with fists and screaming and screaming. Mac still on ground doubled up white as a sheet clutching his hand and saying, 'Bloody hell, bloody hell.'

Beth's yelling heard by Mum, who opened window and shouted for Father. They came out running and everyone was explaining things at the same time. Father made everyone shut up, turned to Grinny for explanation. She said something about the children teasing but Beth tore in again. Father lost temper and hauled her away calling her a brat, etc., etc., if ever any of us behaved like this again he'd chuck us out of house. (Mac ignored – nobody knew his thumb was bust yet.)

Beth turned on Father and screeched, 'Why don't you chuck her out? Why is she still here?' She turned to Mum and asked the same thing – beseeching is the word, Beth was begging them to get rid of Grinny but of course they had the old block, the hypnosis or whatever it is, they *cannot* answer such questions, Grinny has got their minds tied up.

All quiet now, ha ha that's a laugh, all quietly murderous. Mac has been driven to doctor, then home, thumb bust. Beth with me. Like a caged tigress. Wants to kill Grinny, then parents, then anyone handy. Grinny not giving a damn either way because Father and Mum cannot be reached by us about anything concerning Grinny. No doubt she's doing crossword and looking sweet.

After all that twittering I wonder if –

April 19

Yesterday's entry ended 'I wonder if –' Then I had to go downstairs to be bawled at by Father, who is pathetically determined to be master in his own house, etc., etc. If only he knew! But it's not his fault, of course, so I just stood there and let it roll.

What was I wondering if? I was wondering if, after all the Grinnish twittering of yesterday, there would be some response from Out There, the Wild Blue Yonder. So I rang up poor Mac, who is in agony (I got my thumb yanked right back once and know how it hurts) and asked him – if he couldn't sleep during the night – to look out of the window now and then. He took the point at once, but said nothing would happen. I said it might, because things were so obviously coming to a climax and Grinny might need advice.

I set my alarm for two in the morning. I woke up when it rang, set it for three and went to sleep again. I slept through it, though, but luckily woke up at ten to four and set the clock for four-thirty. If I had woken up at three as planned and then set the clock for four I would have missed the whole thing. As it was, I could not have timed it better.

It was there all right. The sky was cloudy and sometimes you could only see a glow behind cloud. But then the clouds scudded by and I saw it plainly, just the same as before. The same shape, the same lights, the same way of taking up a new position in a sudden, instant-acceleration rush. The same spacecraft as before.

I got out of bed quietly and quickly. I did not need anyone else, of course. Except that I was very frightened. I crept down the corridor and got to Grinny's room. When I looked through the keyhole I could see the glow. I started opening the door, turning the handle a millimetre at a time.

Just when I'd got the handle turned (but I was still outside the door) she woke up. Her lighting system dimmed and I heard the bed creak as she sat up. I could just imagine her doing it – straight up from the hips, as if she was hinged in the middle, like the last time.

The difference between the last time and this time was that this time I recognized the sound coming from her mouth even though I was nowhere near her. It wasn't my pulses zizzing and pumping, as I had thought the other time. It was her, Grinny, giving out with some Grinnish. She was twittering to the spacecraft and no doubt it was twittering back to her.

Then I heard something I had not expected at all – her voice speaking in plain English. An old lady's voice, a nice, well-bred old lady's voice, saying something very old ladyish.

'Quite suitable,' she said. 'I see little difficulty. The sooner the better.'

There was a brief pause. I heard some twittering, not Grinny's. It must have been the reply from the spacecraft, it was not at the same pitch as hers.

Then Grinny said, in a low calm voice, 'You may come in now, Timothy.'

April 19 (continued)

I am doing this on my typewriter as there is so much to write and typing is faster. I am taking several carbons and will think later on about where to send them, although I don't suppose it will do the least good.

Which is just what Grinny thinks. 'You may come in now, Timothy,' she said – so I went in. Or tottered in. I could not stop myself shaking. It was not like being frightened, it was more like going to some large and respectable person who you knew was about to tell you in a very correct voice that you were going to die in five weeks precisely, or be expelled from school for some disgusting crime which would be written up in the local papers.

She switched on the little light, settled back on her pillows and said, 'You can sit on the edge of my bed if you wish. Are you cold?'

I said, 'No.'

She said, 'Neither am I. I do not suffer from heat or cold or toothache or any such things, as I think you know. Even if you break my wrist, I feel no pain. And it mends itself almost instantly, which is *most* convenient.'

I said, 'Mac feels pain. You broke his thumb.'

She said, 'You sound upset. If you like, you may break a finger of mine. For Mac.'

She held out her old hand with the fingers spread. '*Any* finger,' she said.

I made some sound or other and flinched back from her.

She said, 'You are afraid, and quite rightly. It is quite correct that you should be afraid, quite in order. You must not mind, Timothy. You must get *used* to it, indeed you must. The strangeness of it all . . . You must accustom yourself to it.'

She still had her hand stretched out. Then she took hold of one of her fingers with her other hand and gave a sudden twist. The finger she broke just split open. The skin parted and it split open. The finger was twisted and it was all out of line with the other fingers. There were little metal bones inside the split skin and some of them stuck out, glinting.

I thought I was going to be sick and was floundering about rather. She soon put a stop to that, however. She said, 'There! You must accustom yourself to it, it is a fact of life, Timothy. I am a new fact of all human life.'

I was still trying to edge away but she grabbed my wrist with her hand – the one with the broken finger – and pulled me towards her. Her hand was like a steel vice with plastic jaws. Its power was awful and unbelievable. She twisted her hand and my wrist so that the broken finger was right in front of my face and I was staring at it.

'Tell me when you are used to it,' she said.

I said, 'All right, all right, I'm *used* to it,' and she let me go. I wish my voice had sounded different.

'Better soon,' she said, almost coyly, looking at her finger. I could not look.

'Poor Mac,' she said. 'That was an accident. You children were very naughty and I found your game most confusing. Looking at me like that . . . Or rather, not looking at me. But there we are, boys will be boys. That is one of your sayings, is it not? It is, isn't it? You must speak when you are spoken to.'

I said, 'Yes.'

'Consider my position,' she went on. 'Think of the difficulties! Imprisoned in this ridiculous artificial body of mine. Even more ridiculous if it were real . . . One must not think of oneself, your difficulties too are considerable. I would not like to be a human, Timothy, really I would not.'

'I wouldn't like to be you,' I said. I wanted to sound defiant but it came out wrong. Sullen.

'A new fact of all human life,' she said. 'This is what you have to face. Things are going to change, Timothy. Change soon, change a great deal. You must accustom yourself. You are young and therefore adaptable.'

'What about my parents?'

'They will find a part to play when things have changed. But they will not be aware of the change, Timothy, that is the important difference. You will know. They will not. But I think you have guessed that.'

'You got at – hypnotized – them. Why not us?'

'See if you can guess,' she said. Again, her voice had that horrible flirty ring to it, the tone of voice you heard when respectable old ladies try to wheedle shop assistants. Perhaps she did not mean her voice to sound that way, but it did and it made everything worse.

Anyhow, she asked me to guess the reason and I replied, 'I suppose you thought that children were too stupid to do you any harm. To put up a fight.'

She said, 'Yes, that was among the reasons, Timothy. *Among* them. After all, it is very difficult for the young. One hardly expects grown people to listen to the arguments of children, let alone allow children to influence grown-up policies and actions . . .'

She left a long questioning pause and I felt I was supposed to say something. I said, 'Well, what are the other reasons?'

She replied, 'I think you have guessed them, for you are

quite intelligent – no, very intelligent, far more intelligent than I would have supposed. Very intelligent.'

I said, 'Thank you kindly, Ma'am,' trying to be sarcastic. But of course this was above her head and she took no notice.

'The most important reason,' she went on, 'is this. When one tries an experiment, one must have what you people might call a "control" – that is, a thing unaffected by the conditions created by the experiment itself. For instance, Timothy, if I were to enter your classroom at school and say to the teacher, "Carry on as usual, take no notice of me, I am merely a visiting inspector!" the mere fact of my presence would be enough to ensure that the teacher and the pupils could *not* carry on as usual.'

'So if you hypnotized everyone, adults and children alike, you'd never know how humans really do behave?' I said. But I was thinking about something else.

'Quite so. We left the children alone. First, because we thought they could do nothing to obstruct us; and second because we had to have free, natural, unaltered actions and responses to observe.'

'Responses to what?' I said. I was still not really listening. I was thinking hard.

'Oh, to anything, anything at all. Everything. After all, a human being is a human being, whether it is aged six or sixty.'

'So we are all the same, are we?' I said.

'Oh, certainly not!' she said. 'That is one of the *many* things I have discovered that surprised me. You are *very* different from each other. Far more different than *we* are, in the place where I come from.'

'So all your prying and peeking in the swimming pool wasn't wasted, then.'

'Oh, how very sensitive you are about that!' she laughed. 'It interested me greatly, your response to my prying and peeking. I looked up some words in a dictionary and tried to make a rhyme about human sex. "Prudery, nudity, rudery, crudity . . ."'

'I am glad you find it all so funny,' I said, trying to sound dignified.

'The *facts* are not very interesting or amusing,' she said. 'But human *reactions* to facts are always interesting. And sometimes very funny indeed. The thing that most puzzles me about you humans,' she went on, 'is the extraordinary contradictions you display. You are the most humorous race we have yet encountered – but the very things about which you make jokes are those that puzzle and distress you. To make your excellent jokes, you must have great insight and knowledge: yet having made the jokes, you remain as ignorant and insightless as ever.'

'There is no such word as "insightless",' I pointed out.

'Impercipient?' she said. 'That could be the word. It was in the crossword puzzle of February the twelfth. How very difficult those puzzles are for a stranger!'

'But we're still a simple little lot?' I continued. 'No trouble at all to super brains like yours?' I was still thinking, in the back of my mind, about how to murder her.

'All the trouble in the world!' she said. 'I never realized, until I came here, how complex *emotions* could be! Reason against emotion . . . any civilization must fight that battle. Your civilization is quite advanced, quite well developed. Yet despite your achievements, your emotions seem to dominate you! You have only two sexes and you make more fuss about them than we do about five. You invent excellent weapons with which to slaughter each other then weep when a puppy dies. Really, Timothy . . . if only you could look at yourself – at the whole of your race – *without* emotion, I think you would agree with me that you are quite – quite – oh dear, what is the word –?'

'Suitable,' I said flatly.

Her manner changed. She stopped being a nice old lady.

'Yes,' she said at last. 'You are a very intelligent boy, Timothy. "Suitable." I wonder how many of my own sons – I have a great number, far too many – would have understood so much from a single word.'

'It wasn't from a single word,' I said. 'It was from all kinds of things.' I was going to say more – to mention her fear of electricity, her speaking 'Grinnish', her worried look when we pretended we had been seeing UFOs for years – but shut myself up in time.

'But it all comes down to one word now, doesn't it?' I went on. 'We're "suitable" so it's game, set and match.'

'I beg your pardon?'

'You have won. And nothing can stop you.'

'That is right, Timothy,' she said. 'Nothing can stop us.'

She settled back in her bed and said, 'Look, my finger

is almost healed. You may go to bed now, Timothy. Goodnight.'

I went to bed and thought. I thought about how to kill her. But then I thought, 'What difference would it make?'

April 20

I see that I have failed to make myself clear in what I wrote yesterday so this time I am going to put down all my conclusions in an orderly manner,

SITUATION

Our so-called Great Aunt Emma is an alien being from another planet, sent to find out how suitable this planet may be for invasion by her species. She is advance guard of an invasion. Her job is to evaluate and understand us – to find out how much opposition we would be likely to offer the invaders, how 'suitable' we are. The thing has been tried before – but other places weren't 'suitable'. Our planet is.

METHOD

To enter our home, Grinny hypnotized all adults she met by using the phrase 'You remember me'. She used this phrase on adults only. She took the children as she found them because she thought that (a) children could not offer effective opposition and (b) because she needed to observe human beings in their natural, unhypnotized condition.

RESPONSES

The children soon discovered that there was something 'wrong' with Grinny and tried to find out what was wrong by laying traps for her. While they were doing this, they felt they were making important and progressive discoveries. What they failed to realize was, that Grinny did not very much care one way or the other. If the children had said, 'There! We have found you out! You are an alien!' she could have replied, 'Yes, quite right – and what are you going to do about it?'

POWERS

Any adult Grinny meets, she can control instantly. Presumably she could do the same with children if she wanted to (she nearly hypnotized me).

She can communicate with her superiors or allies or whatever they are – the beings in the spaceship. But she cannot do this at very long range. If she could, why should the spacecraft have to come within sight of our planet?

She has great physical strength in her non-human body but I do not think this important. Certainly not to her. Her body has been made to measure for the job of posing as a human being. When she has no further use for it, she will assume her own shape and body.

She seems to have great mental powers. Her memory is inhumanly good, for instance. But it does not seem that she has comic-strip, superhuman powers; she has to speak a language, she cannot project thoughts or anything like that. She has to talk 'Grinnish' to communicate with the spacecraft. Sometimes she says things that indicate that all is not well on her own planet. She told me that she has far too many children, for instance. I suppose you could say she is capable of being indiscreet. But then, she is so sure of her powers and the powers of her race that she feels free to say anything she chooses.

I do not know what powers she and her race can bring to bear on us. If her race is capable of equipping Grinny with such a good 'human' body, they can probably make anything they need in the way of weapons. We could never construct a Great Aunt Emma – a walking, talking, cigarette-smoking machine. They can. So presumably they've got the technology to invade us.

WEAKNESSES

Grinny has quite often made mistakes. She even has built-in mistakes – no human smell, skin cannot change colour, many gaps in her programming or 'education' about Earth things and ways. But as I have said, these mistakes cannot be of importance to her or her race.

PROBABILITIES

She told her contacts in the spacecraft that we are 'suitable' (for invasion). She told me that we humans have got to come to terms with 'new facts of human life' – in other words, with the things the invaders will do to us. She was not at all upset when I overheard this.

So presumably the invasion will come soon.

April 22

This evening the showdown came. She started it as much as we did, but we were perfectly willing for it to happen. It was about nine o'clock. The parents were watching the news on TV in the little sitting room and we were alone with Grinny. She sat in the big armchair and we were sitting about uneasily, waiting for things to start.

She said, 'Well. Well, well, well. The time, the place and the loved ones all together. Do you know, Timothy, I think one could conduct the whole range of human affairs solely at the level of quotations! What a wordy lot you humans are!'

'That was a misquotation,' I said.

'Oh, I know, it should be "loved one" – the singular, not the plural.'

'What immortal hand or eye could frame thy fearful symmetry,' said Mac. He had been doing Blake at school.

'That's very apt, Mac,' Grinny said. 'William Blake, isn't it? You are referring to monstrous old me, of course. Well, I cannot pretend to be symmetrical, but I admit to being rather fearful. And also fearless, quite fearless. For what have I to fear from you children?'

None of us could think of anything to say.

'We mustn't waste time, must we?' she said. 'I'm sure you are all bursting with questions – what is going to happen, when, where, what it will be like when it has happened . . . Do feel free to ask anything you wish.'

'Why don't you go away and leave us alone, you beastly old witch?' burst in Beth.

'A good beginning!' said Grinny. 'Why don't we leave you alone? Because we need the space, my dear. Your space. And your amenities – your foods, minerals, water, lands, everything. Yours is by far the nicest planet we have seen.

Ours is quite horrid – rather as yours will become not so many years from now, when you are all standing on each other's shoulders. But we will not permit that situation to arise, of course. You see, Beth, you have come to the end of your time; you humans have had a very long history, far too long. You have done too much, made too many mistakes –'

'While on your infinitely superior planet –?' Mac interrupted. He was twitching with anger.

'But it isn't infinitely superior,' said Grinny. 'As I say, it is quite horrid. Our problem is just the same as yours – over-development and much too large population. The difference is that we can do something about it and you cannot.'

'We won't be allowed to be troublemakers,' I said.

'What happened to the peoples we invaded in the past?' said Grinny. 'They went to the wall (what a strange expression! *What* wall?). They served their new masters and were punished if they did not serve well enough. They were allowed to continue living if their lives were useful. The majority accepted their conquerors – as I hope you will. But those who caused trouble were punished or removed. I trust you children will not grow up to be troublemakers.'

'We won't be allowed to be troublemakers,' I said. 'You'll hypnotize us all, or whatever it is.'

'Certainly not!' exclaimed Grinny. She sounded quite shocked. 'That would be folly! How could mere robots – people living in a trance – learn to serve us as we wish to be served? Oh no, Timothy! The adults, yes, they will be hypnotized . . . just like your mother and father. They are past training, they hardly matter. It is merely a matter of keeping them quiet for a while. But you young people – by which I mean those that have not reached adolescence – you must be encouraged to expand and blossom and grow –'

'Into what?' said Mac.

'Into truly efficient servants! Servants with their own will and intelligence and ability to learn and even invent. But servants who can be formed in the necessary pattern, the pattern we require.'

'It sounds lovely,' said Mac, staring at her. 'Just lovely.'

'If you mean that – but of course you don't – you are greatly mistaken,' said Grinny. 'We will need a great number of things in a very short space of time if we are to survive on your planet. Our own resources will be quite inadequate. Even our machines will not be enough to build what we need. So it will be up to you humans for the first hundred years or so. Two generations, say . . .'

'One and a half,' Mac said rudely. 'A human life is three score years and ten. That's a quotation.'

Grinny looked at him for a moment or two and said, 'A human life will be two score years from now on. You may quote me.'

I could see it all clearly enough. When the invaders came, we would be their slaves. Little children would be 'educated' to serve. Older children would begin doing their work as soon as they were strong enough. An adult would work until he dropped at the age of forty or so. And if he didn't drop, he would be done away with. There would be no place for ageing humans under the new order. No place for the sick, the weak or the brainworkers. No place for my own mother and father.

Beth had not understood all this. She was looking from Grinny to me and Mac with wide, worried eyes. Her face was twisted with fear and hatred into an expression that came out as sheer spite.

She got up from the cushion on the floor where she had been sitting and said, 'I'm going to bed. Goodnight, Mac. Goodnight, Tim.'

She walked over to Grinny in the big chair and said, 'Goodnight, dear Grinny-granny.'

Then she slapped Grinny as hard as she could, right in the face.

There was a complete silence until Mum spoke. We hadn't noticed her, she had been standing in the door with a cup of coffee in her hand. She had seen it all, of course.

Mum said, 'Oh, are you off now, Beth? Well, goodnight, darling.'

And Grinny looked at Mac and me with eyes that were expressionless before she said, 'Goodnight, Beth dear. Sleep well.'

April 23

We met in Mac's house because we wanted to get away from our own house and the feeling of Grinny being all around us.

'Meeting of the GCG called to order,' said Mac. 'Somebody start us off . . .'

Beth made a vulgar noise and Mac said, 'What's that for?'

'For being bloody wet,' she replied nastily.

'You shouldn't say "bloody"! Girls shouldn't swear –' Mac began.

'Bloody, bloody, bloody-blood BLOODY,' Beth said. 'The GCG . . . you make me sick!'

'I second that,' I said. 'It makes me sick too. We've had enough about GAE and GCG and Grinny-Granny. There's nothing for us to be funny about any more, so let's talk seriously. Mac?'

'I want to start,' said Beth.

'All right. Well?'

'I vote we kill her. Tonight.'

'I suppose you're feeling bloody-minded enough,' said Mac, emphasizing the Bloody as a way of ticking Beth off, 'to do it yourself?'

'Yes,' said Beth. She said the one word in a way that stopped anyone else from speaking. She sort of punched it at us. It made me feel sorry for Mac, feeling as he does about Beth. If he thinks she's some sort of fairy princess, that 'yes' must have changed his mind.

'All right – how would you do it?' he said, rather feebly.

She said, 'I'd get the big hammer and a poker and bash it through her head when she's asleep.'

Mac said, 'For heaven's sake!'

'Or I'd push her against an electric fire, that radiant one, the one with the live wires,' she continued. She did not speak at all loudly. Obviously she had been thinking about how to kill Grinny, and these were her answers. Mac and I couldn't think of anything to say. She suddenly noticed the silence and said, sounding like an ordinary little girl again, 'It isn't as if she were human, is it?'

Mac started to say stupid things to her, calling her vicious and so on, until I cut in and said, 'Beth's right. She's been right all along. Mac, you'd better shut up.'

He said miserably, 'All right, then. What *are* we going to do?'

'First,' I said, 'we've got to make up our minds to it – Grinny isn't just some fairy-tale ogre, she's here and she's real and she means what she says. We've got to win against her. But that's not the same thing as killing her.'

'Why not?' said Beth.

'Several reasons. Killing her proves to Them, whoever They are, that we've got a limited amount of power – but only limited. I mean, suppose Mac failed an exam at school, and he managed to get to the man who marked the papers, and did him. All right, the man's clutching his nose and saying, "Don't hit me again! You win!" – but it makes no difference, does it? Mac still hasn't passed the exam.'

'I don't understand,' said Beth.

'Tim means we've got to win a moral victory,' said Mac. 'But I don't suppose you understand what that means,' he added bitterly.

'I do understand, I'm not stupid. Tim means it's no good just bashing her, that's not enough. But I'd like to bash her all the same. Anyhow, there might be more of her.'

'What was that?' I said. And Mac's mouth dropped open. 'You mean, more Aunt Emmas? Ours isn't the only one?'

The idea stopped us cold. We hadn't thought of it before, I can't think why. Then Mac, having thought for some time, broke the silence. 'No,' he said. 'I don't think so.'

'Why?'

'Well, just think of the difficulties. I don't mean the sort of production difficulties, you could just as easily make three of her as one for all we know. But think of the risk! The risk for Them! Think what a chance they're taking planting just one Aunt Emma among us! I mean, we've already found out all about her, and we're not overbright. Suppose they picked someone stronger than us, or cleverer. Suppose, for instance, they planted an Aunt Emma in the right house but the wrong neighbourhood – where there was some stroppy and inquisitive character in the place who wouldn't let go – who'd keep probing and asking questions and – well, someone like Mrs Thrupp was.'

We had a Mrs Thrupp a few houses away and you couldn't stop her. Not only did she know all about everyone, she was quarrelsome with it. She liked picking quarrels about overhanging branches or children playing because in that way she could poke herself into other people's business.

'Or suppose you'd listened to me earlier!' said Beth. Everything she says nowadays seems to have a nasty edge to it, but here again she was right. If Mac and I had been different people and Beth had been the same person, by this time, we'd have done something about Grinny.

Mac said, 'I don't think they'd take the risk of making more than one Grinny. And when she was showing off to us the other night, she didn't give the impression that she had any friends except Them, the spaceship lot. Besides, there's yet another thing.'

'What?'

'It doesn't matter either way. It doesn't matter at all how many Grinnies there are. It's beside the point *as long as we don't kill her*. Killing her doesn't prove anything. Her masters would just write her off and say, "All right, a pity, but we'll go ahead. Anyway, we don't need her any more now!" No, what we've got to do is – make her surrender.'

'Make her surrender!' Mac repeated. 'That's it. She's got to tell them that we're not suitable. It won't do any good coming from anyone else.'

'And once she's told them,' I said, 'it doesn't really matter if there are other Great Aunt Emmas. As far as They are concerned, one single failure is enough. Just one voice saying "Not suitable!" is all we need.'

We were feeling quite pleased with ourselves at this point, having done our little logical exercises and come out with full marks. But then Beth said, 'All right. Now what?' and we were back at the beginning again.

We thought for some time and Mac said, 'What about your parents? Couldn't we make an attempt to get through to them – to break through the hypnosis or whatever it is?'

Beth and I both said, 'No,' at the same time. 'I bet we couldn't, however hard we tried,' Beth said. 'And anyhow, it would take too long. I mean, even if we broke through, we'd still have to *explain*. It would take weeks.'

'We've probably got weeks,' Mac pointed out.

'No we haven't,' Beth said sharply.

'Why not? How do you know?'

'Because I know. And because she's told us so much. Something's going to happen soon, I know it is.'

Neither Mac nor I felt like arguing this point.

'Well, what *can* we do?' said Beth.

'What weapons have we got?' said Mac.

'Only one,' I said. 'The only thing we've ever pulled on Grinny is the Eyes Right trick. I think she still doesn't really understand it. I mean, she knows what it is, and what's been done to her –'

'– But she doesn't know how *much* has been done!' said

Mac. He was getting excited. 'She talked about Eyes Right too calmly! It's like those people who are hypnotized on a show and made to do ridiculous things – you know, pretend they're monkeys and scratch themselves, that sort of thing – and when they come out of it, they just look around modestly and smile politely. Even when they're told what stupid things they did, they still can't believe –'

'It's the only thing we've got,' I said.

'It's not good enough! I wish we could kill her, I wish we could do something to her!' Beth shouted.

I said, 'Shut up, Beth. Unless someone can come up with something better, a new idea, we'll take a vote. Let's all sit still and think for three minutes by my watch. Beginning now.'

I looked at my watch and we started thinking. At least, Mac and Beth probably did, but I couldn't. I was thinking of Beth and wondering if she was really such a bloodthirsty horror as she seemed, or whether it was just Grinny acting on her instinctively female responses – to put it less grandly, her built-in bitchiness. Just once, I've seen my own mother turn into a screaming tearing wildcat. It was when a couple of teenage yobbos got hold of Beth behind the big tree in the playground. They didn't do anything much but when Mum caught them a day or two later in the village street, she just screeched and smashed and flailed. No man could have acted like that, let alone sounded like it. You'd have thought she was mad, but she was right. I thought Beth mad, but she'd been right.

Before the three minutes was up, Mac said, 'It's obvious. Eyes Right, emotions, electricity. They're our weapons. Any argument?'

'No,' I said.

'No, but soon,' said Beth. 'Tonight!'

We talked some more, deciding just what to do, then broke up.

'Tonight, remember,' said Beth. 'Not later!'

April 24

Grinny again in the big chair, holding court. Telling us about the new order. Another instalment of the same nightmare.

We gave her the Eyes Right treatment.

She said, 'Yes, well, this is very amusing but rather naughty of you. I have endured a lot of teasing from you children, all kinds of mischief and tricks. I don't know if it has occurred to you that I have one or two tricks of my own!'

She pulled something out of her handbag. It looked like a large, smooth pocket torch. She held it in her hand.

I think it was this torch thing that started Beth off. We had agreed to push emotions at Grinny as hard as we could go, as well as giving her the Eyes Right. We had even agreed, in a silly sort of way, what emotions each of us would try to project (Beth simply said, 'Hate!'). The trouble was that, apart from Beth, we were beyond emotion. Mac and I agreed that we both felt merely – sick.

Sick with fear, sick with worry, sick with tiredness (neither of us could sleep properly and when we did sleep we had dreams). Perhaps it would have been different if we had known just when the thing was going to happen – just when the spaceship would land, just what the invaders would look like. But we knew nothing and Grinny wouldn't tell.

All we knew was that sooner or later, it would happen. Adults over here, children over there. Get marching. If you didn't march, something to tickle you up and make you. No time for goodbyes – no reason for them, even: the parents would talk about all the usual home affairs – Marjorie's O levels, how expensive good beef is, let's have coffee at eleven on Tuesday . . . And some of the little children would shriek and cry and tug at their mothers' skirts, but mother would just turn round and say, 'Oh, you are being naughty today – run and join the other children over there like a good girl. Mummy will be with you in just one moment.' And there they would be, the hypnotized and the un-hypnotized, the grown-ups chattering away politely as they were herded away together to be wiped out and the children, alone, screaming and yelling and begging in an agony of fear as the world came to an end.

At least, that is how it is in one of my dreams. There are several variations, some of them highly spectacular and bloody. It is just the same for Mac, of course.

Meanwhile, we go to school and do our prep and eat our dinners and lie awake in bed. When you have done this for a week or so, emotions are hard to come by. You just feel sick and rotten and hopeless.

Anyhow, Grinny pulled out the torch thing and Beth tautened like a cat. But she must have still kept on with the Eyes Right. I know I did. I suppose the emotion I put out was fear and anger. The same for Mac. But with Beth it was spitting, violent, killing hate.

It reached Grinny. She went under.

'I have one or two tricks of my own,' she had said. Immediately Beth got at her, Grinny's voice changed. 'Useless!' she grated (she really did grate the word out, right from her throat: you can hear it on the tape, I had the recorder running). 'Useless – how dare you – most certainly not . . . Will not permit . . . most severe and painful punishment . . . painful, terribly . . . I warn you, here in my hand . . .'

She lapsed into Grinnish. The torch thing had fallen into her lap but her hand was still clenched as if she were holding it. We kept up the Eyes Right pressure and I heard Beth muttering. She was saying, 'I *hate* you, I *hate* you, I *hate* you, I want you to *die* and *die* and *die*.'

Then Grinny was talking again. She said, 'A temporary embarrassment. Bring them to order, to heel, discipline . . . in good time, merely temporary difficulty . . . once we are overwhelming superiority will change and subdue, all in charge no further trouble, could not possibly allow . . . (Grinnish) . . . very powerful she is for such a small animal, oh how very powerful she is for such a small animal oh how powerful, oh how uncomfortable it is but still one must endure, merely a temporary situation . . .'

She was talking of Beth and I think Beth knew what was happening. Beth was leaning right forward, glaring at a space one foot to the right of Grinny's eyes, mouthing at her. I glimpsed this out of the corner of my eye – but I could have felt it without seeing it, almost, her hatred was so intense. A solid stream blasting from her mind into Grinny.

I tried to stop my brain from just watching and concentrate instead on projecting emotion at Grinny. I would go back to projecting Muddle. This is as close as I can get to naming my emotion. Confusion, muddle, worry, doubt, all made into a mixture to confuse and weaken Grinny. I suppose I was mouthing away too, saying things like, 'You're wrong, you're failing, you're losing, you're done for, you're frightened!'

Mac had chosen Determination (he is very determined anyway). He was simply getting across the thought, 'You won't, we will. You'll lose, we'll win. We're strong, you're weak.'

Grinny was deep into Grinnish for quite a long time. She must have been greatly weakened. Her eyes were wide open as if she were in a trance. Her mouth was open too. Her fingers were twisted and knotted in shapes I can't imagine in human hands. They were *writhing*.

I thought it a good time to go and get the camera. Part of the plan was to get together as much evidence as possible of the behaviour and nature of Grinny in case we were ever lucky enough to reach some adult who would listen to us and be convinced and even take action.

So, still Eyes Righting, I got to my feet and slowly went to the door. The Pentax was there, fixed up with the electronic flash gear. I came back step by step, being careful not to step across the sightlines of Mac and Beth. I knew the camera was already correctly set for speed and aperture.

I was afraid that the flash would spoil everything, but had to risk it. I took one of Grinny from about six feet, when her hands got into an extraordinary position and her dry open mouth was gaping at me through the viewfinder. The flash went off and she stopped speaking Grinnish immediately.

But she didn't come right out of her trance as I had feared, she just started talking English again. She said, 'Special circumstances . . . not likely to be encountered when we have established our general, overall superiority and ascendancy. Admittedly most uncomfortable, most, most, most, most . . . thrice blessed is he who gets his blow in first, a quotation.'

I felt something touch my leg. It was Mac's finger. He was leaning forward still Eyes Righting Grinny, but he wanted my attention. He flicked his eyes towards the French windows for a split second. I looked out of the window.

The spaceship was in the sky, closer than I had ever seen it before. So close that you could guess its height, only a few thousand feet. Its shape was crisscrossed by the branches of the lime tree in our garden.

I was shaken badly. Mac was too for he began to talk his emotions. He began muttering, 'We're *not* suitable, *not* suitable.' He was doing this to make himself concentrate.

Grinny changed position in her chair like someone uneasily asleep. Her hands began to writhe again and I thought of photographing them because they were so strange and inhuman but I was afraid she might wake up. Then I thought (it was difficult to think and at the same time keep up the Emotion and Eyes Right) I should photograph the torch thing, which might be valuable evidence. I couldn't look at it myself as I had to concentrate on Eyes Right. The spacecraft was still there. I could see it without looking at it as something bright at the edge of my vision. Mac was getting confused too by everything that was going on at the same time. Only Beth was really keeping going.

I suppose it was our weakening that made a change in Grinny. She began talking again, this time much more clearly and with expression in her voice. She said, 'Most severe and painful discipline unless. I have only to give the order and the torch thing the torch thing you called it the torch thing will punish most severe and painful. Your silly tricks. I saw a flash, a flash of light. Your silly tricks.' But the torch thing was no longer there! It had disappeared – gone – vanished.

Beth was saying, 'Die, die, die!' Mac said, 'No you won't, no you won't, we are *not* suitable, *not* suitable!' And I was saying (or thinking, or both) the same thing as Mac – '*not* suitable, *not* suitable!' It was the reappearance of the spacecraft that had brought this phrase back, of course.

Then Mac changed his tune. He began to tell Grinny that the 'torch thing' was no good, useless, she couldn't use it, couldn't touch it, couldn't reach it, etc. I thought this was a good idea of his. It turned out not to be.

Grinny suddenly woke some more. She said, 'Emotion! Emotion! The mind!' Then she looked round about her, just as someone does when they wake up, and said, 'You children are behaving very stupidly. I shall punish you if you continue, with the "Torch thing".'

Mac then said, 'You can't! It's gone!' and Beth screamed, 'Gone! It's gone!' and started screeching with laughter. She was getting hysterical.

Grinny said, 'Don't be so absurd, of course it has not gone!' She spoke as if she was not quite with the situation.

Mac said, 'It's gone. It's out of reach so it's no good to you.'

Grinny looked surprised and puzzled and replied, 'But, you stupid child, *I do not have to touch it, it is worked by the mind!*'

There was a sort of gulf or vacuum for a second or two while the same thought hit all three of us: somewhere, Grinny's punishment machine was crawling round the room waiting for her instruction. When she gave it – when she flicked it on with her mind! –

I yelled, 'Eyes Right !'

We all glared until our eyes were bursting and it worked. She shrunk down again in her big chair and said, 'Triggered by the mind, the mind.' She was quiet for a moment. Then she said, very sharply and clearly, 'Oh dear! I should not have said that! If the nasty children should hear . . . !'

But we *had* heard.

At last, Beth's voice said, hoarsely and softly, 'Punish her.'

We stared at the space one foot to the right of Grinny's eyes. Only Mac and I were in the right position to see the dull glint that appeared under the skirt of the sofa. The torch thing! The glint moved, slid across the carpet like a small rat and silently went towards Grinny.

Beth saw it and I heard her gasp. Then she said, 'Punish her!'

Grinny said, 'Most certainly not, most certainly . . . ! I forbid. I am the master and you will obey me . . .'

The glinting rat stopped.

I hissed, 'Emotions!' We all clutched our minds together and beamed them at Grinny.

The torch thing slid onwards towards Grinny.

'More!' I said. We gritted our teeth and poured the stuff at her. The torch thing slid smoothly up the side of Grinny's chair. She was wrestling with herself now, jumping and jerking in her chair. Streams of Grinnish came from her lips.

The torch thing paused – swayed – then dived into the sleeve of her dress. It went up her arm. It made a rippling hump under the fabric, right the way up her arm.

She made a horrible noise, a horrible noise, not a scream at all, it was like machinery tearing itself to pieces, like metal cutting metal. It went on and on and on until we couldn't stand it. She was flailing and whipping about with her arms in the chair.

I screamed out, 'Stop it! – Stop it!' and everything stopped.

She was still again. Her chair is the wing chair. One of the wings was broken and the cloth on the arms of the chair had been beaten through by her arms. Her sleeves were split and torn. So was the skin on her arms, it was torn. The metal bones showed through.

Yet her face was just the same as ever. The slight grin was still playing round her mouth. Her eyes were steady, her skin was neither pale nor red.

She said, 'Please. Don't do it again. Please don't do it again. You know how afraid I am of electricity.'

Mac said, 'Electricity?'

'Blood,' she said. 'Some humans are afraid of blood, are they not? The life fluid. I am like them . . . afraid of the life fluid . . .'

Her voice sounded so ordinary and old-ladyish and unstrained.

'You would not be so cruel!' she said. Then she repeated it, giving her voice human stresses and emotions. 'You would not be so cruel!'

Mac said, 'What do you mean, electricity?'

I said, 'The torch thing punished her with electricity and she's afraid of electricity like some people – human people – are afraid of blood. Electricity is their life fluid just like blood. Is that right?'

She said, 'Yes. Please, *please* don't do it again.'

Mac said, 'You admit that we win?'

Grinny replied, 'Yes, yes, anything you like. Just don't do it again.'

'You admit our minds – our emotions – beat yours?' I said.

'Oh yes, yes.' She was grinning politely.

Beth said, 'I hate her! Don't trust her!'

I started to remove the flash head from the electronic flash. When you do this you expose a three-pin socket. You can put a variety of flash leads into the body. I took the extension lead and threw it to Mac. He always carries a penknife. I said, 'Strip off the ends, Mac.'

He began to bare the wires. Grinny said, 'What are you doing?'

'We're not suitable, Grinny,' I told her. 'Not suitable at all. We are not going to be invaded.'

'No, of course not!' she said. 'What are you doing?'

'Do you know what Grinnish is, Grinny?'

'No. What are you doing?'

'Grinnish is the language you speak when you talk to the thing out there.' I pointed out of the French windows. The spacecraft was no longer visible, but that made no difference. She knew what I meant.

'You're going to speak Grinnish, Aunt Emma. Now. You are going to tell your people that we're not suitable. Now or ever.'

She began to knot her fingers and shift in her chair.

Mac said, 'Catch.' He threw the lead to me. I pushed the plug in. The three wires coming from it had shiny, raw ends. I opened my hand and held it, palm out, towards Grinny. Then I put the three raw ends in my palm and closed my fingers over them.

'If I pressed the button now, I'd get a shock,' I told her. 'Lot of volts. I don't know how much voltage that thing puts out –' I pointed to the torch thing – 'but I'll bet this compares quite well. And it isn't controlled by the mind, it's controlled by a little red button.' I showed her the button.

She said, 'No. Please!'

'So if I put these wires in your hand, Grinny,' I went on, 'and if I tell Mac to press the red button, you'll get a shock of electricity. And there is nothing you can do to stop it. If you try to hypnotize us, you'll be too slow. If you get the torch thing going, you'll be too slow. If you blow the whole world up, you'll be too slow. Mac will still press the red button.'

She said, 'You mustn't, you mustn't.'

'Say something in Grinnish, Aunt Emma,' I said.

'I can't. I can't think of anything.'

'Say "the rain in Spain stays mainly in the plain". It's a quotation.'

'I can't. There is no word for "Spain".'

I went over to her and said, 'Give me your hand.' She held it out. I looped the wires over her middle fingers and twisted them tight. 'Say it,' I told her. 'And when you come to "Spain", say that in English.' I caught Mac's eye and nodded towards the tape recorder. He went over to it. She looked at me with her emotionless eyes and said, 'All right.'

Then there was a split-second burst of Grinnish.

'Again.'

Another burst.

'Again.'

A third burst.

'Play it back on the slowest speed, Mac.'

He played it back. Even on the slow speed, it was impossible to catch the syllables. But one thing was certain. The three bursts of sound were identical; and in each, there was the spitting sound that could have meant 'Spain'.

'We're not suitable!' said Beth. 'Make her say that! Make her! Make her say it!'

'But I cannot possibly say it!' said Grinny. Her voice was loud and passionate. She must have concentrated hard to get so much human feeling into it. 'They will be angry, very angry . . .'

'Make her!' said Beth. She jumped up and gave the wire a little tug so that Grinny's finger jerked. '*Make* her!'

I said to Grinny, 'You better tell them.'

She said, 'But I can't, I dare not.'

'Tell them we are not suitable. Tell them we have weapons they can't defend themselves against. Tell them our planet won't be invaded.'

'They will punish me –'

'Do it.'

She spoke Grinnish for perhaps a second.

'Again. Tell them again.'

She talked Grinnish again. Then she said, 'Please take the wire off my finger. I have told them, I really have.'

'How am I to know that?'

'I could make the spacecraft appear again. That would prove I have been talking to them.'

'Give them the message for the third time and make the spacecraft appear as well. But only for a short time. Make it appear for three seconds.'

'Then will you take the wire off?'

I said yes, and she said words in Grinnish.

Almost at once, the spacecraft appeared. Mac and Beth ran to the window to look at it but I stayed by Grinny and said, 'I want to ask you questions about your planet and what were you planning to do to us. And about the torch thing –'

She said, 'Oh, I forgot it! Oh!' She leapt to her feet and clumsily ran round the room, searching for the torch thing. She kept saying, 'Oh! Oh!' in a metallic squawk. It almost sounded like an electronic signal, not a human cry of fear. But then she said, in a human voice, 'I can't *think*! How can I control it if I can't *think*?' I understand what she meant. She meant that she had no control over the torch thing, her mind was too hysterical to give it orders.

She stopped darting about for a moment, to grip me with her terrible little steel hand and said, 'You children! Think at it, stop it! Stop it, you must stop it, they will turn it on me!'

But even as she spoke, I saw the torch thing. It was behind her. It slid fast across the carpet then leapt at her hand. I saw it on her hand like a big metal leech – but only for a split second, for she started running, staggering, blundering round the room. She crashed into the standard lamp and it went down. There was a flash from the socket as something fused and the room was suddenly almost dark.

Then she was on the floor and there was the metal-cutting noise again and her screams, but they stopped just as they were becoming unbearable. I couldn't see much of what was happening and what I could see I could hardly believe. She seemed to be tearing herself to pieces, you could see fragments of cloth and patches of her skin and the glinting metal of her bones. There was a sort of drumming noise. It was her heels and elbows on the floor.

Beth was screaming, 'I don't care, I'm glad,' and sobbing and shuddering. Her eyes were completely round, she was staring at Grinny on the floor, still hating her. I thought she shouldn't be watching and put my arm round her, trying to push her head into my chest so that she couldn't see, but she just clawed my arm aside and went on looking. Mac was trying to get the lights to work. I am glad he failed.

And then all the noise and flailing motion stopped: there was just a small dragging, scraping sound. It was one of her arms. It was separated from her body. It was being pulled towards the French windows by the torch thing.

It went on like this, on and on. We three just stood there, cold with horror, while she was dismembered. The limbs and bits of machinery weren't so bad – it was the clothing that made you feel sick. Old lady's clothes, human clothes, with some busy, vile, alien machine inside them making them heave and twitch and bulge as it cut and ripped. The torch thing was as busy and unstoppable as a rat, never pausing from its nibblings and humped-up scurryings and lunges and tugs.

At last it had finished. What had been Great Aunt Emma was a pile of rubbish outside the French windows (it was Mac who opened them – I'd never have found the courage to get so near the horrors on the floor). Only one thing remained, gleaming on the carpet: a beautiful and elaborate metallic lattice-work cage about the size of a football, trailing filaments of metal thread like gold and silver hairs – spider-web hairs, like gossamer. No wonder she had been so frightened of our coarse electricity.

The torch thing arched its back and attacked the cage. There were sharp little clicks as the latticework was snapped or bitten through. A hole was made. The humped thing's back heaved and tugged industriously and something was pulled out through the hole.

It was another torch thing.

The two things seized the remains of the cage and hustled them to the pile outside.

They did not come back. The sky lit up and the spacecraft came closer than it had ever done before. I suppose the craft picked up the two torch things.

And I suppose one of them was Great Aunt Emma.

YOU REMEMBER ME!

THE ROLLERS

27 June, afternoon

The Roller Rally came down the street. The yobs were ready.

The Rollers carried nothing but banners – big, simple, well-printed banners in Dayglow yellow with plain black lettering.

The yobs carried bricks, rotten fruit and vegetables, bottles, chains, knives and stinkbombs.

The Roller banners each carried a different message. The first read:

R.O.L. R.O.L.
RULE OF LAW
JOIN US!

That banner always led a Roller Rally. Rule of Law – R.O.L. – 'Rollers'. The whole nation knew the words, the initials and the nickname.

The second banner read:

R.O.L. R.O.L.
<u>PROTECT</u>
THE THINGS THAT MATTER
JOIN US!

Other banners read:

R.O.L. R.O.L.
<u>ACTION!</u>
DECENCY
DISCIPLINE
DEDICATION

R.O.L. R.O.L.
<u>BRITISH</u>
– AND PROUD OF IT!

There were eleven banners, three hundred Rollers and one six-piece Dixieland-style jazz band. The musicians wore Union Jack blazers and straw boaters with ribbons boldly patterned with R.O.L. R.O.L. R.O.L. They played cheerful tunes, like 'When the Saints Come Marching In' and 'I Want to be Happy'.

They played very well. The Roller Rallies were always well organized.

The yobs waited until the band struck up 'Side by Side' – a favourite with the Rollers because it contained the lines, '*Rolling* along, singing a song, side . . . by . . . side'. On the word 'Rolling' the musicians made a dipping, sideways, rolling motion and smiled; and everyone in the Roller Rally shouted the word, very loudly, all at once. It sounded like a good-natured battle cry.

'*Rolling* along, singing a song,' they began to sing – and the yobs moved forward, yelling.

Between the yobs and the Rollers walked policemen. The police were spaced at fairly wide intervals. Their faces were blank. They gave no impression of power: they did not wish to. Their orders were to accompany a public procession for which permission had been granted by the Authorities. The marchers had a right to march and the police were there simply to see that they marched unmolested.

Nevertheless, the first casualty of the Roller Rally was a young policeman. A bottle hurled by someone in the yelling crowd hit him in the side of the face and broke his cheekbone. If he made a sound, no one heard it above the yells and catcalls and the music of the band. The policeman put a hand to his face and fell to his knees. Blood jumped out between his fingers.

Two other policemen half carried and half dragged him into the crowd. The injured man tried to help them by walking but his legs were gone, they made awkward, gangling movements. A knot of yobs, in the place where the bottle had come from, set up a chorus of hooting jeers.

One of the yobs had his head shaven bald but for a central ridge of hair ending in a pigtail with a ribbon. The pigtail stuck out behind. A big woman with a shopping bag reached forward and grabbed it. She pulled. The yob yelled but she would not let go, her plump fingers were locked in the hair and her red face was set like a mask with protruding eyes.

The yob yelled and jerked. His mates reached over each other, trying to land downward punches on the woman's face. Some punches reached her but they had no force. Besides, there was another sound, a sort of surly growl, all around the group. It was the sound of the crowd.

The growl grew. The crowd closed in on the yobs. Men, women and even children hit out at them. The shopping woman never let go of the pigtail, though her lower lip was puffed and bleeding.

The yob's face was soon in a worse condition than the woman's. Fingers, nails and fists from the surrounding crowd had managed to reach it. Already, he was pouring blood from his nose.

His mates tried to break free, scatter and lose themselves in the crowd. Their progress was marked by a moving pattern of rising and falling arms. The yobs had to run the gauntlet. Those who got through no longer ran: they limped and staggered. One even collapsed.

The Roller Rally kept moving. In the early days of the Roller movement, the yobs had won hands down. Even five weeks ago, in a seaside town, the yobs had beaten the Rollers to their knees and stopped the Rally. There had been fifty-three casualties, forty-four of them Rollers and three of them policemen. But that was five weeks ago.

Since then, there had been Roller Rallies all over the place. In a London suburb, three hundred Rollers had set out – but the Rally ended with three thousand or more marchers. JOIN US!, the posters said; hundreds and thousands of people accepted the invitation at every Rally. They fell in behind the marchers. Sometimes they linked arms. Always they roared out the chorus, '*Rolling* along, singing a song, side . . . by . . . side!' Always, the word '*Rolling*' crashed out like a great wave breaking.

Now, today, people were already leaving the crowd to join the Rollers; housewives, men of all types and ages, girls in jeans, pensioners – anyone.

A girl with a hairstyle like a cockatoo's deserted a group of yobs and joined the marchers. The yobs howled at her and thrust through the crowd, trying to grab her and pull her back. Furious-faced, she yelled, 'You can stuff it! I've had enough!' One of the yobs threw a Coke can at her.

The can missed her and hit a man who looked like a pensioner. The can must have been full, the man staggered and clutched his shoulder. The girl picked up the can, flung herself into the crowd and jammed the can into the face of the punk who had thrown it. He ducked, jeered and hit the girl with his fist.

Again, there came that growling, snarling sound from the mass of the crowd. Then the mass heaved and swarmed in on the yobs. They were submerged.

Missiles still occasionally arced out of the crowd to hit the marchers, and sometimes the police escorting them. But the storm had died down. At first, the escorting police had waded into the crowd to pull out the throwers. Now they did not have to, the crowd itself seemed in control. Constantly, more people broke from the crowd to join the Rollers.

At the rear of the procession, a new noise came from the crowd. It was a cheerful, roaring 'hooray!', the sort of noise you hear when royalty passes. The sound followed the movement of a Rolls-Royce. It was an open, silver-grey convertible. Union Jack pennants flew from its front wings and a big Union Jack flapped over the boot lid.

When this car passed before you, you could hear what the waving, smiling crowd shouted – 'Good old Mona Lisa!' 'We're behind you, gal!' And the hissing 's' of the name Lisa. For standing by the driver, one hand holding the windscreen and the other waving, was Lisa Treadgold. She looked marvellous.

Like the band, she wore a boater with R.O.L. ribbon round it. The boater was perched right at the back of her golden head. It did not hide her face. Her Union Jack blazer was not buttoned up. You could see her I'M A ROLLER! T-shirt and the curves of her figure. She smiled and waved vigorously. You could just hear her voice, sometimes: 'It's only *hired*!' she shouted, jabbing a finger at the Rolls-Royce, 'Honest! It's *hired*!' The crowd laughed and shouted back.

'Come on,' she shouted. 'Join us! Fall in and march!' Many people obeyed. They laid their hands on the Rolls-Royce and pushed. Lisa Treadgold shouted, 'That's right, save fuel!' and said something to the driver. He made a pantomime of removing a bunch of keys from the dash of the car and holding them up. The crowd laughed and kept pushing. Lisa Treadgold laughed delightedly and waved her arms to encourage the pushers.

It was a triumphal procession.

Now no missiles came from the crowd and the voices of the yobs could no longer be heard. Even the policemen looked relaxed. They sauntered and smiled. This Roller Rally was going to be a no-trouble affair. This Roller Rally was going to be a pushover for Lisa Treadgold and R.O.L., the Rule of Law.

Timothy Carpenter, standing near a senior police officer with silver braid round the peak of his cap, heard the man say, 'That woman . . . You've got to hand it to her. She's got *power*.'

Timothy wrote the words down in his reporter's notebook.

CELEBRITY

That was in high summer. Later, much later, when everything went wrong and the dark days came, Timothy spoke to his cassette recorder. Using the machine always cheered him up. Typewriter, tape, notebooks, even a smattering of shorthand – they were all tools of the writer's trade. Timothy liked using them.

But now he frowned. He had to choose his words carefully, it was important to get everything right. He'd probably send a copy of the tape to Mr Fisk, who was his friend and a friend of the family. Mr Fisk was a real author, a man who earned his living by writing. He had encouraged Timothy's ambition to become some sort of writer. Timothy remembered how Mr Fisk had helped in another time of trouble (but what time? – and what had been the trouble? Why couldn't he remember?).

'Get on with it!' Timothy told himself: and pushed the microphone's little button to On. He began talking.

'When Lisa Treadgold first came on the scene – the *national* scene – everyone was beginning to talk about her and the Rollers. And I'd just got my job as a cub reporter on the local newspaper. It wasn't a real job, it was a "Work Experience" scheme. For schoolboys and schoolgirls. A local employer takes you on for a limited period so that you can learn something about Work and the Real World and all that . . .'

Timothy pulled a face and operated the Off button. He did not like the sound of his own voice, trying to be funny. He sat on the edge of his bed, staring at the microphone, frowning. 'Think!' he told himself. '*Think!*'

But that was the trouble. Whenever he tried to concentrate on Lisa Treadgold, the mind seemed to slip sideways. You had to fight to remember. A fog rolled in and blurred the brain. A fog that blurred, smothered, dulled. A fog that clung, grey and damp, inside his head.

'*Think!*' he told himself. '*Remember!*'

Painfully, he began to remember. He forgot the microphone and recorder. He remembered that sunny day in the little town near the village where he lived: the day of the Roller Rally. Taking notes, proud of himself for being a real, genuine, teenage newspaper reporter with a real, genuine reporter's notebook.

Lisa in the Rolls-Royce. The crowd, becoming more and more cheerful once the trouble with the yobs was over. The warmth of the crowd, the family feeling – 'We're all together in this.' And Lisa, lovely Lisa, sailing by in the Rolls. Lisa smiling, thousands of faces smiling back.

Then, when the parade was over, he got on his bike and took what he'd written back to the *Gazette*. Back to Len Sturgeon – gingery eyebrows, ferocious pale eyes, beer-drinker's complexion, fifty-ish, threatening, always on about 'knowing the trade'. 'What's this typeface, boy? Give it a name! Come *on* then!' Or, 'When you make up copy, you use the correct printers' marks. You don't roll your own. *This* is how you tell the compositors that you want a transposition. Like *this*.'

'Yes, Len.'

'Mr Sturgeon to you. Don't look bored. Look keen, willing, attentive, able, eager.'

'OK, Len. I mean, *Mister* Sturgeon.'

'One day, you'll bless me for teaching you your trade. In fact, you can bless me now. Say "Bless you, Mr Sturgeon!"'

'Bless you, Mr Sturgeon.'

'That's better. And don't smirk like an ape.'

Timothy smiled at his memories; then thought of the other reporter. Fanny Bishop. About thirty. Plain. Tried to be tough but cried at funerals and christenings. A good writer, far too good to stay on for ever with a local rag like the *Gazette*. The sort of writer you have to keep reading . . .

'Wish I knew the trick,' Timothy murmured, out loud. He shrugged, switched the microphone to On and spoke into it.

'I met Lisa Treadgold face to face when I went with Fanny Bishop of the *Gazette* to interview her,' he began. 'Lisa Treadgold! The Celebrity! It was a big day for me. And for Fanny, of course. Because Lisa was already a household name. She happened to live in the Vicarage, the big Georgian house on the edge of our village. Enormous grounds and the second biggest monkey-puzzle tree in Britain. I suppose she chose it because it's isolated, private – yet close to the motorway leading to London.

'Len Sturgeon was jealous but tried not to show it. He was the senior reporter, but Fanny was female and got the job. Len pretended to hate Lisa. "That damn woman," he'd say, "always grinning. Like a Cheshire cat." But he'd still stare at photographs of her, waggling his eyebrows and chewing at his pipe. I'd catch him at it sometimes . . . "Thought you didn't fancy her, Len!"

'"Get on with your work, boy."

'"This one's nice, Len. Where she's leaning back. Or do you prefer this one with the smile? But it only shows her face –"

'"Watch it, boy!"

'"Oh, I thought *you* were watching it –"

'Then he'd try and put me head first into the wastepaper basket.'

Suddenly disgusted with himself, Timothy yet again switched off the microphone. 'You're talking drivel!' he said aloud. 'Get down to the real story.' Yet his mind rebelled. He sat back and went on remembering, remembering . . .

He had tried to get Len to discuss Lisa seriously. 'What have you got against her, Len?'

'I don't know, boy. I admit she's a corker . . . And the smile, the famous smile, I can *see* what people *see* in her, but . . .'

'But what?'

'I don't really know. All these photographs pouring in from her agent. All the pressure behind her. All this Roller business. Law and order and discipline.'

'But you keep telling me that *I* need discipline, I've got to learn the trade, I've got to try harder. Isn't that just what the Rollers say? Decency, Discipline, Dedication. The three Ds.'

'It's all right *me* saying that to *you*, but I don't like other people saying it to *me*.' He grinned and noisily knocked the filthy mess from his pipe. 'I suppose,' he went on, 'I just don't trust celebrities. She's a celebrity. Someone famous for being famous.'

'Now the national newspapers are calling her Mona Lisa,' Timothy said. 'You know, the famous smile.'

'Mona Lisa . . .' Len said disgustedly. Tim thought his eyebrows would tie themselves in knots.

'Anyhow, I'll be seeing her tomorrow, actually meeting her,' Tim said. 'Pity you won't be coming,' he added airily.

But Len refused to be drawn. 'Go and make coffee, you young ape,' he said. 'And in cups, not mugs. And without slopping it all over the saucers.'

*

So, in those earlier days, not everyone was mad about Lisa. Len Sturgeon mistrusted her on principle. Tim's father pretended to be bored by her constant appearances on television. His mother used to sniff disapprovingly when the beautiful face appeared yet again on the screen.

The person who really hated Lisa Treadgold was his young sister, Beth. 'I *loathe* her!' she'd hoot, flashing her dark eyes and waving her skinny arms. 'She's a phoney, she's a pig-woman, she's all smarmy and smiley one minute and bring-back-the-birch the next! She's sinister, she's awful, I *hate* her!'

Timothy would pretend to go all love-sick: 'But she's so *beautiful*!' Beth would literally spit, in a sort of fine spray, as she howled, 'She's *despicable*!'

Beth never changes, thought Timothy. She's the same unspoiled baby sister, half hellcat, half shark (she's as greedy as ever). And Mac from down the road still dangles after her, doing his boy-next-door act, being fresh-faced, reliable, honest, nice, always there. I can't think what he sees in her. Or perhaps I can. Whatever you say about old Beth, you've got to admit that she's a goer. She's more like a firework than ever. You light the blue touch-paper (by mentioning Lisa Treadgold, for example) and retire to a safe distance. Then – fizz, splutter, fizz, BANG! THUMP! CRASH! WALLOP! BANG! (That's Beth!)

Timothy smiled: then sighed, cleared his throat and began dictating his report of the very first meeting with Lisa Treadgold. Later, he'd boil down all his talk and write to Mr Fisk. But there was so much to tell . . .

First, he spoke of the house – the old Vicarage. Outside, big trees, lawns, flowerbeds, a kitchen garden, a greenhouse: all in very good order considering the short time Lisa and Lisa's money had been there. Then, the interior. Acres of expensive tiling and panelling. A covered and heated swimming pool, half in and half out of the house; Lisa was said to swim fifty lengths first thing every morning. A kitchen with copper canopies over the electronic ovens and cookers, all satin-chrome and smoked glass. A marble bathroom with gold-plated dolphin taps downstairs (the upstairs bathroom, the 'master bathroom', had a jacuzzi). Clever little telephones that opened and shut like oysters, trilling constantly, urgently.

And Bunny, Lisa's personal assistant – bulging, spotty, anxious, shiny-faced Bunny, loyal, flustered, over-worked, getting more and more behind every hour of every day – Bunny to show visitors the house, the gardens, the dogs, the signed photographs from famous people. Bunny filled in the time between the arrival of Lisa's visitors (the visitors were always careful to arrive early) and the appearance of Lisa (who was always careful to be exactly ten minutes late).

Because she almost ran, Bunny was able to show Fanny and Timothy at least half of the house. There were some surprises: sudden untidinesses, sudden dirtinesses. Areas that looked shop-soiled. In Lisa's own dressing-room, the walls were covered in glowing suede leather. The effect must have been superb when it was completed. But now the suede was scuffed and scratched and stained. Bunny caught Fanny staring at the marks and said, 'Oh, yes . . . isn't it terrible? . . . But what can you do? The dogs, it's the dogs, oh dear . . .' She hurried Fanny and Timothy down to the great living room, muttering guiltily as she led the way.

On the curving staircase, there was a sudden scuffling and hooting as a golden Saluki dog scrabbled past them. The Saluki had a broken leg. It had managed to undo, with its teeth, the bandages encircling a wooden splint. 'Oops!' howled the Saluki: 'Oh!' howled Bunny, running after it.

Timothy and Fanny found themselves alone on the staircase. Fanny raised an eyebrow and said, 'We go in there, I suppose.' She nodded at the green and gold depths of the living room on the ground floor.

Before they could enter the room, Lisa Treadgold was there behind them, at the top of the stairs. 'Oh, hal-*lo*!' she said, 'You're the *Gazette*, aren't you? How exciting! Let's go to the conservatory and have tea!'

Her voice was a delight. And so was her smile.

The conservatory was elaborately Victorian, warm, humid and alive with growing things in enormous oriental jars and pots. Water gurgled and tinkled in a little marble fountain with a bronze cupid in its centre. Lisa sat her guests in great white balloon-shaped lattice chairs, deeply cushioned. She wore a flimsy, many-layered frock elaborately patterned in green and gold. Her jewellery was gold. The flesh of her smoothly perfect arms and legs was another, subtler shade of pale gold. Her hair was carefully tumbled strands of many shades of gold. She glowed richly, a haze of gold relieved by startlingly luminous dark blue eyes.

She smiled. 'Now, you're Miss Bishop, aren't you, and you're Timothy Carpenter. How nice . . . I'm a terrific fan of the *Gazette*, I read it from cover to cover. Especially the small ads! The Classifieds, I mean, you know, things for sale. We've just *got* to have a croquet set here, think how perfect it would be, croquet on the lawn! Bunny's bringing tea – at least, I hope she is, I just live for tea . . . Tea and these Belgian chocolates, do have one, the mocca ones are the best. Bunny, where are you? Bunny! *Bunny!*'

The chocolates were the shape of little buns, individually wrapped in foil. A shiny paper seal had to be peeled off to open the wrapping. 'LT', Lisa's initials, were stamped on each seal. Fanny and Timothy accepted one chocolate each. Lisa took two and immediately ate one, making small yum-yum noises. They were superb chocolates.

Bunny's heavy footsteps thundered in the distance as she ran to answer the front-door bell. 'That ought to be Jim Benedict, our photographer,' Fanny said. It was: Bunny led him in. 'Couldn't get away from Council meeting, very sorry,' he mumbled. He sat down heavily, his two Nikons bashing into each other on his chest.

Lisa dazzled him with a smile and said, 'Tea, Bunny. Lots of lovely tea!' Bunny lurched away, sweating in her heavy sweater. It was very hot in the conservatory.

She returned carrying a massive silver tray. She poured

tea and handed it round. 'China tea,' Lisa said. 'Will that do? Or would you prefer Indian? Bunny could bring a pot of Indian if you'd prefer.' Nobody preferred. Everyone but Lisa drank the scented tea as it came from the pot. Lisa, surprisingly, added two large spoons full of sugar to her cup. 'Bunny,' she said, 'I think we'll need more hot water. Be a dear . . .'

To Jim, she said, 'I can tell you're in a panic, Mr Benedict, press photographers always are! So shall we get your bit done? How do you want me?'

Jim mumbled suggestions. Lisa agreed with all of them – then did something completely different and much better. She seemed to know just where to find perfect lighting, how to place her hands, how to give herself something to do. Jim clicked and clicked. He began to smile, delighted with his good luck in finding such a wonderful and famous model. When he left, he was beaming triumphantly, knowing he'd got some good stuff in both cameras: stuff that anyone, not just the *Gazette*, might pay good money to use. Exclusives of Lisa Treadgold – in her own home!

From upstairs came the noises of dogs running riot. Fanny caught a glimpse of Bunny, anxious-faced, running up the curved stairs. She was half-way up when Lisa called to her. 'The dogs, Bunny!' Lisa smiled ruefully, rolled her eyes comically and said, 'Oh, those dogs! Bunny will cope. Now, let's get down to business, Fanny. May I call you Fanny, or must I call you Miss Bishop? Fanny? Oh, good. I knew we'd be friends. Fire away, ask anything you like.'

Timothy looked from face to face. The difference was astonishing: Lisa so graceful and gracious, so at ease with herself; Fanny so hunched and awkward, so on edge. It was as if they were of different species. Yet both were intelligent women of much the same age.

Fanny caught him staring and said, 'Take notes, Timothy.' He mumbled, 'Oh yes . . .' and fumbled for his ballpoint and reporter's notebook. Fanny's shorthand made him nervous: it was so rapid and assured. Timothy's always let him down. He had to rely on unreliable abbreviations.

'Chocolate, Timothy?' Lisa said and passed the box to him. He reached forward to take it – and his ballpoint jumped out of his hand. He actually saw it burrow itself down among the cushions, as if to spite him. He blushed, took a chocolate, muttered, 'Thanks,' and began the ridiculous business of sliding his hand down between the cushions while trying to appear involved and interested in the conversation between Lisa and Fanny.

'Yes, ask anything you like,' Lisa encouraged Fanny, 'and I'll answer frankly and openly just as soon as I've finished making a pig of myself!' She was eating yet another chocolate, Timothy saw. Her hand concealed her mouth for a few seconds as she munched. How many did that make so far? Five? How could she keep such a fabulous figure when she wolfed chocolates and even took sugar in China tea?

And still more interesting – what did she do with the chocolate wrappers? How did she dispose of them? He watched carefully.

He was just on the point of solving the mystery when his probing fingertips met the ballpoint. This was more important. Carefully, he curled his fingers round the pen and brought it to the surface. Now he could frown intelligently and play the part of the ace reporter making lightning notes. The solution to Lisa's Disappearing Chocolate Wrappers would have to wait: the interview had started.

SCALDING WATER

Fanny's first questions were routine stuff – 'What are your plans, how do you like living in this area,' that sort of thing. Soon, however, she took the plunge. 'D.,D.,D.,' Fanny said. 'You really mean it, don't you, Miss Treadgold?'

'Oh do call me Lisa!' was the reply. Then, 'Decency, Discipline, Dedication. My three Ds. Of course I mean them. *Shouldn't* I? Is there something wrong about them? Because I'm quite sure there's something wrong with people and nations that don't follow the three Ds!'

Fanny cut in. 'Who tells us what's decent? Who applies the discipline? To what or to whom are we supposed to be dedicated?' She blurted out the questions as if they were attacks. Lisa simply smiled for a few seconds.

Timothy inspected the famous smile, thinking, It's just perfect. No flashing of teeth, no wrinkling of the eyes, no hand gestures. It's *economical*, that's what it is. Her lips go into a pretty shape, the smooth cheeks grow rounder, the long eyelashes come closer together – and there it is, the famous smile, the effortless, natural, economical smile. A Saving Grace, that's what she's got.

'You asked me *who* applies the three Ds,' Lisa smiled. 'I think you *meant* to ask, who do I think I am? Am I some sort of would-be dictator, an Iron Hand in a Velvet Glove, a bully waiting for a victim? That's what you meant to ask, isn't it? Well, I don't know . . .' She began to laugh, a flowing, easy, musical sound; then said, 'Tell me honestly, Fanny: do I look the part? Can you see me in jackboots, flourishing a whip? Well, can you?'

From upstairs, the noise of the dogs suddenly became louder. The Saluki's hoots sounded like a ship in a fog. Lisa raised an eyebrow and said, 'We've been talking about *discipline* . . . !' She smiled and added, 'I think I'd better put my own house in order, don't you? Please excuse me for a moment.'

She picked up a copy of the *Gazette*, rolled it up and left the room. Fanny pursed her lips and pretended to review her shorthand. Really, Timothy knew, she was listening intently. The two of them heard Lisa's running footsteps ascending the stairs; then her voice calling, 'Bunny! Bunny! Whatever's happening?'

Then still louder barking as the door upstairs opened; and a slam as it closed.

A short pause: then one enormous, yodelling howl from the Saluki – then a chorus of yelps and howls and barks as all the dogs started up again, louder than ever.

Lisa returned to the conservatory, her face calm, her hair unruffled. 'Where were we?' she said, smiling. She threw the rolled-up *Gazette* on a small table and sat down.

Timothy stared at the *Gazette*. When Lisa left the room, it was a smooth roll. Now it was kinked in the middle as if it had been used to hit something.

Upstairs, the Saluki hooted and howled like a demented banshee. It was almost a comical sound, but Timothy did not smile.

'Ah, yes,' Lisa said. 'We were talking about the three Ds, weren't we? Well, I think we've covered that. So now let's talk about my Big A – Action! A for Action! First, local action: I am in favour of voluntary patrols equipped to deal with vandalism and assaults. I am in favour of capital punishment.'

Before she could say more, Bunny burst in, her face suety with shock. 'Oh, Miss Treadgold! Poor Prince Igor! It's his leg, it's gone again, worse than ever, he can't even stagger!' She saw the rolled-up newspaper and put her hand to her mouth.

Lisa said, 'Hot water, Bunny! Another minute and that tea will be undrinkable!'

Bunny's mouth opened and closed. Her eyes were locked on the dented roll of newspaper. Her footsteps clumped away and clumped back again. Now she carried a big, steaming silver jug of hot water. 'I'll fill the teapot,' she mumbled.

Lisa simultaneously said the same thing. Both bent forward to the teapot. There was a slight mix-up. Their arms collided. Bunny clumsily drew back the silver jug. It hit Lisa's arm.

'Not *yet*!' Fanny said.

'You mean, it's OK for you personally to cry with rage about that old lady, but not OK for a whole gang of people to cry about her. Or to try to do something to stop that sort of thing. Is that what you mean?'

'You should read some history, sonny boy. Read about the Blackshirts and the Gestapo and concentration camps.'

'That's not the same thing as Lisa Treadgold. Hitler was a fiend, Lisa is just a very beautiful woman with strong opinions. Do you *mind* her being so beautiful?' Timothy added innocently.

These words made Fanny so angry that she stopped the car. 'Listen, Dumbo,' she said, glaring, 'I realize that I'm no oil painting and I'm not rich and I'm not famous and no one wants my autograph –'

'And you smoke too much,' Timothy said cheekily, trying to make her smile. Really, he was quite afraid of her at that moment. She looked fierce.

'And I smoke too much,' Fanny agreed. 'But there's one thing I'll tell you, and it's this: *learn to be frightened*. When you see some magic-type person, a public person, hogging the media to talk about bringing back the birch, and hanging, it's time to get a little nervous. Because the person who gets beaten or hanged might turn out to be someone you know. Are you with me so far?'

Timothy said, 'OK so far.'

'But when that sort of person talks about action groups, and banded-together brotherhoods of citizens, and vigilantes – get terrified! Because the person who gets dragged away in the middle of the night for a flogging might turn out to be *you*. Yes, *you* – simply because you're a decent, normal, pleasant, dim human being. The sort of person who just happens to get in the way of the bully-boys and bully-girls. Do you understand, Timothy?'

'I thought I was sonny-boy, or Dumbo,' he said, drawing back from her.

'No, you're Timothy and I like you. That's why I'm lecturing you. Have you understood the lecture?'

He thought about it for a minute, then said, 'Yes, I suppose so. But I don't understand how it fits in with Lisa Treadgold. I mean, she's just . . . Lisa Treadgold, temporary celebrity.'

'*Is* she?' Fanny said. '*Is* she? Do you really think that?'

'I don't know . . . There are things about her, I admit. That dog. Chocolate wrappings. Boiling water. Even her smile. But nothing fits any other thing. I just don't know.'

'Well, think about it till you do,' Fanny said. She slammed the Cortina into gear and drove back to the *Gazette* almost in silence. Once she said, '*Chocolate* wrappings?' Timothy decided not to answer.

But the unanswered question stayed in his mind. Where did Lisa's chocolate wrappings go?

August. Breakfast time. The Carpenters' house

'Of course I'm a proper TV star,' Mr Carpenter grumbled. 'Just look at my profile.' He turned his lined face sideways and stuck out his chin.

'You're saggy,' Beth said. 'Saggy and baggy. Especially under the eyes. Marmalade, please.'

Mrs Carpenter said to her husband, 'I don't know why you put up with her cheek, Edward. If I had spoken to my father like that when I was her age –'

'I think I'll be a TV star myself,' Beth said, 'I'm just the right age. Pre-teen, I'll be like that movie-star girl, what's-her-name, the American one with the smouldering eyes. She made it when she was eleven or twelve or something. So will I. Father won't, he just *appears* on telly, sometimes. That's not the same as being a *star*, like Lisa Treadgold. Euch! Is there any more toast?'

'I'm sick of Lisa Treadgold,' Timothy said. 'If you want more toast, make it yourself.'

'You introduced the subject!' Beth said. 'You mentioned Lisa Treadgold first, didn't he, Mum? He's always mentioning Lisa Treadgold, just because he assisted at a crummy interview for the crummy *Gazette*! Lisa Treadgold said this, Lisa Treadgold said that!'

Mrs Carpenter said, 'Do you want another rasher of bacon or something, Edward? You've got a long day. Beth, shut up. Timothy, you can't go to the *Gazette* with finger-nails like that, *please* scrub them before you leave, *thank you* very much, *no*, don't argue. Bacon, Edward?'

Mr Carpenter said, 'No, really. There's a good pub near the site, we'll all go there for lunch. Unless we hit on something exciting, that is. There's so much Roman stuff, I can't imagine why . . .'

He scratched his chin then turned to Beth and said, 'The

TV people will be there again, you know. Perhaps you'd better find some excuse to stage a personal appearance, Beth! You never know, you might be noticed. Or then again, you might not.'

Beth pulled a face at him. Timothy said, 'Yes, try it on, Beth! They might have a talent spotter! And you've got spots!'

'I haven't!' Beth said – and anxiously felt her face with her fingertips. Timothy chuckled. He'd got her that time.

There was a knocking at the back door and Mac came in. He escorted Beth to school. When there was no school, he still turned up. As usual, he hovered at the door, neither in nor out of the room, carefully not looking at Beth. He said, 'Good morning,' and eyed the toast. Beth followed his eyes, picked up a piece of toast and dangled it in front of him. 'Did he want his second brekkies, then?' she teased, not all that pleasantly. 'Was he a greedy lickle boy? Beg for it, then! Come on, sit up and beg!'

Mac grinned uneasily. Timothy said, 'She's in one of her moods this morning, Mac. Something to do with spots. She's got spots, you know. All over.'

Beth clawed at him. Timothy said, 'Big mauve ones, with yellow bits in the middle!'

Mrs Carpenter said, 'That's enough, will everyone please *go*. Goodbye, Edward. Goodbye, Timothy. Goodbye, everyone.' She bustled everybody out and stood watching her husband's long, gum-booted legs folding themselves into the Land Rover. 'He's getting very grey,' she thought.

She looked in the mirror and touched her own hair. No grey. She went about her housework humming.

BURNS AND FLOWERS

It had been Lisa Treadgold at breakfast time: it was Lisa Treadgold in the *Gazette* offices.

Len Sturgeon was saying, 'You're irrational, Fanny – oh good *morning*, Timothy, nice of you to turn up – irrational. You agree, don't you, that delinquents and criminals get away with murder; but then when someone like Lisa Treadgold comes along and says, "Let's do *something* about it!" you say, "I can't stand her, I don't like her, I don't know why but I just don't fancy her!" I mean, that's irrational, you don't make sense!'

'Just what I was saying!' Timothy interrupted. 'My sister Beth's like that too. She says, "I can't stand her, she's phoney, I loathe her!" Yet when the yobs thump someone –'

'Coffee, laddie,' said Len Sturgeon. 'We'll consider your invaluable opinions when you've made coffee.'

Timothy made coffee and frowned. Not because of Len Sturgeon – he liked and understood Len. It was his thoughts about Lisa Treadgold that worried him. Why was Fanny so vicious about Lisa? Why did Beth hate her so much? With Fanny, it could be just jealousy. With Beth, it couldn't be; with Beth, it was just plain cat-and-dog enmity. Of course, Beth was barmy.

The electric kettle – it had been boiling furiously without Timothy noticing – went POINK! and spat out its plug. Oh Lord, Timothy thought, I hope Len didn't hear. Nervously, he tried to push the plug back into its socket. It went in all right but then pushed itself out again.

'Really, laddie!' Len said. He had ghosted in to stand behind Timothy. His eyebrows waggled sarcastically. 'While I show you how to mend electric kettles,' he said, 'you can tell me the names of all the typefaces in this advertisement. Proceed.'

'The headline is Cooper Black,' Timothy said hopefully.

'Wrong,' said Len. He was bent over the kettle, forcing the plug in. 'Wrong, but a good try.'

There was a spitting bang as the plug in the wall short-circuited and spat blue fire. Len jumped back, frightened.

'Wrong,' Timothy said, cheekily imitating the man's voice. 'Wrong, but a good try'.

For a minute or so, Lisa Treadgold and everything else was forgotten as Len Sturgeon stalked Timothy, trying to back him into a corner near the big wastepaper basket. He would put Tim head first in the basket, if he caught him.

But then Fanny Bishop came in. She had been to the florist's and carried a large bunch of flowers wrapped in paper and cellophane. 'All right, you two,' she said. 'Playtime is over. Back to business. Follow-up to the Treadgold story. Who's going to see to it? Any volunteers?'

Len looked with distaste at the flowers and said, 'Ah. Well, no, I am particularly busy.'

'So I saw. Someone's got to do it,' Fanny said.

'Do what? What do you mean, follow-up?' Timothy asked.

'Mona Lisa,' Fanny said. 'Flowers, good wishes, how are the burns, that sort of thing. The *Gazette* really cares,' she said, fluttering her eyelashes. 'It had better,' she added. 'There's a lot of mileage to be got out of Treadgold. Right, who takes the flowers to her?'

'You,' said Len.

'I told you, I can't stand her. Come on, Len, be nice.' She pushed the flowers at him. He sat down at his desk and started typing very fast. 'Too busy,' he said. He read out what he had typed: 'Sex-Change Vicar in Mercy Bid Dash.'

'That leaves you,' Fanny said, fixing Timothy with a hard eye. 'Go on. It's all experience. On your bike. And don't crumple the tender blossoms.'

'I'm supposed to be learning reporting, journalism –'

'And now you're getting a botany lesson,' Fanny said, 'for free. If she's gone to London or something, bring the flowers back. Understand? I could use them in my flat.'

So for the second time, Timothy found himself on his way to the home of Lisa Treadgold. But this time on a bicycle.

On the way, he met Mac and Beth, also on bicycles.

'Flowers!' Mac said in a squeaky falsetto. 'Oh, how well they suit you! How sweetly pretty!'

Timothy muttered, 'Shut up,' and tried to ride on. Beth wheeled across him and prevented his escape. 'I thought you were a reporter, not a delivery boy,' she said. 'No, wait . . . ! Flowers! Who for? Lisa Treadgold, of course! I'm coming too! So's Mac!'

Timothy tried to prevent them but failed. So all three of them were at the front door of Lisa Treadgold's mansion when Timothy rang the bell.

ALL FALL DOWN

He rang once and, in the distance, all the dogs started barking. Nobody came to answer the bell.

He tried again and yet again and heard the thumping footsteps of Bunny, the housekeeper/secretary.

When she opened the door, her face was shinier and her eyes more goggling than ever. Her mouth opened and closed.

Timothy said, 'Flowers. For Miss Treadgold. From the *Gazette*. You probably don't remember, but I'm from the *Gazette*, too. I was here the other day –'

'Flowers,' said Bunny dazedly. 'Flowers, yes. The *Gazette* . . . Oh, dear.'

'We don't want to come in, or anything,' Timothy said ('Oh yes we do!' Beth said fiercely in his ear), 'but we all wanted to know – all of us at the *Gazette*, I mean – if Miss Treadgold's all right. The hot water, the burns . . .'

Bunny's staring eyes were still fixed on the flowers; and still her mouth kept opening and closing. At last she managed to say, 'Flowers . . . yes, she's quite all right. She's wearing a long skirt, you can't see anything. She's quite all right . . .'

Then, like a factory chimney coming down, Bunny collapsed on herself and ended in a clumsy limbs-and-body mass on the floor.

Beth reacted instantly. 'Inside!' she hissed. 'Close the front door!' Her eyes glittered. 'Oh come *on*!' she said to Timothy, digging her fingers into his arm, 'You're supposed to be a *journalist*! And this could be a *story*! Come on, come on, get her up! Water, splash some water on her!'

They dragged and carried the half-conscious Bunny through the house. Beth's eyes darted sideways all the time, taking in every detail. 'A-tishoo, a-tishoo, all fall down!' she mumbled. 'Where do we go?'

'Over there,' Timothy grunted. 'Conservatory. Gosh, what a weight!'

Before they reached the conservatory, Bunny came to. For a second, she stared wildly from face to face. Looking at Timothy, she said, '*Gazette?*'

'That's right,' Timothy told her. 'I was here with a real reporter, I'm just a –'

'Oh, I remember all that,' Bunny said wearily. 'Yes, flowers for Miss Treadgold. How nice. She had a late night last night – the TV personality dinner.' She rubbed her forehead with the heel of her thumb. 'I gave her breakfast in bed,' she continued. 'She slept late, you see.

I took it up just now.' Again, the dazed expression clouded her face. 'Just now, I can't seem to remember what happened just now, I can't seem to remember . . .' She shook her head.

They helped her to a chair, made her comfortable with cushions and wiped her brow with water from the fountain.

As soon as the water touched her, she gave a small hoarse scream – jerked in the chair – cried, '*No! That's impossible! No, no, no! I don't remember that!*'

Then she became unconscious again.

'Don't do that!' Timothy said. He was trying to stop Beth flooding Bunny with water. The small girl, her mouth set like a trap, was trying to shock the big girl back to life. It took a long time to bring her round.

When she was conscious, Bunny sat up, pulled at her soaked sweater and looked miserable. 'Tell us what happened!' Beth whispered urgently in Bunny's ear. She whispered because she had heard sounds from upstairs. First, the barking of hysterical dogs; then, light, fast footsteps; finally, Lisa Treadgold's clear, pleasant voice calling, 'Bunny, where are you?'

'Keep quiet!' Beth whispered to Timothy and Mac. 'Ssh!'

Lisa Treadgold's footsteps suddenly became sharp and ringing as they left the stair-carpet and met the marble-like tiles of the hall by the front door. 'Bunny . . . ? Bunny! Oh, blast, I'll get the car myself . . .'

The front door opened and slammed shut. Now Lisa's footsteps crunched on gravel. Then they were gone.

Bunny said, 'I ought to be out there to see her off . . .'

'You stay here with us!' Beth said sharply. 'Tell us what – no, wait a minute, why have the dogs stopped barking?'

'Oh, the dogs . . .' Bunny said. She still looked puffy, miserable, damp and lost as she sat on the floor. 'I don't know, the dogs don't seem to like her,' she said. 'They always make a fuss when she passes their door. I mean, I have to lock them in . . . but usually they're outdoors . . . Oh, Lord . . .'

Beth, helped by Mac and Timothy, got Bunny to her feet. 'You've soaked me!' Bunny said, pulling at her sweater. 'I don't suppose it matters, it will dry out . . . I don't know what came over me –'

'I do!' Beth said. 'You were frightened! So frightened you passed out! Bunny, tell us: *what frightened you*?'

Bunny said, 'I've got to walk the dogs, it's their time!' Then, suddenly, she collapsed again, this time into a chair, and burst into noisy tears. 'I *didn't* see it!' she howled. 'I *couldn't* have done!'

And then Beth was bent over her, pulling at her, and Timothy and Mac were shamefacedly saying, 'Beth, leave her alone!' and trying to disengage Beth's claws from Bunny's sweater; and Bunny was saying, 'It was a trick of the light! I thought I saw it but I couldn't have!'; and then she was hysterical and saying things that made no sense; and then the front door bell rang and it was all over. Bunny jerked to her feet and said, 'Oh Lord, the video cassettes!' and ran to the door.

There was a motorcycle messenger standing outside,

jigging his booted feet and whistling through his teeth. 'Here you are, love!' he said – thrust a parcel at Bunny without looking at her – and was gone in a blatter of exhaust.

Bunny stared at the parcel and said, 'Oh gosh, she was supposed to take these with her, I forgot to tell her, oh Lord, she'll be *furious*!' She was crying again, damply, no longer hysterical. Beth bit her lip and glared, knowing that the parcel was all that mattered to Bunny now.

Timothy said, 'Why don't you phone for another motorbike messenger and have him deliver the stuff?' Bunny said, 'Brilliant! Oh, why didn't I think of that!' She rushed to the telephone and made complicated calls.

Timothy looked at Mac and shrugged. 'Better leave,' he said. Beth followed reluctantly. She wanted to stay and dig her little claws deeper into Bunny.

They closed the front door behind them, mounted their bikes and looked back at the big house.

'Well!' Mac said. 'What was all that about, do you think? What frightened Bunny?'

Timothy said, 'Who knows? One of life's great unsolved mysteries.' He prepared to ride off but was stopped by Beth's voice.

'Wait a minute!' she demanded. 'Haven't you guessed what happened? Do you really mean you *don't know*?'

'Course I don't. Nor do you.'

'But you *must* know!' Beth stormed. 'I mean, it's so obvious! You can't be that dim! Mac, tell him!'

'Tell him what?' Mac said. 'I don't know what you mean.'

Beth rolled her eyes disgustedly and said, '*Stupid*!' She almost spat the word. Then she rode off, her back very straight, not looking back. 'So *stupid*!' they heard her say as she disappeared round a bend in the drive.

Mac laughed uncertainly and said, 'Good old Beth. What's she on about, do you think?' Timothy did not answer. His head was full of foggy thoughts. He rode off frowning, not looking where he was going. He nearly rode into the iron drive gates.

Timothy's typed notes that night

I get embarrassed: Beth doesn't. That's the difference. I mean, she takes everything in while I'm just standing there wondering if I'm doing the right thing. She'd make a better reporter than me. She'd get a front-page story out of an oyster . . .

But getting back to today – what did Beth think and see? What have Mac and I missed?

This afternoon, I cornered Beth and said, 'All right, I'm dim, but what did you mean this morning when you said it was all obvious about Bunny?'

Beth: 'Oh, you're just stupid, I don't want to talk to you,' etc. etc. I kept on at her.

Having told me for the umpteenth time

how stupid I am, Beth said, 'You just don't listen, do you? Didn't you hear what Bunny said, when we'd just arrived?' I said no.

Beth glared and said, 'Bunny told us that Lisa Treadgold had a late night, surely you remember that?'

I said yes, because of a TV affair.

Beth then said, 'And Bunny told us that Lisa T. *slept late* and Bunny gave her *breakfast in bed*. Breakfast in bed, which means that Lisa was *asleep* when Bunny came in with the tray. And then we arrived and Bunny came down the stairs frightened out of her wits and fainted all over us and all that! *Now* are you beginning to see the light?'

I gaped at Beth, not understanding. She sort of poked her face at me and said, 'Seeing the *light*, stupid! I'm giving you a *clue*, oh do *wake up*! That's a clue too, when you come to think of it!'

I still gaped at her and she stomped off, refusing to speak to me any more. Which is pretty cool from a kid sister of ten or eleven or whatever she is. She really is a pain. And typing out her conversations is a pain, you have to back-space all the time to underline every other word she speaks. Perhaps it would be quicker to use CAPITALS, LIKE THIS. But then it looks funny on the page. Len Sturgeon is always going on at me about trying to visualize (visualise?) the words as printed: using crossheads and all that. Right, we'll have a crosshead –

YAWN YAWN I'M TIRED

There's an attention-getting crosshead for you. Really, I'm not achieving anything by just sitting here banging away on the typewriter but I suppose it sounds impressive to the family. They're below me with the TV on. Lisa Treadgold's on the TV. Why can't I *think*?

This is riducilous (try again – ridiculous) – I still can't work out what Beth means about Bunny and the breakfast in bed. Bunny took breakfast in to sleeping Lisa. Then something about light. So? Was it a *light* breakfast? Ha, ha, ha.

Why isn't my brain working better? Beth said I'm stupid but I'm just sleepy. If I keep typing it will all come clear. It's hard to concentrate with the telly on. I can just hear it from downstairs but not hear it properly. Lisa T. is talking.

```
  Now is the time for all good men to
come to the aid of the party. The quick
brown fox jumps jumps over the lazy dog.
The quikc brown.
  The quick brown fox jumps ovre
  Oh hell
```

LISA'S LEGS

Gazette office next day

Len Sturgeon told Timothy, 'You're supposed to be in the facts business. Newspaper reporting is factual. When you come in here, you leave your imagination back in the nursery, where you belong, you horrible infant.'

Timothy said, 'What have I done wrong now?'

'You and Fanny, I don't know which is worse. All that malarkey you two were giving me about Mona Lisa and the boiling water.'

'That was a fact! Boiling water, all down her legs! Ask Fanny, she was there, she'll tell you just the same thing!'

'Ah, there's another one with a lively imagination. She saw it too, didn't she? Big silver jug, all full of boiling water! Then – oops! – over it goes, all that red-hot water, scalding Lisa's lovely legs. Oh, yes!'

'I don't know what you mean, it happened! It's a fact! And when I glimpsed her the other day, she was wearing a long skirt right down to her ankles. To hide the bandages on the burns!'

Len Sturgeon nodded his head several times, staring hard at Timothy. Timothy stared back and began nodding his head in time with Len's. It was one of the best ways of cheeking Len: either the man laughed or tried to up-end the boy in the wastepaper basket. You never knew.

This time, however, Len merely stopped nodding and said, 'Right: if you're so hot on facts, give me a weather report. Go on, look out of the window and report what you see.'

Timothy said, 'If I look away, you'll come at me!'

Len said, 'No I won't. Cross my heart. Give me a weather report.'

Timothy looked out. 'Showery periods, visibility good. Strong wind from the south-west. What's all this about?'

'Strong wind, laddie. Gusty and blustery. Bad weather for a lady wearing a flimsy skirt.'

'What lady?'

'Lisa Treadgold. I saw her this morning. Getting out of a taxi at the station. Digging in her purse for change, both hands occupied. Then, whoosh!'

'Whoosh?'

'Whoosh. Wind blows, up it goes. Her skirt. And there's poor Mona Lisa without a hand to spare.'

'You averted your eyes, of course,' Timothy said.

'Of course,' said Len.

'Pity about the bandages,' Timothy said. 'That must have spoiled it for you.'

'No bandages,' Len said. He beetled his eyebrows at Timothy and repeated, '*No bandages.*'

'Well, marks, then,' Timothy said. 'Burn marks.'

'No sign of them. A flawless epidermis, Mister Carpenter. Flawless.'

Timothy leaned forward. 'You're joking,' he said.

'You don't joke about Lisa's legs,' Len told him.

'But they had to be marked, or bandaged, or something –'

'No, laddie. Definitely no. The lady's not for burning. The lady's legs are flawless.'

Timothy said, 'Leg make-up . . . There's a sort of lotion women use . . . she must have had that on!'

'No lotion, Mister Carpenter. It was all Mother Nature and Lisa Treadgold.' He studied Timothy's face and said, 'You look perturbed, young sir. Have I said something to upset you?'

'Yes,' Timothy muttered. 'I mean, no. Look – is this all some sort of joke that I'm supposed to be too young to understand? It is a joke, isn't it? Did you really see her legs? This morning?'

'No joke, Timothy. Sober fact.'

'Above the knee? You saw them above the knee?'

'Most certainly above the knee: I'm not complaining. Does mention of a lady's legs always make your eyes pop like that, Mister Carpenter? I thought that the younger generation of today was –'

Without knowing he did it, Timothy impatiently cut off Len's words with a wave of his hand. He rose and stared out of the window, looking at the trees blowing in the wind. He shivered.

Len saw his face. 'Is there anything wrong, Tim?'

Timothy said, 'I'll make coffee,' and walked out. Len watched him go and pulled at his chin. 'Perhaps I shouldn't tease him,' he said to himself. 'He's a good lad, and bright. I keep forgetting how young he is.'

He fed paper into his typewriter and started working.

Timothy's typed notes, that evening

Looked up burns in Library. All too technical/medical, no help. Asked Dad if he had ever scalded himself, he gave me long rigmarole about boy at school who tipped a kettle over himself – ghastly scars, etc. etc. – and showed me pinkish, shiny area on inside left forearm. Strange I'd never noticed it. He did it years ago when camping. Boiling water. Asked him, how long did it take to heal? He said weeks: first blisters, then peeling skin, then hard pink scar.

Fanny away from *Gazette* for two days so could not ask her to confirm what Lisa T. was wearing that day – but do I have to? It was a soft, draped dress. No protection against boiling water.

Was the water boiling? Yes.

Did it fall all over Lisa T.'s legs? Yes.

Could dress protect Lisa T.? No.

Yet Len says no scald or burn marks.

Was Len teasing me? Yes, but only in his usual way, nothing special.

He says Lisa's legs showed no signs of burns and I must believe him.

Timothy's typed notes, next evening

Couldn't keep it to myself any longer so told Beth everything about Len seeing Lisa's legs with NO injuries or bandages. Which is impossible.

BETH: Oh, you're so stupid, you're so dim, etc. etc.

ME: Look, I know all that, you've mentioned it once or twice before. Let's just leave it that you're always right and everyone else is stupid, OK? Now, what about Lisa and the boiling water?

BETH: Oh what's the use, how can you be so dim, etc., etc. It's all perfectly obvious if only you think! Look, I'll try and explain it in simple terms so that even you can understand, right? Listen closely. Suppose you told everyone you'd had a fight with some enormous yobbo . . . you'd had to fight him to save an old lady being thumped by him . . . but you hadn't really had a fight at all, you were trying to draw attention to yourself to make yourself sound brave and noble – well, suppose that happened, what would you do to make your story sound true?

ME: I can't imagine.

BETH: You'd give yourself some sort of injury, wouldn't you? You'd clonk yourself in the eye with a milk bottle to give yourself a shiner! Or you'd crunch your knuckles against a brick wall to make it look as if your poor little fists had been doing brave things –

ME: All right, all right, I get the point. I'd make myself look as if I'd been having a scrap. What's that got to do with Lisa T.?

BETH: Now suppose the other thing. Suppose there was a *truth* about you that you didn't want known. What would you do?

ME: Fake some evidence in the form of a lie, I suppose. So as to hide the truth.

BETH: Well, there you are then!

ME (baffled): Where am I? Sorry, you've lost me.

BETH: Or take her dogs. They bark whenever she passes their room. Didn't you hear Bunny say that?

ME: Yes, but . . . Dogs can be like that, they bark because they hear their owner and get excited. They think of food or walkies or something.

BETH: Who do you suppose feeds the dogs? And walks them? Do you honestly think it's Lisa? Do you?

ME: No. I suppose it's Bunny most of the time.

BETH: *All* of the time. Yet they bark when your precious Lisa goes near them. Right, now think about Prince Igor and that rolled-up newspaper. (I'd told Beth about this earlier.) What exactly happened then? Go on, tell me!

ME: I don't know. You don't know. I mean, we didn't see anything, we weren't there.

BETH: And you don't want to guess? Go on, have a guess. Have three guesses if you like, I'm feeling generous. Dog barks, Lisa smiles. She smiles, she's always smiling! – and goes upstairs with the paper –

ME: Paper . . . . And there were those choc wrappings . . .

DISCIPLINE

Beth didn't know about the Lisa trick of making choc wrappings disappear and she got unduly excited about it – eyes wild, clutching fingers, the lot. Then I say, 'Perhaps it's just an idea of mine, perhaps I wasn't watching properly, let's talk about her miraculous now-you-see-it-now-you-don't burns!' But Beth won't play. She just stares at me, shaking her head accusingly. Then she bursts out, 'You know, don't you? You do know, you just won't admit it! But I know you know! It's all beginning to happen again, only this time it's Lisa!' And I try to calm her down, I even put my arm round her, but she's genuinely shaking and shivering, it's not an act.

We end up sitting on the edge of my bed, she hunched up and sobbing into my handkerchief and me beside her, stiff and awkward, stroking her head and back, being nice. We don't talk properly, she's too upset, but she does say one thing I remember:

'*I'm the only one with sense enough to be frightened*!'

Before I can make her explain herself, she tears herself away and blunders to the door making a sort of choking noise. At the door, she recovers herself. She turns and gives me the full glare and says, 'You *know*! But you won't admit it, perhaps you can't! Perhaps she does something to get you all stupid and confused, rays or something, thought waves, I don't know – but she's not going to do it to me!'

I say (and I mean it), 'Please explain! Please stop making me into some sort of enemy!' But she just sobs, 'Oh, what's the use, you've got it all down in plain words in front of you, you type it all out night after night and still you won't understand! Why don't you read what you've written?'

I say, 'Why don't you just *tell* me what you mean, in plain words?'

She replies, 'It won't work that way, you've got to see it for yourself!'

Then she leaves me. Clueless.

All right, I'll read what I've written. Read and re-read it. Yet even before I begin, I know I'll soon get tired and confused and the words will blur and run into each other. There's something in my mind, it's there all the time, something simple yet too difficult for me. Something about Lisa T., of course. No, that's not right, it's not her, there's someone else too. Someone in the past. Beth said, 'This time it's Lisa!' But who was it *last* time?

Wait! I think I remember! Concentrate! Sit back and think!

What's the use . . . When I stop typing and look at the things I've written, my eyes go funny. Or my mind. Fog. Yet as soon as I start typing again I'm fine, I can see everything perfectly well. I can even see the slight furriness you get on typed characters and the way the full stop bites into the paper.

Beth could tell me. Why doesn't she?

I'm fed up with this. They're watching TV downstairs, I can hear it booming away. Think I'll join them.

THE TV PROGRAMME

' . . . So we can expect the showers to die out, I think, and warmer, brighter weather to spread from the south and west . . .'

'About time,' Mr Carpenter growled, staring accusingly at the girl weather forecaster. She smiled back uneasily from the screen and was faded out. Mrs Carpenter said, 'There's a play, it sounds rather interesting. Or perhaps it doesn't. All about deprived children in urban environments . . .'

'Or there's *Opinion*,' Mr Carpenter said, in a neutral voice. 'With that blasted woman of yours, Timothy –'

'If you mean Lisa Treadgold,' Timothy said, 'she's *not* my blasted woman. I couldn't care less about her. Can't we watch that American cops and robbers film?'

Beth, hunched by her mother's armchair, said, 'Let's watch *Opinion*.' Her voice sounded foggy. Timothy was not surprised: Beth was always in a tizz recently. So was his mother. She looked anxiously at her daughter, prepared to ask her what was wrong, changed her mind and said, 'Oh, all right. We'll watch *Opinion*. Who's got the thing?'

Timothy found the thing, pointed it at the set, pressed its little buttons and watched the word 'Opinion' form itself from a series of moving coloured patterns. Under his breath, he chanted, '*Boring, boring*,' to show that he did not want to watch the programme.

In fact, he wanted to watch it very much. Because of Lisa Treadgold. His father, he knew, felt the same way.

It was a dull programme that even Lisa Treadgold's beauty could not enliven. The speakers would not stick to the point. They were supposed to be discussing new industries for Britain; instead they kept harking back to old, out-of-date grievances. The union man said this, the industrialist said that and the presenter's face became a smiling, frustrated mask as he tried to drag his panel out of the past and into the future. Lisa Treadgold took no part in the dreary talk. She sat looking composed, intelligent and lovely.

The industrialist said, 'But surely you must agree that many of our troubles stem from the unions – their refusal to accept the facts of commercial life, their refusal to stick to agreements –'

The presenter succeeded in cueing a camera to himself and interrupted.

'Yes, well, of course there is a great deal to be said for that point of view,' he said, talking too fast. 'But perhaps we should bring in Miss Treadgold at this point.' He stopped speaking, having lost himself.

'To say what?' Lisa Treadgold asked, coolly and unhelpfully.

'Well, this point about industrial discipline –'

'Oh, *discipline*,' Lisa replied. She seemed to be enjoying the confusion and the knowledge that she alone could calmly and elegantly put the programme back on its tracks. She stared at the glass of water in front of her; touched the glass with a fingertip; then, very lightly, said, 'I'm not sure I have much to offer. After all, you remember me on discipline!' She smiled, sat back and toyed with her glass.

She had said nothing: she had said everything. A silence fell on the theatre. It was as if everything and everyone was stilled and frozen.

The presenter forced himself to move and speak. 'What?' he said – and managed to stumble on. 'What did you say, Miss Treadgold? You said – I thought you said –'

With a jerk, another camera cut in to show the man's face. His mouth gaped. His eyes showed their whites. He seemed to be choking.

He said, 'I think you said . . . You were going to say . . .'

Another untidy cut brought in another camera. The screen showed the union speaker with a finger in his collar. He too seemed shocked, gasping. The industrialist poured himself water with a hand that shook.

The programme's director switched shot yet again. Now Lisa Treadgold's face filled the screen. 'I think,' she began, serenely and beautifully in control of each syllable she spoke, 'that we should be talking of the future, not the past. Of what we can do instead of what we've failed to do. Don't you agree?'

And suddenly everything was all right again. The presenter smiled his practised smile, the industrialist and union man settled cosily into their familiar arguments, the studio audience nodded or shook heads as the words poured out. Cameras were smoothly cued in and out, sound levels were gently balanced –

Beth rose to her feet, her eyes wide. '*Now* don't you see?' she stormed, raking her wild eyes from face to face. The faces looked back at her mildly.

'But you *must* see!' she almost screamed. Mrs Carpenter said, 'See what, dear?' and looked anxious. Mr Carpenter asked, without much interest, 'What's up with you, Beth?' and before she could reply, looked back at the TV screen.

'Tim, Tim!' Beth cried, reaching out her hands to her brother. 'There's only you! Please say you understand! Please! Please!'

And just for a moment, Timothy thought he did understand. For a second, he thought he saw and remembered things from the past, a face, a feeling –

But then Beth ran from the room, sobbing. And Tim's pictures blurred.

Mrs Carpenter did not even turn her head when the weeping Beth ran out. She said, 'Oh dear, poor Beth,' in the same tone of voice she would have used to say, 'Oh dear, I forgot to bring in the jam.' Timothy stared at his mother. His mother stared at the TV screen.

His father, surely, would have seen that something was very wrong. 'Dad,' Timothy began. But his father waved him to silence. He too was absorbed in the television programme. 'Got to admit that that woman sometimes talks a lot of sense,' he said mildly, as Lisa Treadgold, smiling, gave her views on conscription for young people. She was in favour of it.

Timothy wanted to stand up and shout – to wave his arms and yell, 'Look! Listen! Something's happening, Beth says so, I think she's right!' He felt a great need rising inside him like a bubble, a need to straighten things out, to solve a mystery, to make a decision –

Lisa Treadgold smiled at him from the TV screen. Lisa Treadgold's pleasing, reasonable voice was warm and soothing in his ears. The bubble inside him shrank and softened and subsided. The great need died away. Timothy, too, slumped back in his chair. His face, like his parents' faces, became mild, accepting, docile, vaguely pleased.

Lisa Treadgold gave her opinions on corporal punishment in schools. She was in favour of it. Bring back the cane.

Timothy nodded agreement.

TUG-OF-WAR

Yet, in the night, he lay awake, wide awake, his brain playing a tug-of-war that he could not control.

He had timidly entered Beth's room to say goodnight to her. 'Oh, go *away*, leave me *alone*!' she moaned. She lay across her bed, her face in her pillow.

'But, Beth, I only –'

'Get out, you're *stupid*, you're *awful*, get *out*!'

Timid Timothy got out and went to bed.

As soon as he turned the light out, his brain started on him. The tug-of-war. Lisa seemed to be pulling one way, Beth another. He could not understand what either of them wanted. He wished they'd go away, leave him alone (no, that was Beth talking). He wished Lisa would stop smiling at him: but her smile was lovely, warming, reassuring, a perfect smile, not too little, not too much, just right. Yet all wrong.

Downstairs, the little clock on the mantelpiece went 'Ding, ding, ding'. Three o'clock in the morning. Timothy grunted, sat up in bed and said out loud, 'I'll write to Mr Fisk. This time, I'll actually do it.' Just writing to him might help Tim sort things out in his mind – might cut through the fog that kept rolling over his brain whenever it tried to concentrate on certain questions. Questions about Lisa, and someone else, someone the fog wouldn't let him remember. Someone belonging to the past.

Yes, he'd write to Mr Fisk; and get back a helpful, lively, amusing, practical letter. From one writer to another.

Yet Timothy did not get out of bed. His eyes itched with tiredness. He could not use his typewriter, the noise would wake people. And his bed was warm.

He sighed and pulled the bedclothes over him. He began to compose a letter in his mind, an amusing letter, a bit cheeky here and there yet still straight to the point –

But what *was* the point?

Timothy swore, switched on his bedside light, wrote a letter, put it in an envelope, stamped it and left it ready for posting. The letter was short and sweet. It gave news of all the family, then said, in effect, 'I don't know what is happening to me – to the family – to the people I work with. I'm confused. It all stems from Lisa Treadgold. Is something happening to us all? Is something happening to you? *What*?'

Once he had finished the letter, the tug-of-war stopped. He slept. Next day he posted the letter.

The answer came by return post.

Mr Fisk's letter was not so much a surprise as an

astonishment. Normally, his letters had a flavour to them – even a texture, loose and friendly and familiar, like a favourite old coat. But *this* letter! . . .

Dear Timothy,

Many thanks for your letter. I am very pleased to hear from you that you are applying yourself seriously to your journalistic work.

I am afraid, Timothy, that you will have to work even harder! Your writing still exhibits a carelessness and looseness that does you little credit. It does not do to begin a letter, even to so old and understanding a friend as myself, with the words, 'Well, nothing much has happened since I last wrote.' And 'Father is fine, Mother likewise' is not a happy choice of words.

In your penultimate paragraph, you write – 'Beth is making us all RATHER anxious, she seems RATHER hysterical', etc. You are prone to such repetitions and must strive to avoid them, even in friendly correspondence.

In your last paragraph, you use the word (if it is a word – I hope it is not) 'telly'. This is slang of the most degraded kind.

I was about to warn you of the dangers of over-enthusiastic use of the exclamation mark, but I see that I have used the mark myself. So I will spare your blushes – and my own – and take the rebuke no further. The last thing I want is to chill the warmth of our friendship.

I note that your real concern in writing to me is to elicit my opinions regarding Lisa Treadgold. I am not in the least surprised that you find her impact disturbing: so are the reactions experienced after being inoculated against smallpox and other unpleasant diseases. One must endure discomfort in order to achieve a long-term protection, a future benefit. You are passing through the discomforting stage. I passed through it some time ago.

My first opinion of Miss Treadgold was that she was yet another artificially created Television Personality – a woman of no importance.

I now consider her to be a wholly admirable phenomenon. All the more so since I have had the privilege of reading her written words (my publishers are to produce her forthcoming book and I was consulted in the capacity of publisher's reader). She is astonishingly clear and frank about the implications of the three Ds. We must strive, she writes, to restore *Decency* to our personal, local and national lives; *Discipline* ourselves to accept various restrictions (but these restrictions are, as she points out, really our 'freeways to a greater liberty'); and above all we must *Dedicate* ourselves to a concept of Obedience – which means that we must *act*.

She admits that some of the actions we must take will leave a bitter taste, at first. People living in what they think to be a democracy do not like the idea of reporting on the activities of their neighbours; or of physically enforcing law and order. But these and many other surrenders must be made if the greater good is to be attained. You, my dear boy, must prepare your mind for some considerable changes. As for Beth! – well, I do not think we need bother ourselves unduly about such juvenile and hysterical outpourings. However, please extend to her my usual good wishes.

With cordial regards to yourself and the family,
Yours sincerely,
Nicholas Fisk

When he first read this letter, Timothy thought, 'This is some sort of spoof. It isn't Mr Fisk writing. Or if it is, he is playing a game with me . . .'

He read the letter again, and again; and it seemed to come into focus. The words he had at first thought stuffy and pompous – words that had bored him, numbed him – began to make some sort of sense.

He read the letter yet again and seemed to see Lisa's face behind the paper, nodding and smiling at him, approving, giving her blessing.

He read the letter for the last time and suddenly shouted 'Bosh and twaddle and drivel!' at the top of his voice and flung the piece of paper from him.

The letter was the first of many confusing, contradictory experiences . . .

PEOPLE CHANGE . . .

'Kindly switch it off,' Mr Carpenter said, pointing his finger at the TV set. 'It is quite disgusting.'

'But it's your favourite programme!' Beth said. 'You love Lenny Mount!'

'Kindly switch it *off*!' Mr Carpenter said.

Beth was still too surprised to obey. She had reason to be surprised. Lenny Mount had a whole season of fifty-minute peak-period shows. They were naughty, clever, fast-moving and filled with sketches of the kind in which pretty girls' skirts get blown over their heads. Lenny Mount himself made rude jokes with an innocent look on his face. It was the sort of programme that, done badly, makes you feel depressed; but done well, as Lenny Mount did it, it was silly and cheerful and very often witty. To Mr Carpenter, the show was a sort of release. He was a considering, conscientious man: Lenny Mount's show was a holiday from himself and his work.

Yet now his face showed only anger and disgust.

'Switch it OFF!' he barked.

Beth obeyed. Lenny Mount's face and a cluster of girls in underclothes suddenly shrank to a bright dot – then vanished.

'Disgusting!' said Mr Carpenter.

Beth turned to look at Timothy. He always watched the Lenny Mount shows. Beth knew that, though he pretended not to, he liked the pretty girls. Yet his face, too, was set in an expression of lofty disgust. 'That sort of thing,' he said loudly, 'is exactly what we don't need.'

'I quite agree,' said Mr Carpenter.

'But why?' Beth demanded, 'Only last week, you were saying, "Come on, hurry up and finish dinner, I don't want to miss –"'

'I do not enjoy watching the sort of entertainment,' Mr Carpenter began, 'that deliberately degrades the values by which our society should try to live.'

'But last week, and the week before, you were laughing away like anything –'

'We live in serious times, Beth,' Mr Carpenter continued, deliberately not hearing her. 'The nation must put its mind to the higher things of life.'

'Decency,' said Timothy. 'Discipline. Dedication.'

Mr Carpenter nodded his head. 'Timothy is right, Beth,' he said. 'You are, perhaps, too young to understand; but not too young to obey! In this house, there can be no time for foul-mouthed, slack-minded, frivolous exhibitions. We must dedicate ourselves to higher purposes, Beth!'

'Decency,' said Timothy. 'Discipline. Dedication.'

Father and son nodded their heads, slowly and solemnly.

Beth looked from the one to the other. Her lips parted as if she were about to speak. But then she thought better of it. She left the room, her eyes glowing like coals.

'My gawd, I don't believe it!' said the director of the Lenny Mount show, two days later. He waved the viewing figures for the Lenny Mount show under the research girl's nose. 'Ratings down sixty-seven per cent! *Sixty-seven per cent!*'

'I wish you would not use that expression,' she said.

'What expression?'

'"My gawd". I find it offensive.'

'*You* find *that* offensive?' he said, amazed. The research girl, Wilma, could be a bit of a raver. The director stared at her. As he stared, his expression changed. His face became clouded and uncertain. 'These figures,' he said. 'They're impossible! I mean, we've dropped through the floor! I mean, they're *glued* to the box when Lenny's on! People never switch off on Lenny!'

'People change,' said Wilma quietly.

'Not by sixty-seven per cent,' the director said.

'People change,' Wilma repeated. 'I know *I've* changed. Have you?' She returned his stare.

The director was confused. 'What do you mean, have I changed?' he said. He thought about it for several seconds and then said, almost to himself, 'Well . . . Have I?'

He had, of course. Beth could have told him. But Wilma could not.

Letter from Mr Fisk, five days later

Dear Timothy,

I am glad to hear from you that you observe in yourself, and in those around you, the evidence of change.

In your last letter, for instance, you wrote of a new spirit in the conduct of affairs at the office of the *Gazette*. To me, this seems yet another example of a widespread and very important change: a change of heart; a change of purpose; a change of direction.

We, as a nation, are ripe for this change, as I am sure you will agree, Timothy. There is a new spirit abroad. A spirit which, if carried by every one of us as a brightly burning torch is carried, may – no, *shall*! – lead us onwards to a great and worthy goal.

But first we must, each and everyone, as did the knights of old, dedicate ourselves anew. We must forget the darkness of the past and turn our faces to that brightly burning torch of the future.

Do you agree with me, Timothy? Will you, like me, renounce the darkness and seek the light? Will you, too, join the Crusade?

I hope and trust you will. I have made a start by pledging my service – and one third of my income, present and future – to the R.O.L. I trust you will make a similar act of dedication: and endeavour to persuade all those around you, within and without the circle of the family, to act as you act – to support, in whatever way she asks, the purposes of the R.O.L. and Lisa Treadgold.

And Timothy: let there be no delay!

Yours,

Nicholas Fisk

Dear Mr Fisk,

I have, as you knew I would, taken the steps you suggest. Both I and Mac have joined the R.J.L., the newly formed Rollers Junior League. All the older boys have done so. We are proud to wear our R.J.L. badges and pleased to see so many other young people wearing the buttons, badges and armbands. Lisa Treadgold herself found time to drop in briefly on our R.J.L. Recruiting Rally in the Parish Hall two days ago and said a few words. There was total silence while she spoke and three rousing cheers at the end of her address, which I will always remember. As you say, there is a new spirit abroad.

I wish that Beth (and the young children in the village) could experience and share in it! She is sullen and silent except when the Rollers and Lisa Treadgold are mentioned. Then she says insulting and wicked things, often ending her outburst with tears. It makes me, Mother and Father very sad, for we are all completely loyal to the Cause. It is the same at the *Gazette* offices. There is no more larking about, just steady work – much of it in support of the Rollers!

I must close now as I am attending a Roller meeting

this evening to discuss the adoption of a suitable R.J.L. uniform. The Mayor is to be one of the speakers.

Yours sincerely,

Timothy Carpenter

MAD, MAD, MAD!

Beth's diary of that same day

. . . everyone has gone mad, mad, MAD, that is the only explanation. Lisa this, Lisa that, and Rollers for breakfast, dinner and tea, they are *stupid* all of them, why can't they see? And nobody will listen to me, oh of course not! I am just a stupid infant, nothing I say counts.

I shouted it out last evening at the top of my voice, I said, LOOK! DON'T YOU SEE, LISA T. IS GETTING AT YOU, IT IS LIKE *GRINNY* ALL OVER AGAIN, THE ONLY DIFFERENCE IS THAT THIS TIME IT IS LISA T. AND THE ROLLERS! But they just look at me as if I am mad and Mum said, 'Would you lay the table, dear,' as if I had not spoken. Yet I was *yelling*.

It is the same all over the village & everywhere else I dare say, everybody has gone Rollers MAD & going around looking like ghastly stupid SHEEP rolling their eyes all pious and goody-goody & moaning on about Decency Discipline & Dedication, that is the 3 Ds, fancy my own brother (and Mac too) believing such rot but then they are the right age, it is the same as it was with Grinny, everyone over 13 or 15 or so goes MAD and worships Lisa Treadgold. There is nothing on the telly but Lisa Lisa Lisa even our stupid old local rag the *Gazette* is all Lisa Lisa Lisa. To think my own brother works for it, it is dreadful.

What Lisa does, she hypnotizes everyone whenever she says 'You remember me' then they all sort of shake their heads for a split sec then say 'Oh yes' & from then on they are TRAPPED, they just do whatever she wants them to do. She said it on that telly programme, *OPINION*, just those three words and everyone looked like sheep all of a sudden, it started then. *The same words Grinny used!*

YOU REMEMBER ME
you remember me

There, I've written it down and stared at it for hours, it does not work on me at all however long I look at it, I don't feel anything or get hypnotized. It's only grown-ups and teenagers and they get hypnotized. I thought Tim would see through Lisa's trick and remember Grinny and everything by himself, but no, he's too deeply hypnotized, I've had to spell it out for him: LISA IS GRINNY. But he won't hear me.

There are animals called Lemmings they follow their leader Lemming and if the leader runs towards the edge of a cliff all the Lemmings follow & they all go over every one & are killed dead. That is what is going to happen to the HUMAN RACE if Lisa T. is not stopped.

I am not just hysterical I really mean it, we will all go over the edge of the cliff and that will be the end.

So I am writing my Secret Thoughts and Plan of Action in this diary I have never kept a diary before what a time to start (!!!) But I must get my thoughts clear & besides when everyone is dead someone may find this Diary and understand. At least they will know that there was one Sane person left on Earth & that is me, Beth Carpenter age eleven.

I know what I will do, I will start a Secret Society it will be called the Anti Lisa Society. Anti Rollers. Antiroll. Sanity Legion.

That one is best, ANTIROLL. ANTIROLL is secret enough the other names give it all away.

I will now list the founder members:

Mona Ratcliffe
Darren Nisbett
Fi and Peter Mathews (but NOT Alec)
Matthew and Melinda H
Asha & Ram Patel

<u>President and Founder,</u>
Beth Carpenter.

Now I will write letters to these founder members telling them to join the Society and we will swear secrecy and go into ACTION.

That man Mr Nicholas Fisk what a FOOL he must be I thought writers were supposed to be so *clever* Ha ha but he is just the same as the rest, Tim has been showing his stupid priggish grotty letters to everyone & saying 'There you are, my friend Mr Fisk is on Lisa's side too.' But he is just another Cleverstick. Never mind, wait until ANTIROLL gets going we will see who is clever then.

That is enough for now I must start on all the Society letters using carbon paper and so I will close my Diary now.

Next day, breakfast time

Timothy told Beth, 'You really must stop it. You can't say things like that about Lisa Treadgold, you just can't. I mean, your behaviour yesterday evening. Shouting and yelling!'

Beth took another piece of toast and said, 'I will say just what I jolly well like and you can lump it. And *please* will you pass the *marmalade*, how *kind* of you. Anyhow, nobody even notices what I say, I mean I was screaming and yelling last night yet nobody took any notice. Anyhow, I'm not going to stop saying what I think.'

Timothy scratched his head and wrinkled his brow. Watching him, Beth was almost sorry for him. She knew he did not know how to answer her; and that he was disturbed and upset by her behaviour; and that he was fond of her. Well, so he should be, she told herself. After all, we are brother and sister.

Timothy looked up at her and said, '*I* took notice of what you said yesterday evening. You were attacking –'

Before he could finish, Beth pounced on him with, 'What *did* I say, Tim? Can you remember any actual words I said?'

'You were shouting and yelling . . .' Timothy said, uncertainly. 'The exact words don't matter. You were attacking the Rollers and Lisa Treadgold.'

'Yes, I was and I meant it and still mean it. Do you remember any of the – *listen* to me, don't just fiddle with that spoon! – do you remember what words I used? What I actually *said*?'

She leaned forward, waiting for his answer. It was important to her. She had to know if he could hear her properly – if any of the grown-ups could; she needed to know just how deeply the hypnotic phrase 'You remember me!' dug itself into the minds of the people, more and more of them, that Lisa Treadgold controlled.

'Well?' Beth said.

Timothy's face was still twisted in a puzzled frown. But he pulled himself together and answered Beth. 'I don't think you understand,' he began, 'just how important Lisa Treadgold and the Roller movement are to the future of this nation –'

'*What did I actually say*?' Beth shouted, reaching forward her thin hand to clutch Timothy's arm. But he was not listening to her now. He seemed to be hearing an inner voice.

'Without decency, discipline and dedication – without punishment that fits the crime – how can we make ourselves worthy to enter the Bright Gateway of the Future?' Timothy recited. He no longer frowned. Now his head was up and his eyes were round and solemn.

And Beth no longer clutched his arm. Now she stared at her brother's face with a look of horror. 'What you said just then . . .' she murmured, 'those were the very words that Roller man on the telly said last night! His very words!'

'We are all of us instruments,' Timothy said, staring through and beyond Beth. 'Instruments for good. Instruments of tempered steel – surgical instruments of bright steel that can cut away, ruthlessly, the rotten, diseased parts of our society!'

Beth, white-faced, silently got up and left the room. At the doorway, she looked back at her brother.

Now he was nodding his head in time with his words. 'We must be prepared for the New Dawn,' he said. 'The New Dawn is coming.'

ANTIROLL

The Rollers marched down the High Street. In the town, in the village, the Rollers were marching, almost daily. The *Gazette* gave front-page coverage to every march.

Three boys and a girl, all seemingly about ten or eleven – but they were a long way away, Timothy could not see them properly – kept threading themselves in and out of the watching crowd lining the street. The children appeared and disappeared like diver ducks in a pond. 'Berks!' they yelled at the marchers. 'Morons! Fools! Wake up!'

The crowd placidly ignored them. No one hindered them, even when they darted at the marchers, snatching at armbands and trying to knock off the newly issued forage caps. The armbands and cap-bands were embroidered with R.O.L. R.O.L. R.O.L.

Like the crowd, the Roller marchers took no notice of the children. They simply stepped out to the music of the boater-hatted Dixieland band. The boater hats' ribbons read R.O.L. R.O.L. R.O.L.; so did the banners stretched across the street. Before, the band had been a six-piece. Now it was a ten-piece, better, brighter and brisker than ever. Timothy wrote in his reporter's notebook: 'To the stirring music of the band and the applause of the great crowd –'

He stopped writing and frowned. Those children were at it again. He saw that there were two groups of three, not just one group. The second group sprang out of the placid crowd just a few yards away from him. The children shouted, 'Wake up, wake up! You're hypnotized! Drugged! Wake up!'

One child shouted these words in the ear of an elderly woman. He tugged her sleeve and bellowed. The woman looked down at the frantic boy and nodded her head as if in agreement. Her face was mild and kind. She spoke. Timothy could read her lips. 'That's right, dear,' she began – or something like that – then, quite certainly, she said, 'Decency, Discipline, Dedication.'

She smiled down at the boy. He shook his head disbelievingly – gave up – and darted back into the crowd.

Timothy kept writing. The children did not matter. They were just stupid, minor interruptions to the big parade.

But the children had not finished. Here came a child, waving a big, untidy placard on a pole. The placard read:

ANTIROLL
Society

WAKE UP!
YOU ARE ALL HYPNOTIZED!
WAKE UP!

People smiled at the untidy placard, wobbling about on its shaky stick. Timothy smiled too. Then stopped smiling. The child holding the placard was a girl and the girl was his sister Beth.

He called her name, loudly and angrily. She did not hear. He shouted again, furiously, and she heard. She turned her head. He saw her face. She wore her crumpled blue canvas hat, her favourite hat with tin badges on it. Under the hat her face was small and young and defenceless. There were tears running down it, tears of rage, agony and frustration.

All at once, Timothy knew he had seen this face before, in another time, a time that surely had never happened.

And yet – and yet it seemed so real, that time, it was like scenes from a film or TV programme running in his mind, running very fast, too fast for him to keep up with or understand: but too real and true and interesting to be just a story on a screen . . .

There had been an old lady in an armchair, the armchair in the living room at home. The chair under the standard lamp. Beth, almost crouching, her face a spiteful mask, faced this woman and spat words at her, words full of hate and menace. Timothy himself was there. So was Mac. But it was the old woman in the chair who mattered.

No, that was wrong: she was not an old lady at all. She was a darting, hump-backed silver rat – the clothes were a disguise, even her bones and flesh and face were just masks and costumes.

The silver rat – and Beth: her hatred and fury had been true and real. Now the silver rat was tearing the old lady to pieces and Beth was glad. And Mac was glad. And so was he, Timothy.

'ROLLING along,' the marchers shouted, 'singing a song, SIDE BY SIDE!' Timothy was back again in the High Street, back to reality, free from the sudden dream. Timothy the reporter! Timothy the serious, sensible, disciplined young man, notebook in hand, ballpoint busy, recording important events!

But no, wait – *she* was still there, right in front of him, his bad little sister! And still her tear-stained face was pointing at him like an accusing finger and her mouth was opening and closing. She was saying something to him, he could not hear her above the noise of the band and the singing and cheers of the marchers. It was a good thing he could not hear her, he did not want to hear.

'SIDE . . . BY . . . SIDE!' bellowed the band: the drummer added his final *barra-BAM*! It was the end of the tune.

In the silence that followed, he could not fail to hear what Beth was saying.

'You do remember!' she wailed. 'You do! I know you do! You *know*, I know you know!'

The words pierced Timothy's mind. He gaped at Beth and dropped his ballpoint. His thoughts and memories and emotions choked him.

He found himself nodding his head stupidly, agreeing with Beth, ashamed of agreeing, ashamed of even knowing this ragamuffin girl with her silly hat and stupid placard.

'Yes!' he found himself saying. 'Yes, I *know*.'

RAT THING

Hours later, in Beth's little room, they talked. Beth kept clutching at him with her spiky fingers – kept thrusting her vivid dark face at him – kept insisting that Timothy said words he hated saying.

'Grinny,' he muttered. 'I remember Grinny.'

'Go on,' Beth insisted. 'Tell me about Grinny.'

'She was our great-aunt Emma. She came to the door, we took her in. She smiled all the time. We called her Grinny because she smiled. We didn't know where she came from. She just came, and lived with us, and sat in her chair and smiled.'

'And then, one evening,' Beth prompted, 'we did something to her, didn't we? Because we'd found out about her. She was in her chair in the living room –'

'The silver rat thing killed her!' Timothy said. 'We didn't do it, did we? It was the silver rat.' He rubbed his forehead; then said, his voice tired and uncertain, 'What was the silver rat?'

'It was Grinny!' Beth shouted. 'The thing inside her that made her work! Because she wasn't real, only the rat was real!'

Timothy shook his head protestingly. Beth would not let him go. She said, 'Listen, Timothy: was Grinny good or bad?'

'Bad. She was bad, I suppose. Because she was sent here to test us out. To find out if we could be invaded. Our world was to be invaded by *them*. And Grinny was the advance guard, we were her experiment. But it didn't work because we beat her –'

'We won!' Beth said. 'And now we've got to do it all again.'

Timothy shifted in his chair. 'I don't see . . .' he began. 'It can't be true, it just can't be . . . About Lisa Treadgold, I mean. Lisa Treadgold is good. The Rollers are good. Decency, Discipline, Dedication . . .'

Beth had to shake him by the shoulders, as if he were drugged or drunk. '*Who is Lisa Treadgold?*' she hissed.

Timothy tried to fight off the question but Beth was too strong. His head rolled as she shook him. '*Tell* me! *Say* it!'

At last he obeyed.

'Lisa Treadgold is Grinny,' he said. 'Grinny come again. But Grinny died! . . . didn't she?'

'Of course she did. But now there's Lisa. Who is Lisa?'

'Grinny come again . . .' He was talking like a sleepy child.

'So – come on, come on! – What are we going to do?'

'Fight her. Stop her. Whatever you say.'

'Yes, we're going to fight her. Stop her. Kill her.' She let go of his shoulders and stood back to look at her brother. What she saw – the drowsy, listless, dull-faced figure – made her despair. 'Oh, Tim!' she said, 'Tim, *please*! Please come back! Oh Tim . . .'

She began to cry angry, despairing tears that spurted out from between her black lashes. He stared at her, his mouth half open, dull-eyed. Lisa Treadgold still owned more than half of his mind. 'You remember me!' Lisa Treadgold had said: and most of his brain was still locked to Lisa by that phrase. Yet –

'Your hat!' Timothy said, suddenly. Now his face was half alive.

Through her tears, Beth said, 'Never mind my stupid *hat*! Oh, Tim, please come back!'

Timothy looked at the hat on her battered and stained bedside table. He picked it up, gazed at it and touched one of the fading tin badges. 'This afternoon,' he said, 'you wore it then.'

He took the hat in both hands; approached Beth; and, as if it were a coronation ceremony, carefully placed the blue hat on her head.

'*Real*,' he said. He sounded amazed. His face was beginning to come alive. '*You*, in your *hat*!' he said, as if making a great discovery. He adjusted the hat to exactly the right angle; then, for a long time, studied the effect.

'YOU were crying then, too,' he said at last. Beth nodded so hard that tears flew from her cheeks. Still Timothy studied her. Now his face was alive.

'Listen, Beth,' he said, 'I've worked it all out! About Lisa Treadgold and the Rollers!'

'Go on,' Beth whispered.

'Do you know what I think?' Timothy said excitedly. 'Lisa is just Grinny! Grinny back in another form!'

'Go on!' Beth repeated.

'But, Beth, don't you see, she's deadly! We've got to do something! We got rid of Grinny all right, but this time it's different – different and much worse! I mean, Lisa T has got the Rollers, the media, TV, everything! And people are queuing up to join her! – just begging to be allowed to line up for their own destruction! This time it's not just one family, it's the whole nation! We've got to stop her, Beth!'

'Go on, go on!' Beth said. She leaned forward, nodding at him, her eyes bright. But no longer with tears.

Beth's diary, two days later

. . . I just don't know, some of the time I think Tim's himself again and quite all right and the rest of the time he's rubbing his forehead and is gone all dopy again I wish I knew. It was so terrific when he snapped out of it – that was only 2 days ago & he was his old self again and it was lovely but it didn't last, next day it was all Lisa T. and D-D-D I could kill that woman I *will* kill her but how can I do it alone? If only Tim would come back to me properly & be the real Tim.

No, wait, I have a plan, we will somehow go to Lisa T., and I will somehow make Tim see her as she really is.

A trick, like the tricks we played on Grinny. Grinny could not stand electricity, that is how we got her in the end, frightening her with electricity. We will try that on Lisa T.

No wait none of this is any good because Mac is not with us, I tried and tried, argued and argued but he does not hear he just looks STUPID & *literally does not hear*.

Never mind, we will get into Lisa T.'s house somehow again, and I will think of something I will play it by Ear. But how do we get in her house? HOW? I will think and think & write down all the ways to try, we MUST get in her house . . .

AMAZER-LASER

Early September

Had Beth only known, getting into Lisa's house was to be the easiest thing in the world: for Lisa had already invited the *Gazette* to visit her. The *Gazette* included Timothy. And where Timothy went, Beth could easily find an excuse to accompany him . . .

Bunny delivered the note of invitation. 'I have the beginnings of a news item for Miss Bishop,' the note ran. 'Nothing important – but the *Gazette* has been so helpful in the past that I'm sure you won't mind . . .'

'*Mind!*' Fanny Bishop said. Her face was nun-like as she stared at the precious letter. For Fanny, like Len Sturgeon and almost everyone else, was completely converted to Lisa Treadgold and the Rollers.

'I'm coming too!' Timothy shouted. 'She must mean me to come too!'

'She doesn't say so,' Fanny said, jealously holding the invitation. She wanted the Lisa interview all to herself.

'Well, she must have meant to! I'll ask Bunny, she'll tell you I'm right, I'm invited too!'

'Bunny's already left,' Fanny said smugly. 'At least five minutes ago!'

'Well, I'll run after her and sort it out!' Timothy said. He rushed out of the *Gazette* office, flung his leg over his bike and pedalled off at full speed in the direction he knew Bunny must have taken: straight along the High Street, then turn left, then straight on through the country roads to Lisa's house.

He never caught up with Bunny. She seemed to have vanished.

Instead, he met Mac, on his bicycle. Timothy said, 'Look, I'm chasing after Bunny, she must have come this way, have you seen her?'

Mac stared at Timothy strangely. 'Seen her?' he said. 'You bet I've seen her! It was weird, really weird!'

'What do you mean, weird? Where is she? I've got something important to say to her –'

'I don't think she'd *hear* you, the state she was in!' Mac replied.

Now Timothy stared. 'What's been happening?' he said.

Mac said, 'I was going along the High Street. I needed a thirteen-amp fuse so I turned off down Water Lane to go to Lectronic. Bunny was there. She was standing outside the shop.'

'So?' Timothy said. 'What about it?' He pictured Lectronic in his mind. A small shop in a street of small shops. None of them lasted long. Lectronic was typical – cheap hi-fi stuff, disco lighting sets, all kinds of electrical bits and pieces but never the one you needed.

They'd got this window display: flashing disco lights and what they called AMAZER-LASER. Rods of light like laser beams, all different colours. For parties.

Mac said, 'She was standing there with her mouth half open. She looked funny. Funny-peculiar. She just stood there, like a soldier, with her bike blocking half the pavement.'

Timothy said, 'What do you mean, like a soldier?'

'All rigid. Standing to attention. Not moving at all. Staring straight ahead of herself.'

'Staring at what?'

Mac said, 'She was staring into the shop window. She looked sort of shocked. Her eyes were wide open, sort of bulging and her face was all shiny. And she was talking to herself. It was weird.'

'What was she saying?'

'Well, that's the funny thing. She was saying what she said before, that day at Lisa T.'s when she fainted. She kept saying, "I didn't see that! I couldn't have done!" And then she said, "No, no, they're not real. I don't see them at all, they don't exist!" She said things like that. She was barely moving her lips, it really was weird.'

'What did you do?'

'I tried to snap her out of it. I said, "Bunny! Bunny! It's me, Mac, how are you?" Things like that. But she kept muttering. Then I saw what she was staring at. It was the Amazer-Laser display, you know, those rods of light.

'There was one rod sticking straight up, she was staring at it so hard you'd have thought her eyes would have rolled out on the pavement. She didn't even blink, she just stared and stared at this rod of light.'

Timothy said, 'You can hypnotize chickens with a chalk line. You put the chicken's head on the ground and draw a chalk line from its nose, leading into the distance. The chicken just stands there, head down, with its beak touching the chalk line. It will stand there for ever, they say. Perhaps the Amazer-Laser had her hypnotized.'

Mac said, 'Yes, it was like that. She was the chicken and the Amazer-Laser was the chalk line. It was spooky.'

'What happened next?'

Mac said, 'I kept trying to get through to her, but she took no notice. I shook her arm, things like that. I felt a fool. Still, hardly anyone shops in Water Lane so I don't suppose anyone was watching us. I said things to her. Things like: "Don't you want to get back to the High Street to do some shopping?" But nothing worked. Not until I said, "Look, Bunny, please, look at me! I'm Mac! You know, Tim's and Beth's friend! You remember me!"'

'And that did it?' Timothy asked.

'Oh, yes!' Mac replied, heavily sarcastic. 'That did it just fine! As soon as I said, "You remember me," she snapped out of it. She certainly did!'

'What did she do?'

'She slapped my face! *Wham!*'

'What do you mean?'

'She just swung her mighty hand in a wide, graceful

curve and slammed me one in the chops. She hit me so hard my teeth rattled like dice!'

'Look, Mac, come off it!'

'All right, you say she didn't slap my face. I say she did. A real cracker. And while I was still getting over it, she lurched off, pushing her bike, getting her feet tangled with the wheels and that sort of thing. One minute she'd been standing there like a paralysed chicken, the next thing she shoved off . . .'

Mac went on talking. Timothy stopped listening. He thought over the story Mac had just told him.

Bunny outside Lectronic. Bunny stares at a rod of laser-like light. She's hypnotized, she says the same things she said on that day she fainted – things about not believing what she is seeing. But when Mac says a certain thing to her, she suddenly comes out of her trance – and gives Mac a slap in the face.

She does that because Mac spoke certain words. Certain words. Certain words. *What* words?

He couldn't remember. Yet Mac had only just finished speaking those words.

Then why not ask Mac to repeat them?

Because, somehow, he didn't want to. Mac was still talking. It would be rude to interrupt him. And besides . . .

A fog curled and spread in the corners of Timothy's brain. Now Mac was saying, 'Hey! I must go! See you later, then?' And Timothy heard himself reply, 'Fine. Later.'

Mac was gone and the fog rolled in and on and over.

But that evening, Timothy pushed the fog away and sat in front of his typewriter, determined to get everything down on paper. What mattered, he knew, was to write the words – the three short words – that Mac had spoken to Bunny. He believed Mac's story. He wrote it down. Just when he was reaching the important part – the part where Mac said the three words – there was a banging on his door. Beth was outside his bedroom. She was in a temper.

'You've pinched my mask and snorkel!' she shouted. 'Oh yes you have! I know you've got it and I want it back now, it's mine!'

'Oh belt up!' Timothy shouted back. 'I'm busy, go away!'

'You're just pretending to be busy, dabbing away at your typewriter! – you're not *really* busy! Where's my mask and snorkel?'

'Where you left them,' Timothy said. 'On the bird-bath in the garden. I can see them from here. Really, Beth . . .'

'Oh,' Beth said, in a very different voice. 'Well, we all make mistakes . . .'

'And I really am working,' Timothy said. 'So go away.'

'You're not working, you're just pretending to work, I know you!' Beth said, working herself up. She hated to be proved wrong about anything.

'I am *busy*,' Timothy said. 'Tomorrow is a *big day*, understand? Please *go away*.'

'Why is tomorrow a big day?' Beth demanded. 'Where are you going? To Lisa Treadgold? Is it Lisa? Is it?'

'It so happens,' Timothy said grandly, 'that the *Gazette*

has been invited to Miss Treadgold's home. And I will assist at the interview.'

'Oh, super, so will I!' Beth said. 'I hate that woman! So I'm going to be there too!'

'Oh no you're not,' Timothy said. Now he was alarmed.

'Oh yes I am!' Beth replied. Just you try and stop me!'

Timothy cursed himself for being an idiot: and forgot all about the three words Mac had spoken to Bunny.

THE DRUNKEN BANJO-PLAYER

Next morning, they set out in Fanny's car for Lisa's house. Fanny's car no longer smelled of cigarettes. She had given up smoking. Lisa Treadgold did not approve of smoking. Fanny wore a tweedy sort of shooting hat with a Roller hatband pinned round its crown. Lisa Treadgold approved of people who 'showed the world they were Rollers and proud of it'. So Fanny wore her hatband and Timothy wore his R.J.L. forage cap, with the big, bold R.O.L. R.O.L. cap-band.

Fanny was too excited to say much as she drove. Twice, she said, 'I wonder what she wants us for?' Each time, Timothy replied, 'As long as she *wants* us, that's good enough for me!' He smiled. Fanny smiled.

Their contentment did not last long. A quarter of a mile from the house, they overtook Beth. She was pedalling her bike towards Lisa Treadgold's house. Fanny beeped the car's horn and Timothy, his heart sinking, wound down the near-side window. 'Hey!' he shouted to Beth. 'Where do you think you're going?'

'Same place as you!' she shouted back, without bothering to look at her brother. 'Lisa Treadgold's! Try and stop me!' She pedalled on without turning her head.

Fanny muttered. In the old days, she would have sworn. 'How did that awful kid sister of yours know where we're going?' she demanded of Timothy.

'Well . . .' he replied feebly.

'You didn't *tell* your sister, did you? Well, *did* you?'

'Well . . . yes, I may have done,' Timothy said.

'You blabbermouthed oaf!' Fanny said, and drove through the gates and into the drive of Lisa's house with her face set in an expression of disgust.

They rang the bell. Nobody came.

They rang the bell again and heard it jingling a long way away. But again, nobody came. Nobody but Beth, that is, who pedalled up the drive, leaned her bike against a tree, close to a big, battered van, already parked; and gave Fanny and Timothy a bright smile and a calm 'Good morning'.

'*Get out!*' Timothy replied in a ferocious whisper.

'*Go home!*' Fanny Bishop said, whispering also. For now they could hear approaching footsteps. Footsteps running, heavily.

The front door jerked open a few inches and Bunny's face filled the gap.

She looked worse than ever – more heated, more spotty, more anxious. 'Oh!' she said. 'Oh, gosh! It's you! Oh, gosh, I'd quite forgotten, she'll be furious, oh Lord, it can't be quarter to eleven *already*! – you'd better come in, she's got someone with her, everything's gone wrong this morning –'

Fanny and Timothy found themselves once again in the conservatory. Too late, they discovered that Beth, too, had slid herself in. They stared at her coldly. She stared back, poker-faced, then flipped the brim of her old hat with a cheeky finger and said, 'I know: two's company, three's a crowd. Too bad.' Then, coolly, she asked Bunny, 'How long will Lisa Treadgold be before she gets round to us?'

'Oh dear, I suppose I ought to – everything's running late this morning, it's all my fault –'

'Who's with her now?' Beth said.

'Oh, it's awful, she's furious, people are always letting her down, this time it's the Band, I mean one of the Dixieland Band, the sort of leader – well, anyhow, the one that makes all the *arrangements* –'

Timothy looked up, interested. 'Banjo?' he said. 'Banjo Heatherington?'

'Yes, that's the one and I think he's half *drunk* or terribly hungover, he shows no *respect*!'

'No respect for Miss Treadgold?' Beth asked innocently. 'But that's impossible, isn't it, Timothy? Isn't it, Fanny?' Timothy and Fanny looked at her blankly and nodded.

Bunny twisted her hands and kept looking at the ceiling. 'They're up there!' she said dramatically. 'He's a *dreadful* man . . . !'

Timothy looked puzzled when Bunny said this. Banjo Heatherington had never struck Timothy as a dreadful man. He had met Banjo twice. Both times, Timothy had been helping prepare stories about the Rollers Dixieland Band. Both times, he had sought out Banjo because the man was a frets player, a banjoist, and Timothy was trying to learn guitar. It had turned out that Banjo's great interest was the guitar, not the banjo; and he had shown Timothy some runs of chords. He had even written them down. Banjo had been loud and beery; he had also been patient, encouraging and kind.

'He says he wants more money,' Bunny said. 'More money or he'll leave. And he says the band will go with him, but I can't believe they would. They couldn't desert Miss Treadgold, she would never allow it . . .'

Now, above their heads, they could hear the sound of pacing footsteps; and Banjo's voice. He was shouting and laughing. The laughter was a sort of weapon, to drown argument. There were quicker, lighter footsteps; a door opened; and Banjo and Lisa were coming down the stairs. He was still shouting and laughing. 'You've got to be out of your tiny mind!' he bellowed. 'A hundred and eighty? We'd want twice that – *and* proper accommodation! Listen, lady –'

'I am Lisa Treadgold,' said Lisa. 'You remember me. *You remember me!*'

Beth saw Timothy's jaw drop: saw Fanny's face lose its colour: saw their eyes widen. She could almost see the fog rolling over their minds.

Yet outside the room, Banjo's voice was strident and unchanged.

'Oh, *that*!' Banjo jeered. 'The magic phrase! Listen,

Madam Treadgold, you can fool most of the people most of the time but you can't fool all of the people all of the time! "*You remember me*" . . . Yeah, it's terrific, it's hypnotic. But it doesn't work on me! You're playing in the wrong key! I've got a key of my own, I can block you out! I *am* blocking you out!'

'Oh dear, oh Lord!' Bunny whispered. Her face was shining with shock and terror. 'He can't talk to her like that, he doesn't understand . . . ! What shall I do?' She looked desperately from Timothy to Fanny, from Fanny to Beth. Lisa Treadgold and Banjo Heatherington were right outside the closed door of the conservatory now. 'She'll *do* something . . . !' Bunny whispered. 'She'll *hurt* . . . !'

Beth, her face pinched with excitement and tension, said, 'I want to see! Open the door!' Bunny could not summon the courage to obey. Beth had to open the door herself.

The opened door revealed a frozen set-piece. Banjo had one foot on the lowest step of the flight of carpeted stairs. Lisa was above him. He was staring, with fixed intensity, into Lisa Treadgold's eyes: challenging her. 'I'm blocking you out!' he said, in a low, steady voice. 'What are you going to do about it?'

She said, 'You remember me!' Her voice was quiet and controlled and steadier than his. She was smiling her small, controlled and beautiful smile. She descended a single step, seeming to glide towards him. 'You remember me!' she said.

Banjo flinched and moved backwards perhaps three inches. Sweat seemed to squeeze itself from the pores of his red face. 'You're wasting your time,' he grunted. 'I told you: you're off-key! I've got a key of my own!'

Lisa's face moved another inch closer to his. 'Ah, you're a strong man,' she smiled. 'A most unusual man. You have strength. Strength. Such strength.'

Very slowly, she extended her right hand as if to touch him. '*Don't!*' Bunny said, in a sort of choking gasp. No one heard her. Everyone watched the pretty arm and hand weave forward. Tim had a sudden picture of a cobra.

Banjo began to shake. The droplets of sweat on his face ran together and poured down. 'I'm taking the band to Amsterdam,' he almost groaned. 'You're not going to stop me . . .'

Lisa nodded her smiling head. 'To Amsterdam,' she agreed. 'Such a shame. But we part friends, Mr Heatherington. You remember me – as your friend. Shake hands.'

Automatically, Banjo put out his right hand. Again, Bunny gasped, '*Don't!*'

Lisa took his big hand in her own ivory fingers. The fingers closed. Her fingers gripped.

'Strength, you have a good, strong hand, Mr Heatherington!'

Her fingers tightened on red flesh. The red flesh whitened where the ivory fingers clasped it.

'Oh, I admire strength!' she said. She gave a little laugh. Her fingers tightened. Banjo screamed hoarsely and fell to his knees. His eyes bulged.

'Strength and discipline!' Lisa said, the words clear and sweet – and tightened her grip.

Banjo raised his head and howled like a dog. The sound was so strange that it broke the spell that froze the watchers. Bunny screamed, 'No, no, NO!' and ran forward, blindly and uselessly snatching at the space surrounding Lisa, never touching her, never affecting her. It was as if she was plucking at a ghost.

Timothy said, 'I think we ought to be going soon, Fanny. What do you think?' He looked at her earnestly. His voice was quiet and normal, yet the pulses in his temple beat wildly, as if to burst through the skin.

Fanny said, 'Yes, if Miss Treadgold is satisfied that we've got everything necessary.' Her voice was normal. Her face was chalk-white.

Only Beth truly saw what there was to see: the man, gasping, sometimes shouting his agony as he twisted and writhed on the floor; the woman calmly smiling, her hand clamped like a vice on the crushed, white and scarlet hand of the man. The cool, gracious little smile of the welcoming hostess; the twisted, sweating agony of the face of her guest. Yet he spoke no words of protest: and his eyes were accepting, obedient, dog-like.

Bunny still battered with clumsy hands at the space surrounding Lisa – still shouted, 'No, no, no!' – but Bunny did not matter, Bunny was somehow not real. She did not belong in the picture that only Beth could see.

Beth jerked herself forward, small fists raised, as if to join Bunny in beating against the non-existent and invisible wall surrounding Lisa Treadgold. But then Beth's courage failed. She backed away: gave a great, despairing howl; and ran.

She ran from the house, ran through the grounds, ran through the gates and into the road. She ran until her muscles failed her, then tripped and fell, slamming her head against a thick branch lying in the grassy verge.

Now she lay silent and still. The long grass that had grown all summer waved over her, whispering mildly in the warm breezes. Little insects investigated her, found her uninteresting and went on their busy ways.

Eventually, Fanny and Timothy drove along the road in Fanny's car. Fanny saw the sprawled body of Beth. She did not even slow the car. A soothing sponge, a wraith of fog, wiped her mind clean of what she saw.

Timothy saw nothing. He stared ahead of himself, frowned, gnawed his lip and tried to think. But his thoughts were wisps of the same fog, scurrying fragments of obscurity. His mind was as blank as his eyes.

BUSTER

Lying in the grass, the unconscious Beth had a strange dream. She was being eaten alive, from the head down, by a rather pleasant dog.

The dog's tongue was sometimes cool, sometimes warm, but always wet. Beth did not mind the tongue – indeed, she quite enjoyed it. But she wished the dog would not bite her so savagely. Each time its teeth sank into her scalp, there was a burning pain. Not agony: pain. And the pain interrupted the soothing feeling of the cool, warm, wet tongue.

She woke up to find that her dream was about eighty per cent true. There was the pleasant dog – she even knew its name, Buster, and its owner, Lisa Treadgold. And the dog, a small Dalmatian, was methodically licking the top of her head. It was not biting her, however. The pain came when Buster's tongue touched the big bruise and cut she had suffered when she fell forward and hit the log. She remembered all this and sat up.

'Do you *mind*?' she said to Buster. 'That happens to be *my* blood you're licking.'

The dog looked apologetic and licked her hand instead of her cut head. Beth gently explored the cut with her fingers and offered a fingertip slightly smeared with blood to Buster, who gratefully licked it clean. 'I suppose I'll get a terrific headache,' she told Buster. 'Amazing I haven't got one now.'

The dog looked sympathetic and began scratching itself. Beth got to her feet and tried to remember further back. She succeeded and her expression changed. 'Oh!' she gasped. But before she had time to be horrified by her memories, she heard the voice of Bunny calling, 'Buster! Buster!', and saw the girl running heavily towards her along the little road.

'He's with you,' Bunny gasped, clutching Buster's collar. 'Thank heavens! She's furious with me, she's always furious when any of the dogs get on the road. But what am I supposed to do? I can't control – gosh, what's happened to you? How did you bang your head?'

Beth explained, realizing that Bunny was incapable of listening to her words. She kept talking to give herself the chance to study Bunny's face. It was a frantic face. It was falling apart. It shook as if chilled, sweated as if roasted. And Bunny's eyes continually darted back along the road, towards the gates of the big house.

'So I sort of knocked myself out,' Beth was saying when Bunny interrupted.

'There'll be murder,' Bunny said. 'I'll murder her or she'll murder everyone . . . Poor Banjo, how's he going to drive his car away with one hand? Oh, I wish I knew what to do!' She collapsed into the grass beside Beth and began to cry, wetly and noisily.

Beth waited until Bunny ran out of sobs, wiped herself with a crumpled handkerchief and sat knees apart, head hanging down. 'It's hopeless!' she said. 'I just don't know what to do! Ever since that day –'

'Yes, that day!' Beth cut in sharply. 'The day you gave Lisa breakfast in bed. The day something happened and you were scared to death and passed out. *I* know what happened!'

'You don't,' Bunny said feebly. 'You can't!'

'Oh, can't I? Well, let me take a guess. You took her breakfast in to her. The room was dark, right? And there was a light of some sort –'

'Like a rod, a whip!' Bunny said eagerly. 'No, it was more like a sort of pencil of light, it came straight down from the ceiling – right through the ceiling – and on to her bed –'

'And into her brain,' Beth said.

'Yes! From above, right through the roof and ceiling and into her brain! Blue light or perhaps it was violet . . . And it flickered, very fast, all the time – flickered on and off –'

'And her eyes, Lisa's eyes, they were open, weren't they?' Beth said. She was on all fours, her face thrust right into Bunny's face, her energy feeding the big, slack body of Bunny.

'Her eyes were open,' Bunny said. 'Wide open. And she was sitting up in bed, all rigid. And her eyes . . . her eyes . . . they were *alight*! On *fire*!'

'Her lips were moving,' Beth prompted.

'Her lips were moving,' Bunny echoed. 'And sounds were coming out. Mad sounds. Impossible sounds. So fast! Like thousands of starlings when they settle down for the night . . . They wheel round and round over Trafalgar Square, millions of them, all screeching and twittering at once . . . I've been to London, you know. Oh, yes. Her voice was like Trafalgar Square and the starlings.'

'What do you think was happening?' Beth said. 'Come on, Bunny! What's the answer?'

Bunny shook her head like a child refusing a dose of medicine. 'How am *I* supposed to know?' she whined. 'What's it got to do with me? Why always me?'

'Come on, Bunny, out with it!' Beth said. Now her fingers were firmly dug into Bunny's arm.

'Suppose she can hear us!' Bunny said, staring with terrified eyes at Beth.

'She can't,' Beth said flatly. 'Go on. Tell me what was happening when the light came and Lisa's eyes lit up and she talked that way.'

There was a long pause as Bunny again tried to refuse the nasty medicine. She hid her head, let herself surrender to hopeless tears, tried peevishly to pull away from Beth's claw-like grasp. Then, suddenly, she gave in. She lifted her head, stuck out her lower lip and said, 'She was talking to *them*. *Them*.'

'Fine!' Beth said. 'Who's *them*?'

'*Them*, out *there*!' Bunny said loudly. Suddenly her voice was raucous and defiant. 'She talks to *them*, and *they* talk to *her*!' she almost shouted. 'They give her her orders or she gives them theirs. I don't know which, and they talk through that rod of light! I've seen it more than once, but I didn't want to see, I told myself, "No, it never happened." But, it did happen, it does happen. They're out there all the time, they're out there now! They *use* her!'

'What for?' Beth said softly. She knew she was nearly there.

'To trap us!' Bunny burst out – 'To make slaves of us! It's got to be something like that, it stands to reason! And one day, perhaps soon –'

'Quite soon,' Beth said, 'they'll come. When Lisa tells them we're ready! They'll come, all of them. And almost all the world will be waiting to welcome them, do what they say – form *queues* to obey them, *beg* to become slaves! Unless we stop her. And them.'

'We can't stop her,' Bunny said dully. She had slumped forward – had lost all her pride and strength again. 'You don't understand, you can't possibly know, you don't *live* with her as I do!'

'But I *did*!' Beth said. 'Me and all my family! She was in our house, living with us. She looked different. She had a different name and body, she was an old lady we called Grinny. But it was her all right! And we beat her. We killed her. Timothy and me and Mac.'

'Oh no you didn't,' Bunny said. 'Lisa can't be beaten. I know. She's hardly human, you don't understand! Listen – you remember that day when I spilled the boiling water –'

'Oh, that,' Beth said. 'That was because she's a machine. I mean, you won't hurt a mincing machine by pouring boiling water over it. But you can still jam its works!'

Bunny was not listening. 'The poor dogs!' she blubbered. 'I mean, *they* know what she is, so why can't everyone see and understand? Humans, I mean. Dogs always *know* . . . that's why they're terrified of her – not just because she's cruel, though she broke Prince Igor's leg deliberately, did you know that? – but because she's inhuman and evil and horrible. Yet to begin with, I worshipped her . . .'

She cried noisily, with her head between her knees.

Beth let her cry. She thought, 'In Grinny's time, we saw the spaceship that controlled Grinny. There's been no talk of UFOs this time. I suppose they work at longer range, or something. They've become cleverer.'

When Bunny's sobs died down, Beth said, 'We're going to kill her. Just as we killed Grinny. The one before Lisa Treadgold.'

'How?' said the muffled voice of Bunny.

'I don't know yet. But you're going to help.'

'Oh no I'm not! I'm probably dead already. If she's heard us talking –'

'You're going to help us kill her.'

'How? How, *how*, HOW?'

'I don't know yet. But it begins with you joining the Society. It's a secret society and you have to join and promise not to tell anyone.'

For a brief moment, Bunny's sobbing ceased. But then it started again, in a different way. Now the sobs were mixed with hysterical laughter. 'Secret society!' she half-laughed, half-cried. 'A secret society . . . to kill . . . Lisa Treadgold!' She hiccoughed and bellowed with laughter. 'Oh, you're marvellous!' she cried, helplessly rolling on the ground with laughter. 'You're a scream, Beth!'

She fell forward on her face, racked with agonizing laughter. She clutched at the grass as she laughed, thrashed her legs, drummed her feet.

Buster the Dalmatian poked his nose into the heaving bundle of Bunny and looked anxiously at Beth, asking for guidance.

THE STRANGE DIET

'There's me,' Beth thought. 'I'm the most important, because I don't go all foggy half the time, like Timothy and Mac. They can't be *relied* on . . .'

The stalk of grass, mushy where she had chewed it, went into her mouth millimetre by millimetre.

'There's Bunny,' she thought, 'But she's a wreck. Lisa has shattered her. She probably still can't believe or understand that Lisa is really and truly a machine-monster.

'All the same, she does know more than anyone else about Lisa – just as we knew more than anyone else about Grinny. So we need Bunny. But –'

As if she had been listening to Beth's mind, Bunny suddenly said, 'I can't go on. I'm *finished.*' She dabbed at her eyes and sat up in the grass, her big face slack and hopeless. 'She *did* for me, Lisa Treadgold did,' she said. 'I mean, I was just made for her. She interviewed half a dozen of us for the job of being her Girl Friday, but of course *I* had to get it! It had to be big, clumsy, loyal, hardworking, ugly, stupid old Bunny!' Her words ended in a despairing howl of self-pity.

Beth said, 'That's nonsense. She hypnotized you. She said, "You remember me" – and Bingo, you became her slave.'

Bunny hardly listened. She said, 'She was my Pash, like in those old schoolgirl stories. Gosh, I suppose it's funny, really . . .'

'It's not funny at all. It's deadly serious. For the whole world!'

'And your secret society is going to change it all, is that it?' Bunny said, suddenly peevish. 'Pardon me while I have a good laugh! Gosh, how old are you? About ten or eleven? But you're old enough to save the world?'

Beth said, 'I'm old enough not to keep saying "gosh" all the time.'

Her sharp nastiness silenced Bunny. She rubbed her damp eyes for some time, then said, 'It was all right at first. I mean, Lisa's so terrific, so super-glamorous. She seemed to know everything, be everything, do everything. I just doted on her –'

'What went wrong?' Beth said.

Bunny thought hard before answering. 'Nothing went *wrong*, exactly,' she began. 'It was just that . . . that no *human* could stand up to Lisa's demands. I mean, humans aren't machines. And Lisa is like a machine –'

'She *is* a machine,' Beth said. 'I keep telling you.'

Bunny said, 'I just couldn't cope: it was as simple as that. I couldn't keep up. She ran me into the ground – flattened me – got me into a state where even "You remember me!" had no effect any more. She expected the impossible of everyone else – and got it. But I was with her day and night, I just couldn't cope . . .'

'And then you saw the light,' Beth interrupted. 'The light in her bedroom, I mean. And before that, she broke Prince Igor's leg. And now she's given Banjo the D.D.D. treatment.' She chewed her grass stalk, then said, 'Why does she keep eating chocolate? Grinny didn't do that. What else does she eat?'

'That's another weird thing about her,' Bunny said. 'She *doesn't* eat! I mean, if I hadn't been hypnotized, that alone would have told me . . . She hardly eats at all! She just goes through the motions of eating. She stirs the food about on her plate. Nobody's ever noticed. Except me.'

'But you gave her breakfast in bed, the day you saw the light,' Beth said. 'She *asked* for breakfast in bed.'

'Oh, that. If you want to know what I think, she asked for it simply to get a news story out of it. "Lisa's Day Off", that sort of thing. She'd got the press coming that day, I think. And anyhow, she didn't eat the food, just the lemons.'

'The *lemons*?'

'Oh, she sucks lemons. Gosh, I can't watch! Slices of lemon, like a rugby player or something. One minute lemons, the next chocolates. Sweet and sour. She never seems to eat eggs or toast or anything like that. Sometimes I wonder if she flushes the real food down the loo.'

'Those chocolates,' Beth said.

'Yes, she *wolfs* chocolates! That's the thing she's really greedy about, those special chocolates. Gosh, you'd never believe, we get *crates* of them delivered each week! From Fontenville in Bond Street. To her special order.'

'No one can eat *crates* of chocolates each week,' Beth said.

'No, I suppose not. But Lisa certainly tries! Still, I suppose she gives a lot away – you know, Lisa Treadgold Special. Instead of signed photographs or personalized ballpoint pens. Anyhow, she's a complete pig about her chocolates, she keeps them in every room and in the car. She takes them in her grab-bag, too. That little sling bag she carries. I have to remember to pack them for her but she always checks for herself. She *hogs* them.'

'And the wrappers?' Beth said, 'Who clears away the wrappers? Does she? Do you? Timothy thinks there's something weird about the wrappings. Is there?'

To Beth's surprise, Bunny began to giggle. 'Gosh, weird's not the word!' she said. Her giggling voice took on a spiteful edge. 'You'll never believe this, but it's true all the same: she's such a sow about those chocolates that she even eats the wrappings!'

'You don't mean that!' Beth said.

'I do! She didn't know I saw, of course.' Now Bunny's mouth was twisted into an old-womanish expression of gossipy spite. 'But I jolly well did! She was on the lawn, you see, with her cassette recorder, dictating; and stuffing herself with chocolates at every other sentence, as per usual! She was gabbling and stuffing, stuffing and gabbling – and she got a bit confused, poor dear! *In* went the chocolate, silver wrapping and all – then *on* went the mike and she continued yacking away into it! Oh, it was priceless, you've never seen –'

'But she spat it out,' Beth said, 'She got rid of the wrapping somehow. How?'

'But she *didn't*!' Bunny said triumphantly. 'That was the cream of the joke! She was so full of yacketty-yack and chocketty-chocolate that she never even noticed! And that wasn't the only time! I've seen her swallow down her precious chockies, wrappings and all, more than once!'

Bunny hugged herself at the memory of Lisa Treadgold's greed. Beth mused silently. Then she said, 'What does she drink?'

The question inspired another delightedly spiteful response from Bunny. 'Oh drink!' she said, her face old-womanish again. 'Well, tea and coffee and all the usual things . . . fancy putting *sugar* in China tea, but *she* does! . . . but *also* – and wouldn't the media be pleased to know about it! – she *also* has a fancy for the strong stuff!'

'The strong stuff?' Beth said. 'You mean, spirits? She gets drunk?'

'Drunk? Lisa Treadgold? Oh, my gosh, my *dear*, you've got to be joking!' Now Bunny was rolling her eyes, wagging her head, bursting with clumsy malice. 'Oh, not our Lisa, our golden girl! How could you even think such a thing! Lisa *drunk*! Oh, perish the thought!'

Her expression changed. 'But I'll tell you this – if you swear to keep it secret! – anyone else would be drunk on the amount she gets through! Stoned out of their minds!'

'What does she drink?' Beth said.

'Vodka!' Bunny cried. 'What else but vodka! Almost pure alcohol, which means she can get good and stoned nice and quick! And of course it's colourless and odourless, so people can't see what's she's up to! I mean, anyone seeing her taking a swig would think it was water! But if anyone asked me, I could tell them the *truth* about Luscious Lisa. She's simply a *lush* . . . on vodka!'

Beth chewed her grass stalk and scowled. She could not make sense of what Bunny had just told her. She thought it might be important, but could not think why or how. Had Grinny been like that? She tried to remember. Probably yes. She could not recall Grinny's eating habits – only the French cigarettes she smoked all the time. But that had been to hide her absence of smell. Chocolate? No, Grinny had not been a chocolate-guzzler, like Lisa. What was the chocolate about? And the lemon slices? And the vodka?

Bunny interrupted Beth's thoughts by saying, 'So I'm not really surprised by her bickies.'

'Her bickies?'

'*Charcoal* bickies! By her bedside! Very special, of course. Charcoal biscuits in a tall round tin with lots of writing on it. She's always at them.'

'What do you mean, charcoal biscuits? I've never even heard of them.'

'You take them for *wind*, dear. Like medicine. The

charcoal's supposed to absorb digestive gases.' Bunny began to giggle. 'Bet it never occurs to all the Lisa worshippers that their idol might occasionally burp! Belch! Rumble!'

'On her diet,' Beth said. 'You know – lemons, chocolate and vodka, I'm surprised she doesn't blow herself inside out.'

'No such luck,' Bunny said. All at once, she lost her spiteful pleasure in telling the awful truths about Lisa Treadgold. Beth saw her turn her head towards the big house. Her shoulders dropped. 'Oh, gosh,' she said, 'what's the use? I've just *got* to go back, there's no escaping her.'

Beth said, 'There's another thing you've got to do: you've got to join my Society. Antiroll. All right, it's just stupid kid-stuff, that's what you think. But what else have you got? We beat Grinny. Smashed her: and we'll beat Lisa Treadgold.'

'Just how?' Bunny said.

'I don't know. I'll have to think. You've told me lots. We'll find something, a weakness . . . Grinny was terrified of electricity. Is Lisa? Does she go all funny near electrical things?'

'No. Never. She spends half her life in TV studios. She couldn't do that if she were afraid of electricity.'

Beth threw away the last three inches of her soggy-ended stalk of grass. 'She's got to have a weakness,' she told Bunny. 'And we've got to find it. You've got to help. That's why we need you in the Society. We'll tell you where and when. I'm going now.'

Bunny watched her go. Beth was small for her age. Her favourite hat made her look still younger. She walked towards the gates of the big house; obviously she was going to collect her bicycle.

But Lisa was in the house! Bunny wanted to shout a warning to Beth – to say, 'Don't go in there! Come back!' She did not. There was something about Beth that said, 'I'm not frightened. I'm not a loser. I'm *me*.'

Sure enough, after a few minutes Bunny saw Beth, head high, spine straight and thin legs pumping vigorously, leave the big house on her bicycle. Beth waved. Bunny got to her feet, slowly and heavily. It was all right for Beth: she was leaving the house. But Bunny had to go back.

'Oh, gosh,' she muttered. And made herself start walking.

That evening

'Chocolates contain sugar and sugar is a source of energy,' Timothy told Beth. 'Why this sudden interest? Are you doing biology or something?'

'No, I just want to know. Why can't I ask you a simple question without you –'

'Well, that's the answer. Sugar equals energy, OK? Now leave me alone.'

'What sort of energy does sugar equal?'

'Animal energy. Human energy. We convert sugar into energy. That's one reason why we give horses lumps of sugar. A reward of energy.'

'A girl I know says you can make a battery out of half a lemon.'

'What's that got to do with sugar?'

'I don't know. You put sugar in lemonade . . . I just thought of lemons because you were talking about sugar.'

'You were talking about sugar, not me.'

'Can you make a battery out of a lemon? An electric battery?'

'Yes, you could. But you wouldn't get much power.'

'Don't you have to stick something into the lemon for the lemon juice to act on to produce the electricity?'

'Of course you do. Something metallic for the acid to destroy. And you have to have something to carry the electricity out. Carbon, or metal of a different potential. Something like that.'

'And that's how you make an electric battery? Acid, metal, carbon?'

'Well, not nowadays. I mean, that's the simplest sort of battery. Proper modern batteries are much more complicated.'

'Wouldn't it be funny if there was a sort of living battery, that could walk about?'

'There is. You're one. I'm one.'

'Honestly? No kidding? We really are batteries, making electricity?'

Beth sounded so surprised – and it was so unlike her to be excited about such things – that Timothy looked into her face. He sat at his desk. She stood above him. Her expression was open and ordinary, but he thought he could see something hidden underneath it. He said, 'What's all this about?'

'Oh, nothing. You know charcoal? Is charcoal carbon?'

'Of course it's carbon, it's wood that's been *carbon*ized. You really are ignorant, aren't you?'

'Yes,' Beth said innocently. Her face was suddenly very cheerful. Timothy could not understand why. 'But then, I've got such a clever little brudderkins, haven't I? So good at explaining!' To Timothy's surprise, she bent down and kissed the top of his head.

'What's that for?' he demanded.

'Euch!' she replied. 'You want to wash your hair! What a pong! You'll get mange, like dogs do.'

At the door she turned and said, 'You're *sure* that charcoal is carbon?'

He glared at her, hoping he looked ferocious. In fact; he was not even annoyed. He liked Beth – more than ever these days. He was so often in a fog. He knew it but could do nothing about it. Beth was his best landmark in the fog.

'Charcoal is a form of carbon,' he grated at her.

'And we're all walking, talking batteries,' she said. 'Even re*volt*ing Lisa Treadgold. *Volt*. Joke. Get it?'

He said, 'Ha ha, very funny,' and threw a book at her. But the door was closed. She was gone.

Beth's diary, next day

. . . so Timothy was right, you can make a battery that way and we are all batteries in a way because all our most complicated and clever bits are really electricity. And our brains work by electricity although of course there is the skin stuff and blood and everything but it still all comes down to electricity. Mr Wells at school explained it all but he kept giving me funny looks, I don't blame him, I mean, someone like me taking so much interest. He said, 'Electricity is the life fluid as much as blood.'

I asked him about spirits (thinking of Lisa's vodka) but I couldn't understand what he told me, it is very complicated, something about chemical reactions & sugars & starches. I wish I understood it it could be very important. Let me think, he said sugar = energy and he said spirits help to convert sugar. But I still don't see how that helps Lisa's battery, if she's got a battery.

Of course she *ought* to have her own battery to make electricity. When she was Grinny she was terrified of electricity but now she is Lisa Treadgold she doesn't mind electricity at all. Which proves that Lisa is the new improved Mk II Grinny complete with do-it-yourself power station built in inside her.

And the chocolate. Mr Wells said he didn't see how chocolate has anything to do with batteries, he gave me another funny look because one minute I was asking about electricity & the next about chocolates. He must have thought I was trying to be funny. But then he got all broody and said, 'Ah, wait a minute,' and went on & on about biological energy & fats & more about sugars. I just gave up. I could not follow him at all. But chocolate is sugary.

But the chocolate *wrappings* are all right, they fit in with the Battery idea because the foil is metal. What I mean is, suppose it is lead foil, you can have lead in batteries. Or zinc or copper. And besides, almost any metal will do, the acid eats the metal. The acid is in the lemon juice of course so that fits. The acid is the Electrolyte.

I wonder what the actual chocolate is for, though? Wouldn't it be funny if Lisa T. was filled with chocolate-coated batteries, I suppose some would be hard centres and the others soft centres, bags I the 12-volt coffee cream. Big joke. Mr Wells is nice but he is married with two sons & 1 baby girl.

Oh I am bored with this stupid diary all I want is to GET Lisa T. I want to KILL her. I will hold a meeting of the Society, we will make plans. We will plan how to use Bunny. She is All Washed Up but all the same she is in Lisa's house & that could be just what we need. I wish I had a plan. I wish I knew what to DO instead of writing in my stupid diary. Now let me think . . .

Mac is all right he will help. But he is foggy. Banjo is not foggy I wonder why but he is gone.

Timothy is getting better he is out of the fog quite a lot he is not hypnotized by Lisa all the time & that is a good thing.

Roll on ANTIROLL we will win in the end we will get her somehow just you see.

Timothy's diary, same evening

. . . and there she is, scribbling away in her room next door to me and banging her foot against her writing table. Poor old Beth, determined that Lisa T. is the Arch Villain of all time.

I wonder what is wrong with Mr Fisk. His letters are always so dull, nothing but platitudes about Lisa T. Perhaps he is getting old – suddenly becoming senile. His letters read like sermons by some stuffy old Victorian preacher. Nothing but Duty and Service and Obedience to Lisa. D.D.D. Of course Lisa is right about everything but Mr Fisk doesn't half go ON about her. Still, I suppose that's worse than what the kids do. Kids like Beth make rude jokes about Lisa T. Even Mac said something rude about her the other day. And he didn't turn up for the Junior League Rollers' meeting. I did, of course, wearing my uniform as usual. It wasn't quite as good as most of the meetings, too many people talking like Mr Fisk. They said nothing new, just kept on hammering away at Decency, Discipline and Dedication. And a very long speech about Being Ready When The Great Day Comes. I quite agree with that, but *what* Great Day? *When* is it coming?

Ah, thank goodness Beth has stopped banging her foot against her table leg. Now she's heading for the bathroom. And so to bed. Peace and quiet at last. Strange how she went on and on about batteries and electricity.

Why? Why would she do that? And why does it make me think of Grinny? I think of her often these days. Grinny was frightened of electricity. But Lisa T. isn't, so what's the connection. I bet there isn't one.

In fact, nothing is connected to anything in my brain. I feel things are changing in my mind but I don't know what things. I am sitting here typing away only to keep myself company, so to speak. It's as if there were two of me. Perhaps I am a Schizophrenic, have I spelt that right? (And which is correct, SPELT or SPELLED?) 'Goodnight, Timothy,' said Timothy. 'See you in the morning.' So he shook hands with himself and went to bed. Joke, ha ha.

Early September

Beth spread the newspaper cuttings in front of her. There were not many but there were enough. For they all told the same significant story . . .

LOCAL MAN SPITS
ON NATIONAL IDOL

The cutting came from the *Gazette*. It was about Mr Caswell. Beth knew him. He framed pictures and boarded dogs in his kennels. He was a bit weird but nice enough. About fifty. Rode a big old bike. During a Roller parade in the town, he had jumped out of the crowd and spat at Lisa Treadgold. 'She's a menace, don't you understand, she's a murdering menace!' he shouted. The Court fined him £25 and costs.

LISA
DOES NOT PLEASE HER!

The story was about a district nurse, somewhere in the Midlands, who, like Mr Caswell, had tried to disrupt a Roller parade by shouting insults at Lisa. Fined £15.

CHURCHMAN CHIDES 'BRAZEN IDOL'

A very small story in the national evening paper. 'There is but one God,' the Reverend had said, 'and His Holy name is not Lisa Treadgold.' He had gone on, during his sermon, to compare her with a Brazen Idol. His superiors in the Church said that the matter was under inquiry.

MAN DRIVES CAR AT LISA'S ROVER

The man was a commercial traveller, aged twenty-nine. He said he wanted to kill Lisa Treadgold before she killed him and everyone else. Fined £100 and costs, licence endorsed.

LISA SAYS 'I WILL NOT PROSECUTE'

A woman of thirty-three, an advertising copywriter, was accused of sending offensive and obscene letters to Lisa

Treadgold. The police wished to prosecute but Lisa (shown smiling and holding up a handful of letters) refused to take the matter further.

TREADGOLD, TREAD WARILY!

A university student with a .22 rifle was found on the roof of a building overlooking the entrance of a London hotel sometimes used by Lisa. The man, 'in a highly excited condition', talked of 'ridding the world of its most deadly menace'. He was given a suspended prison sentence and a heavy fine.

The Lisa incidents had occurred in widely spread parts of the country. The people concerned had nothing in common except for a hatred of Lisa Treadgold.

'So not everyone's mad,' Beth said. 'Not everyone's hypnotized. There are sane people left, but not many. All the same . . .'

LETTERS FROM LISA

Mid-September

Banjo, to his amazement, got a letter from Lisa Treadgold in her own handwriting. It read:

Dear Banjo,

I feel quite awful about what occurred at our last meeting. I am entirely to blame, both for refusing your not unreasonable request for an improved scale of charges for the band; and for the painful and unnecessary trick I played on you.

Can you – *will* you – come to my home to discuss money matters? I don't think you will regret it – I have a most remarkable proposition from an international recording company! I suggest 24 Sept at 11 a.m. Telephone me or my secretary if this is suitable.

With repeated apologies, I remain
Yours most sincerely
Lisa Treadgold

Fanny Bishop, to her surprise, received a letter from Lisa Treadgold. It read:

Dear Miss Bishop,

Do you still have that very pleasant boy, Timothy Carpenter, working for you at the *Gazette*? I think I have something on the boil that could be truly helpful to him personally – and to young people in general.

Alas, this is not a proper, grown-up 'news item', but if anything of interest to you and the *Gazette* arises (as it well may) I shall give you first bite of the cherry!

If Timothy wishes to bring his intriguing sister (Beth, isn't it?) and their mutual friend, Mac or Jack (?), they will be welcome. You see, it's very much a young-people sort of thing. The more the merrier! Do come yourself if you can spare the time.

Time and Date: 11 a.m., 24 September. I feel it to be only polite to extend the invitation through *you*, but he can accept or refuse my invitation himself.

Yours sincerely,
Lisa Treadgold

Fanny was at her *Gazette* desk when she read this. Timothy was busily searching some proofs for mistakes. Fanny called out, 'Oi! An exclusive for you!' And handed him Lisa's letter. He read it carefully and said, 'Wow. Well, I must go, mustn't I?'

He was surprised by Fanny's expressions before she

answered. First, he saw confusion: then doubt: then a forced brightness. 'Of course you must go!' she said. 'It could be your first step on the ladder to *Fame* and *Success*!'

She laughed, but there was no pleasure in the sound. Timothy wondered why. Like Len Sturgeon – like himself – Fanny had changed. She was more like her old self some of the time. But not all of the time.

'Are you coming?' he asked Fanny.

'Yes. I mean, I'd be a fool not to. Anything to do with Lisa Treadgold . . .' She lit a cigarette. She had taken up smoking again.

Timothy telephoned Bunny and made his acceptance.

On the day, Banjo hitched a lift from Fanny. Banjo's hand – the hand Lisa had crushed – was in plaster. 'Driving's out till it gets better,' he said as he rolled his big body into the car. He looked and sounded grim. 'I'm going to get that cow,' he grunted as he settled himself and his bulging briefcase in the front passenger seat.

Fanny stubbed out the cigarette she had just lit in the messy ashtray and said, 'What? What cow?' Timothy, sharing the back seat with Mac, could see she was tense and a bit flustered. He could think of several reasons why. Like half the people he knew, Fanny was confused. Fogged.

'Yes, I'm going to get Madam Lisa, the cow!' Banjo said. 'Bust my hand, would she? Then write a soapy letter, half bribe and half apology. The stupid, hypocritical –'

'You can't speak of Lisa Treadgold like that,' Fanny said primly. She drove carefully to the big house.

Mac said, 'Where's Beth, then?'

'She's going on her bike. Travelling under her own steam,' Timothy replied. 'As usual.'

Fanny said, over her shoulder, 'How are your parents, Tim?'

'Fine,' Timothy answered. Well, they *were* fine. His father was still slaving away on the Roman site. Often, he went to London to talk about a new TV series. When he came back he was generally quietly angry. He pretended he was cross about the programme's complications. In fact, Timothy knew, he was worried about his whole life. Lisa had 'got to him'. Lisa ruled more than half his mind. His mother's too.

They reached the gates of Lisa's house. 'See this brief-case?' Banjo said. 'It's full of lawyer's stuff. I've got my lawyers on to Lisa. But I'll need witnesses. That means you and you and you. I can count on you, can't I?'

Fanny was so alarmed by this remark that the car swerved and clipped the edge of the lawn. But there was no time for her to say anything. Bunny stood outside the pillared, fan-lighted front door, waiting for them. The dogs tumbled and chased around her. 'Oh!' she said, 'oh yes . . . you're so punctual, I haven't finished with the dogs. Oh dear . . . Come in – down, Buster, stop that! – Oh, and here's Beth.'

A bicycle bell tinkled and Beth was with them. She got off her bike, pinched the rear tyre and said, 'Feels like a slow puncture. Hallo, everyone. Well?' She put her hands on her narrow hips and stared from face to face.

'Well . . .' Bunny said, 'we're all here. Let's go in, then.'

They went in. Lisa Treadgold was coming down the stairs, smiling. She looked marvellous. 'Lovely of you to come!' she said. 'And dead on time! We've got so much to talk about,' she said. The famous Lisa Treadgold smile widened.

DEAD ON TIME

'We'll start,' Banjo announced, 'by talking about Assault. Here's a letter from my lawyers. Read it. There'll be more to come.'

They were in the big lemon-and-amber living-room – a long, many-windowed room, as cool and elegant as Lisa herself. She smiled and took the letter from Banjo's good hand. She read it, always smiling, and said, 'I love lawyers' English, don't you? But these people should buy new type-writers. The E is broken and the N isn't in line. It spoils the professional effect.'

She offered to return the letter to Banjo. His face swelled and purpled with fury.

'Take it,' Lisa said. 'Go on, take it.' She stepped forward and neatly tucked the folded letter into the top pocket of his jacket. 'There,' she said. 'You've got to learn to take it. I dish it out, you take it.'

The humour of her voice, the curve of her arm, the fall of her many-layered, filmy frock, the radiance of her perfect smile, defeated Banjo. He made a furious choking sound.

Lisa said, 'We're here on business. *Real* business, Banjo, not letters from stuffy old lawyers. *Big* business.'

Banjo sullenly said, 'If you think you're going to bribe me with all this talk of offers from international recording companies –'

'Oh, bigger than that!' Lisa said. Her head was on one side. Her hand toyed with the heavy, tasselled Victorian gold chain round her neck. 'We're here,' she said, always smiling, 'to discuss matters of life and death. As I said, you're dead on time. And now's the time.'

She twiddled the tassels on the end of the chain, letting them wind and unwind round her finger. 'So down to business,' she said. 'We'll start at the top. That means you, Beth.' Beth stared expressionlessly at Lisa and did not move.

Timothy was lost. 'But your letter said something about Young People . . . a plan, or something,' he said feebly.

'Oh, that. Well, Beth's young,' Lisa said. 'Very young. Therefore very important. And I've got a plan for her. Tell them, Beth. Keep it simple and easy for them.'

Beth, still expressionless, got up from her chair and looked from face to face. 'Her plan is, to murder you all,' she said. 'No, it's worse than that. She's going to sort of kill you inside. Then use your bodies. Everyone's. All over the world.'

Her face was very white and her eyes huge. Her voice failed her. 'Don't you see?' she said. 'Don't you understand? She's just the first! When *she's* got us ready, *they're* coming!'

The faces stared back at her blankly.

Timothy's mind spun in his head like the golden tassels on Lisa's finger.

Lisa Treadgold said, 'The letters were just excuses to get you here, Timothy. Well, isn't anyone going to say anything?' She smiled into Fanny's face, a stupefied mask; into Mac's, but his eyes were fixed on the swinging tassel; into Banjo's blotched, starting eyes, but he could not answer; into Timothy's startled, urgent eyes. He managed to speak. 'She's right,' he said. 'Beth's right.'

'Good!' Lisa cried. She clapped her hands softly, applauding Beth. 'We're getting down to business! More, Beth! You tell them! They'll never believe it from me. I'm far too lovable and beautiful.'

Beth was almost crying. She had to jerk the words from herself in gasping spurts. 'She's a pig! Filthy pig robot, not real, a machine, hateful! . . .'

'Excellent!' Lisa said. Now the tassels of the golden chain were slapped gently and rhythmically by the right hand into the palm of the left; a soft, heavy sound, like the ticking of a clock.

'She's the first,' Beth said – and now tears started from her eyes, yet she was not truly crying. 'She softens us up, she pretends she's human, she's *mad*e like a human, but she's *not*, she's a robot machine, evil . . . and the others, they're out there telling her what to do, there's a rod of light they send down from space – Bunny saw it, it's all true! – and Lisa's here to get us ready for when *they* come. . .'

'And when they come?' Lisa prompted.

'It will all be over and no use, everyone will be their slaves, we'll just go round like zombies doing whatever they tell us! And they'll kill the old people, even when they're not all that old! They'll kill anyone who's ill or old or not what they want!'

Banjo, in a daze, said, 'Hang about! Look, you talked about an offer from an international recording company, that's what all this is about, isn't it? Well, isn't it?'

Nobody paid him any heed. The golden tassels went slap . . . slap . . . slap, richly and softly. 'Well, go on, Beth!' Lisa encouraged. But Beth could not. She let herself fall into a crouched heap at Timothy's feet.

Mac was the first to speak. He lifted his strained face to Lisa and said, 'Beth's got it all wrong, hasn't she? What she's been saying is lies . . . Isn't it?' It was more an appeal than a question.

Lisa gave her low, pleasant laugh. 'Oh, you know better than that, Mac! Lies? Of course she's not lying! You remember Grinny, don't you?'

Mac nodded miserably.

'Well, first there was Grinny, Now there's me. *You remember me!*'

As she spoke the words, Mac's face clouded. He shook his head, trying to clear his brain. When he looked at Lisa again, his expression was mild and cheerful. 'Of course I remember you,' he said. 'You're Lisa Treadgold. You invited us here. It's nice . . .'

Lisa laughed. 'You see, Beth!' she said. 'It's up one minute, down the next. I work their minds like puppets on strings. They're all my puppets. Everyone but you. You, young people – and a few others: a few flukes, the very few people who don't fall under my spell; who resist my fatal charm.' She made a charming little self-mocking face. 'This time, even most of the children are bewitched, Beth. They join the Junior Rollers, don't they? Last time we deliberately left the children out of it. This time, we haven't bothered. So lots of them are in it. Right up to their little necks. They believe. They obey. They're ready for the Great Day, Beth! But not you. And not Banjo – at least, not often. Poor Banjo. Poor *anybody* who tries to resist! Because the Great Day's almost here, Beth! Just about to dawn!'

Beth was crying now. Her muffled voice said, 'Why, why? Why can't you leave us alone?'

'Oh, don't be silly, Beth! You know why. Nothing has changed. Our own world is finished. We must have a new home. Earth will do very nicely. Earth is perfect for our purpose. And so are you earthlings! What marvellous servants you'll make!'

'I know what you lot are like,' Beth said indistinctly. 'Robot pigs! Foul, filthy, horrible machines! I can just imagine –'

'No you can't, Beth,' Lisa said. 'You can't imagine us at all. But we can imagine you! We can do it so well that *I'm* here, in human form, worshipped by millions of humans just like you! Lovely Lisa Treadgold!'

She pirouetted like a mannequin so that the folds of her skirt lightly brushed Beth's bowed head. Then – 'Oh, chocolates!' she said. 'Do have one, Beth. No? Well, offer them to the others. You won't? Then I will. Mac, a chocolate. That's right. Timothy, a chocolate. No, take one. Take it and eat it. There's a good, sensible boy. You'll be obedient, won't you, Timothy? And you too, Miss Bishop. Or may I call you Fanny? Yes, take the nice chocolate. Now unwrap it and pop it in your mouth. Oh dear, why do you female humans use lipstick? Answer me, Fanny.'

'To make ourselves attractive,' Fanny said, speaking like a machine.

'Well, it doesn't work. But never mind, you won't have to worry about "looking attractive" in the future. Nothing but Decency, Discipline and Dedication. Banjo, eat your chocolate.'

He swore and threw the silver-wrapped chocolate at her. She touched it with her toe and said, 'Now, now, Banjo. Eat your chocolate. Or I will crush your other hand.'

She did not bother to see if he obeyed her. She walked to a bell-pull, a long embroidered strap in the corner near the door, and pulled it. Bunny obeyed the call and hurried into the room. 'Yes, Miss Treadgold?'

'Lemon juice, Bunny. And tea for my visitors. They need refreshment. I have been telling them the new facts of life. Do I need to tell you, too, Bunny, or have you guessed?'

Bunny went red, then white, and said, 'Invasion. You're invading. Very soon.'

'Quite right, Bunny. Continue to listen at the keyhole, if you wish. Or if you prefer, join our little party. But refreshments first.'

Bunny left. Lisa turned to Banjo. She stared at him. He flinched; unwrapped his chocolate; and put it in his mouth. He looked like a whipped dog.

'Good,' Lisa said. Then she took the silver wrapping from his fingers, crumpled it, thrust it into her mouth and swallowed it.

She wiped her fingers, very deliberately, on the lapel of Banjo's jacket.

DEATH WITH A 'D'

'Yum, yum,' Lisa Treadgold said. 'Lovely chocolate. I'll have one more, I think.'

She picked up another of the expensive chocolates, glittering in its silver foil, and neatly threw it into her mouth, foil and all. Then she chewed vigorously and swallowed. 'Don't look so amazed,' she said. 'I haven't got taste buds, have I, Beth? Machines don't need them. Machines cannot taste. I am a machine –'

'Then why –' Banjo began.

'Why eat and drink, you were going to ask? Well, there are two reasons. First, I am a public figure and if everyone else around me eats and drinks, so must I. But second – and more important – I am largely an *electrical* machine.'

'We'll kill you somehow,' Beth snarled. 'We did it with electricity last time, when you were Grinny. We'll do it again!'

'Not with electricity,' Lisa said, smiling down at Beth. 'Not this time! We learned our lesson from the Grinny affair. Mistake number one – sending me into a *family*. Families are so close-knit, so observant, so clever. You learned far too much about me far too quickly, Beth!

'And mistake number two – when I was Grinny, I relied on an outside supply of electricity for my delicate little insides. Oh, I can laugh now, but it was terrifying at the time! And you children found out, and used electricity to frighten me to death. Literally, to death! Ah, Bunny, there's a good girl, pour tea for everyone. I'll have my lemon.'

She took a large slice of lemon and held it up for everyone to see: then thrust the slice between her perfect teeth. The teeth closed. Lemon juice spurted and dribbled from the smiling mouth. She swallowed and the lemon was gone. 'Not sweet, not sour,' she said. 'Nothing. Yet your poor mouths twitch and pucker! But then, you're only animals. While I am a perfect machine, with none of your weaknesses. Watch . . .'

She took another slice of lemon and held it to her eyes. She smiled, opened her eyes wide and squeezed. The juice flooded her eyes and ran down her cheeks. 'Wipe my face, Bunny,' she ordered. Bunny obeyed. 'You see, I'm super-human,' Lisa said. 'It's very pleasant for me.'

'We'll kill you somehow,' Beth said.

Timothy, groping his way through the fog in his mind, said, 'Electricity . . . Your eating and drinking . . . Beth asked me questions . . .'

'She's got a battery inside her,' Beth said. 'Her own battery. Mr Wells explained but I don't really understand.'

'Clever Mr Wells!' Lisa said. 'He was right, of course.

I am a walking power station! But on a very miniature, low-power scale, naturally. Timothy! Wake up and explain how I work! Lemon juice is – come on, Timothy! – lemon juice is . . . ?'

'The electrolyte,' Timothy mumbled. 'Like acid. Well, it is an acid. And the silver foil on the chocolates is the cathode or anode –'

'And my charcoal biscuits are the other half,' Lisa said sweetly. 'But what about the chocolates, Timothy? Why chocolates? And sugar?'

'Don't know,' Timothy said sullenly. 'Don't care.'

'The chocolates make the *cases* for my charming little batteries,' Lisa said. 'Bees use wax to make cells: I use the fats and solids in chocolates to make battery cases. You see, I've a chemicals factory in here too!' She tapped her stomach and smiled. 'What's sugar for, Timothy?'

'Energy,' Timothy muttered.

'And alcohol?'

'Energy.'

'So there you are! Now you all know the secrets of my diet! Sugar-and-alcohol interactions, with some fats and solids thrown in, on the biological side; and a nice, simple battery, always re-making itself, on the electrical side. What more could anyone want?'

'I want you dead,' Beth said.

Banjo said, 'All right, *Miss* Treadgold, you're a great little package, a terrific product. And you're going to conquer the world. But why give us all this advance information? Why tell us anything at all?'

'There will be two main classes of human slaves,' Lisa replied. For once she was not smiling. 'First, those who *don't* understand – who just obey us like robots; who work till they drop or must be disposed of. They will form the main body. Say, ninety-nine per cent.

'Second, those who *do* understand us. Just a little. People like you, Banjo. And you, Beth – people still very young. You will serve us more intelligently, more sensitively, than the mass. Because you will report on the mass and help us to use them efficiently.'

'You mean, we'll be your spies?' Banjo said. 'Your informers? Your Gestapo?'

'That's it precisely,' Lisa said, 'You'll tell us how to put the pressure on your fellow humans. Tell us what *really* hurts them, what *really* frightens them. You'll tell us the shortcuts; save us wasting time on crude methods – pain, terror, grief.' Now she was smiling again. Banjo, shocked into silence, was white-faced and silent.

'I'd never do that,' Beth said. 'Never. Whatever you did to me.'

'Oh, I think you would,' Lisa said. 'I'm sure you could be persuaded. Not just by doing painful things to you – simple physical tortures. Although *we* wouldn't mind trying that . . . No, I was thinking of rather more subtle ways. Suppose, for example, that by obeying us, you could keep your own family alive? And by disobeying us, you would condemn them to death?'

Beth's head dropped. Her shoulders began to shake.

'There you are, you see,' Lisa smiled, pointing at Beth.

'She understands. She's a sensible girl. And you Banjo – and you Mac and you Timothy – you're going to be sensible and understanding. Like dear Bunny, who's always good and obedient, aren't you Bunny? Yes, you're all going to be good as from now on. D.D.D., remember! Death begins with a D, doesn't it? You'll do what you're told. You'll be good. Or you'll die.

She smiled charmingly: then said, 'There's a Roller Rally tomorrow. You will all be there, cheering and waving. You will also be there to remember the faces and names of those who *aren't* cheering and waving. You understand. You do? Good. Bunny, get rid of them, they bore me; then exercise the dogs. Oh, and give them their tickets for the big show. The final show!'

She smiled warmly and was gone.

Bunny handed them a sealed brown envelope. 'Tickets,' she said. She was trembling and so damp with hopelessness that she seemed to be dissolving.

'Now you'd better go,' she said. They went.

THE CRUSH

28th September

It was not a big Roller Rally. Nowadays, the major rallies took the form of TV programmes, watched by whole nations. This was more of a curtain-raiser to an important Lisa Treadgold TV show to be held tomorrow evening. Yet, though today's Rally was a local affair, pretty well everyone in the town and surrounding villages lined the streets. They smiled vaguely and waved their R.O.L. wavers. Many wore Roller boaters with R.O.L. ribbons round them. The girls looked cute in them.

Antiroll was there too.

Beth, leader of Antiroll, was near despair. This was to have been her chance to show Lisa Treadgold that there were still people strong enough to defy and resist: people like Mac, Bunny, Timothy, Banjo and the Antiroll children, who would shout 'No!' even until the last moment before They came, the beings from out there, the beings who had created Lisa. 'We know the worst now,' Beth told the Antirolls the evening before. 'Lisa has told us everything. But we're not just giving in, are we? We're not, are we?'

'No,' said Timothy bleakly. 'No,' said Mac uncertainly. 'No,' said the others avoiding Beth's burning eyes. 'So it's agreed we'll meet at the drinking fountain tomorrow?' 'We'll be there,' they all said uneasily.

But they weren't there. Banjo wasn't there. Beth was told he had been seen tuning his banjo with the Roller Dixielanders. Timothy stood beside her, busily writing nothings in his reporter's notebook, biting his lip, pretending not to hear her when she talked to him. Mac stood a dozen paces away in the thick of a crowd of mildly cheerful people waiting for the big parade to come into view. The Antirollers – Mona, Darren, Fi and Peter, Asha and Ram – stood in a group on the other side of the road, making faces and shrugging shoulders to explain that it was impossible for them to cross the road, they were very sorry but –

Matthew and Melinda H, Beth saw, had not even turned up.

Beth seethed and tried to think of something to do to bring the Antirolls into action. Bunny – surely Bunny wouldn't let her down? But as she came to the boil, the sound of the Dixieland band was heard and the crowds lining the street began to surge and sway and buzz. The Roller Rally had started. The parade was on its way.

Once Beth saw Banjo, strutting with the other musicians in blazers and boaters – once she saw his eyes flick towards her, recognize her and then guiltily switch away – once she had seen this, she saw nothing else of the parade. Her eyes were misted, filled with tears. 'How could he,' she said to Timothy. He pretended not to hear her. His face was fogged, his eyes clouded.

The band played. The crowd cheered and waved. It was a terrific turnout, considering that Lisa Treadgold was not expected to be there.

Suddenly the cheering raised its pitch and volume and became wildly enthusiastic. For Lisa was there, after all! Lisa in her Roller Rolls-Royce! Lisa radiant, beaming, skimming her plastic boater into the crowd – then putting on another, and another, as they were handed to her from the back of the car by Bunny.

By Bunny! So Bunny, too, had given in.

Laughter, cheers, skimming boaters bright in the sun! The music of the Dixielanders – 'ROLLing along, singing a song, SIDE BY SIDE!' The bright sky, the breeze lifting Lisa's hair, ruffling and rippling her blue and gold dress! Small wonder that every face smiled, every voice cheered for Lisa!

Every voice but Beth's. She jumped up and down to make herself taller. 'PIG!' she yelled. 'ROTTEN FILTHY MACHINE PIG!'

Now the Roller Rolls-Royce was passing right in front of Beth. She made her final, frantic effort. 'I'LL KILL YOU!' she screeched. 'KILL ROTTEN MACHINE PIG WOMAN! I HATE YOU, HATE YOU, I'LL TELL EVERYONE ABOUT YOU!'

Lisa heard. She turned her lovely head and looked down on the jerking, yelling, tear-spraying face of Beth. She smiled her warm and lovely smile; raised her arm, honey-gold in the sun, to her head; and, as if giving a blessing, gently removed her boater hat and tossed it to Beth.

People smiled loving approval and hushed their cheering for the moment. So they heard Lisa's voice – her warm, understanding, gently mocking words – as she said, looking only into Beth's eyes, 'You wicked little thing! But you're rather sweet!'

Then Lisa's gaze shifted to meet the eyes of those surrounding Beth. Lisa's eyes smiled into their eyes. Her lips formed the words 'You remember me!'

And then some other, silent words.

Bunny handed Lisa yet another boater – the Rolls-Royce slid on its triumphal way – and Lisa was gone. Beth was alone again in the crowd, blinded with her tears of rage and hopelessness.

At first, the crowd took no notice of her.

But then, very slowly, it began to move.

They were nice people, kind people, ordinary people, in that section of the crowd. Once the excitement of Lisa Treadgold's unexpected presence was over, their faces relaxed and became mildly excited, pleased and cheerful. 'Didn't she look *lovely*?' 'She picked us out specially, wasn't that nice?' 'Oh, she's a marvel, that Lisa, she'll be the salvation of the country!'

They nodded, chattered and beamed. Sometimes, they cheered the parade. Always, they moved, with little shufflings and shifts, bunching closer together.

They were moving in on Beth.

She felt the amiable, gentle, increasing pressure and an unreasonable terror gripped her. 'Timothy!' she cried. 'Tim! Please! Tim, I want you!' He raised his head from his reporter's notebook and glanced at her, uninterestedly. He was perhaps two or three paces away. She struggled towards him, the terror growing in her. She pushed against plump bodies, thin bodies. 'Excuse me! . . .' she gasped. 'Let me through, please . . . I've got to get to my brother . . . excuse me! . . .'

The bodies did not yield.

She began to push in earnest, elbowing and thrusting, digging into the tight-packed mass of bodies. 'Please!' she shouted, almost in the ears of a plump, short, grey-haired woman. 'Please, I must get through.'

The woman must have heard her: yet she looked down at Beth, gave a cosy smile and replied, 'Yes, she was looking lovely, wasn't she? Like always.' She would not budge.

Now Beth's left arm was trapped between the bodies of two men. She pulled and jerked, trying to free her arm. The men knew what was happening. They had to know. Both looked down at Beth's face. 'Talk about "Side by side!" one of them grinned – and moved forward so that Beth's arm was still more tightly trapped. The other man smiled pleasantly and placed his foot over Beth's. When he shifted his weight as well, crushing Beth's toes, she screamed – pulled and jerked with all her strength – and got her arm and foot free. But still the mass of bodies and smiling faces moved in on her.

The pressure became almost unbearable. But it had one good effect: Timothy was carried to her side. His sweating face had a waking-up expression: his eyes were coming alive. He said, 'Hell! . . . Beth, are you all right?'

'No,' she whimpered. 'Please help me, please get me free!'

Now Beth panted for breath and her feet left the ground. 'Help me get down, Timothy . . .' she choked. She had realized that her only safety lay near the ground: legs are thinner than bodies. But then there were the trampling feet. They were dangerous too.

Timothy, eyes starting with fear, said, 'Right! – Now!' – and used all his strength. His elbows levered outward. The bodies yielded for a second. The second was enough. Beth fell down almost to a kneeling position, surrounded by a forest of legs. Then Timothy was down with her, his elbows still jutting out, sideways; for the feet were shuffling, millimetres at a time, closing in.

'She told them to do it!' Beth told him. 'She hypnotized them! Lisa did it!'

'Do like this!' Timothy gasped. He took up a frog-like attitude, facing Beth. They put their hands on each other's shoulders and braced their spines. Their bodies made a bridge. The feet shuffled and tried to invade their space, break the bridge. Beth and Tim sweated and held on. Above them, the living forest closed in, blotting out the light.

Timothy said, 'Hold on. Look!' They were crouched over a manhole cover, a big, round, cast-iron disc. 'Escape hatch!' he said. 'But we can't lift it!' Beth choked.

'Reach in my back trousers pocket,' Timothy said. 'Get my Army knife!' It was a Swiss Army knife, a multi-bladed instrument of good steel. She could feel the knife – but it was sealed in the pocket by Timothy's crouching position. '*String*, idiot!' Timothy muttered. She found the string lanyard connecting the knife to Tim's belt. She tugged at it. It broke.

It took fumbling, stifling minutes for her to get the knife free: but only seconds to open the strongest, thickest blade, a can-opener. 'Give it me . . . quick . . .' Timothy muttered. He thrust the blade into the little square hole at the edge of the manhole cover and heaved.

The blade broke.

He fumbled another short, thick blade open. All the time, shoes shuffled closer and closer: bony legs pressed against his ribs and spine or nudged his backside, threatening to tip him off balance so that he would fall face forward against Beth. But he still had time to be cunning. This time, he inserted the edge of the blade, not its flat, in the little square hole: and took his time applying lifting force.

The manhole cover moved. A curved, gritty crack showed. Beth thrust the piece of broken blade into the crack to hold it open. Timothy nodded and gave her a skull-like smile. Slowly, carefully, he applied more leverage. The blade held. The cover kept moving until it showed a slit like a long smile. Timothy shoved three fingers into it.

The smile crushed them painfully but, 'We've done it!' he said. 'Give us a hand!'

Beth gave a hand, literally. She too put her fingers into the gap. It was a mistake. The forest of legs shifted closer still. A man's foot trod on the edge of the cover and bore down on it. Beth gave a scream of pain. Timothy swore and jabbed with his knife at the leg above the foot. The leg jerked and the foot lifted. Simultaneously, Beth and Timothy gave a great heave and wrenched the manhole cover up and away.

Beneath them there was a dark, damp hole, crusted with grey; and they could see the top rungs of a crude metal ladder. The rest of the ladder led down into nothingness.

'Go on!' Timothy said. 'Down!' Beth wriggled and crawled between the trembling struts of his arms. Somehow, she got herself into the hole and began climbing down the steel ladder.

Timothy tried to follow. The human forest closed in tighter still, locking him up in a shrinking prison of feet and legs. He pushed frantically at them, even beat at them with his fists. It made no difference. The forest kept closing in.

He clawed at his knife and managed to open a cutting blade. He slashed and stabbed with it. Bloodstained trousers and jeans: blood jetted and dribbled from nylons and bare flesh. Yet however furiously he hacked and stabbed, nobody protested, there were no cries of pain. But slowly, very slowly, the feet and legs uneasily drew back.

Then Timothy's feet and hands were on the steel ladder and he too was clambering down into the dark hole.

THE SEWER

They were in a sewer. The smell was horrific. It choked them.

'Lucky old us!' Timothy said. 'It could have been one of those electrical things – you know, all wires and cables, just a box in the ground, not leading anywhere.'

'I'm going to be sick,' Beth said faintly. And was. When she had finished, she said, 'Will there be rats? I'll die if there are rats. Rats in the darkness!'

'You won't die,' Timothy said. 'Don't be stupid.' But the thought of rats terrified him. He too was sick, for a long time. The open manhole cover above them admitted only a faint gleam of light: the crush of bodies had closed in to seal the hole. The hole dripped and the droplets fell on Timothy's head and shoulders. He finished being sick and looked at the droplets, puzzled. The hole had seemed only damp. Why should it drip?

He suddenly realized the answer. The droplets were blood from the legs he had hacked at. He was sick again.

They moved into the darkness of the sewer. The smell was like a gas, choking and inescapable, filling their minds and bodies. They were afraid to breathe. Yet soon they overcame the horror of it: for there was light ahead. Pale, grey light. They slogged on through the shallow wet filth. The sewer was unusually empty – Timothy could see this from the wet tide line much higher up the curved walls. He wondered why and thought, 'Of course: everyone's out on the streets, nobody's at work or at home.' Hand in hand, he and Beth made for the light.

It came from some sort of air vent or grating. There was no ladder leading up to it, only a narrow, angled chimney. Beth said, 'We've got to go on, haven't we?' Her voice was surprisingly steady. 'But I might be sick again.' Timothy squeezed her hand. Good old Beth: she was brave. 'We'll be all right, Beth,' he said, and was proud of himself for keeping his voice as normal as hers.

They went on into darkness. Timothy felt Beth's hand shake and tremble in his – or was he the one that was shaking? At least there were no rats. He wondered what else there was in sewers. He wondered if it mattered that his feet were squelching in his sewage-filled shoes. Was sewage poisonous? Beth said, 'Well, at least we're better off down here than up there . . . aren't we?' Her voice sounded shrunken.

'Of course we are.'

'And we'll find a way out, won't we?'

'Of course we will. I mean, there's got to be a way out, just like there was a way in.' He spoke gruffly to make sure his voice would not shake.

Again the tunnel lightened. Again it was only another vent or grating, useless to them. And then they saw the rats.

The rats huddled and squeaked in front of them. They formed a knot, a gibbering village of evil, perched on a ledge. The rats climbed over each other and turned their hideous, red-eyed heads to the sound. Beth kept screaming. The rats cocked their heads and listened attentively, unafraid. Some ran off into the darkness. Two ran towards Beth and Timothy, their wet hunchbacks bobbing, their raw tails writhing.

Timothy gave a cracked yell of sheer terror and hysterically flung his knife.

By chance, his aim was true. The knife slammed into the main cluster of rats. There were squeaks and high-pitched yelps, scrabblings and scurryings and splashings: then, suddenly, no rats.

'It's all right,' Beth said. Her fingers were locked rigidly in Timothy's. He was shaking violently. 'It's all right, it's all right, it's all right,' Beth kept saying, mechanically, as she dragged him forward. 'No! No! I don't want to!' he complained, in the high wailing voice of a little child. They staggered forward, slipping and stumbling, each knowing that this was the end, they were going to die in this hideous place. Then the rats would get them.

But now there was a dim little crescent of light above them: and a ladder: and a manhole cover at the top of the ladder: and they were standing in the empty road outside J. W. Noakes, Groceries & Provisions, Families Supplied.

The air was like a sublime drink that you took down in huge greedy gulps. The light of the sun was blindingly beautiful.

That evening

Beth said, 'The TV broadcast is tomorrow, Tim. The Lisa Treadgold special. What are we going to do?'

He said, 'Something. Something really dramatic, something to make people see her as she is . . . But I don't know what.'

They were in the garden. It was late evening. Although they had washed themselves again and again – even hosed out their shoes – they still imagined that they smelled of the sewer; that everyone in the world was their enemy; that their own parents would turn them in, betray them to Lisa Treadgold. That was why they talked in low voices and were in the garden.

It was light enough for Beth to see her brother's face. It was alive, unfogged. She was talking to the real Timothy, the complete Timothy. She was not alone. So there was a spark in her voice as she said, 'I think I've got an idea. A brilliant idea.'

'It had better be brilliant,' Timothy said, thinking how childish Beth sounded.

'It's a good plan, honestly!' she said.

'All right,' he said, shrugging his shoulders. 'What do we do? Cause a riot? Set fire to the studio?'

'Oh, nothing like that,' Beth said. 'We smash her. Do her in. Kill her.'

Timothy gaped and stared at the dark outline of his little sister's face. Her hands rested in her lap. She looked perfectly at ease.

'*Kill* her?' he said. 'Is *that* all? Kill her? Just like that?'

'That's all that's left for us to try,' she said. 'Kill – or be killed. Well?'

Timothy said, wearily, 'I'm sure it's a brilliant plan. You must tell me all about it some time.'

'I want to tell you now! Listen, Tim –'

'Some other time,' Timothy said. And walked along the dark path through the palely luminous late roses, back to the house.

In his bedroom, he leaned out of the window and felt the dew in the dark air against his face. Above him he saw the stars: a thousand worlds, a million, all cold, remote, none of them caring. Around him there was a fringed silhouette of trees and the lights of houses – houses with people in them, families, children, old folk, the lot. To all of them, this was just the end of another day.

He got into bed and lay on his back, wide awake, staring at the ceiling. There had been Romans and Egyptians, Shakespeare and Charlie Chaplin, world wars and village fêtes, crucifixions and being kept in after school. How could it all just *stop*?

A long way away, someone whistled to a dog. A car driver changed down a gear for Mall Hill. From downstairs, his father's voice said, 'Boomboom, boom-oomer boom?' and his mother's voice, an octave higher, went 'Oop – oop, oop, oop,' in reply. Timothy had known those sounds all his life. This time tomorrow, it could be all over. The whole human story might have a line drawn under it. A line and just two words: *The End*.

TV SPECTACULAR

'Why's *she* got a ticket, *I* haven't got a ticket!' the large woman in the fur jacket said loudly and angrily, glaring at Beth. '*Despite* having applied in good time,' the woman said.

'Applied in good time,' her little husband echoed. He was almost invisible in the press of heads, bodies and legs in the foyer of the theatre where the big Lisa Treadgold show was soon to be screened.

The crush in the foyer was nothing to the crush outside, beyond the plate glass doors. The whole world, it seemed, wanted to be part of Lisa Treadgold's live audience. 'Ruddy kids get everything these days,' said the big woman. 'Pampered, they are. Expect everything served up to them on a plate.' 'Pampered,' said her husband, bobbing his angry little head above the shoulders pressing in on him. 'On a plate.'

Beth giggled. She was in wild good humour, like someone running a high temperature. She was being towed by a policeman. There were dozens on extra duty, controlling the crowds. '*If* you please,' this particular policeman kept saying. '*Thank* you very much. Ticketholders only. *Make* way, *if* you please.' Behind Beth, Timothy and Mac shuffled forward too, thankful for the policeman. Without him, even though they clutched their tickets, they might never have reached the foyer, let alone their seats in the theatre.

Outside, even the cars in the streets seemed excited. They nudged, hooted, heaved, whirred, flashed their lights. Occasionally an over-excited car bumped into another; the small collisions left droppings of broken glass and plastic on the tarmac. CAR PARK FULL said the notices. Attendants waved torches and arms trying to shoo the cars away. But still they came. Beth, Timothy and Mac had come in the Carpenters' car. They had parked it a mile away and walked the rest. They had been wise.

'*If* you please!' said the policeman, for the hundredth time – and suddenly they were in the auditorium, vast and cool and dimly lit. 'Blige me . . .' said the policeman, running a finger round his damp collar. He winked at a pretty girl usherette and said to her, 'Here you are then. More customers. See you after the show, right?' She gave him a flirty look and said, 'I told you, I've got a regular. He's an all-in wrestler.' The policeman grinned and left, no doubt to escort more ticketholders to the auditorium – which gave him another chance to chat up the girl. She said, 'This way, follow me. Row B! Right up front! Well! You must have friends in high places!'

'Lisa Treadgold is my mother,' Beth replied grandly. 'We're her illegitimate children. Don't tell anyone.'

They settled themselves in their plushy seats and looked round for their parents. They had been separated from the children by the crowd, long ago. 'They'll turn up,' Mac said. 'Anyone got any sweets or anything?' He was his old self, Beth saw. Timothy too. Lisa had lifted the fog on this special evening. Would she bring it down again during the programme? Of course she would. But when? How? Why?

Beth thought, 'Time to act.' She got up, said, 'Excuse me,' and started pushing past Mac's knees.

'Hey, where are you going?' he said, surprised.

'To kill Lisa Treadgold,' Beth said, in a low voice.

'What did you say?'

'Back in a minute,' Beth said. Now she was clear of the seats and standing in the aisle. Her head was lowered and her face half hidden by her dark hair. She was looking into the open handbag she held in her hands, apparently checking its contents.

'Where did she say she's going?' Timothy asked.

'She didn't. The Ladies, I suppose.'

They saw Beth close her bag, straighten her shoulders and start walking. 'She's going the wrong way,' Timothy said. 'The toilets are at the back.'

Beth walked towards the curtained stage. She moved briskly, almost jerkily. There were small flights of stairs leading up to the stage. Beth walked up one of them. Nobody noticed or tried to stop her – not even when she stretched out her arm, pushed aside the edge of the glowing stage curtain and disappeared behind it.

Mac and Timothy stared at each other speechlessly. 'She's gone bonkers!' Mac said at last, 'She said she had a plan . . .' Timothy replied uncertainly.

Behind them, the buzz of the people – the seats were filling up rapidly now – almost drowned the canned music flooding the theatre.

Behind the curtain, Beth stood, very small, her eyes very big, waiting her chance. Her lips moved. You would have to have stood very close to her to hear what she was saying.

'Lisa Treadgold,' she whispered. 'Kill Lisa Treadgold.'

•

There were so many people milling about on and around the stage that Beth was soon discovered.

'For God's sake,' the assistant stage manager, a girl, said, 'what are you doing here?'

'Miss Treadgold invited me,' Beth said, staring right back into the ASM's furious face. 'Here's my ticket.' The ASM was too angry to look at it. 'Look, I don't care if –' she began.

'Here's her letter. Read it,' Beth said. She held out a letter from Lisa Treadgold. It was Fanny Bishop's letter. It meant nothing. But it had Lisa's famous signature at the bottom of it. The ASM groaned and repeated, 'Look, I don't care if –'

'I'm part of the show,' Beth said, speaking slowly and distinctly.

'I'll call the floor manager!' replied the ASM. The floor manager, a man, had a face that seemed to be boiling between the earphones he wore to link him to the director in the control booth. 'Who in the name of –' he began, pulling at his earphones which squeaked urgent messages. 'Part of the show,' Beth said calmly. 'Friend of the big star. That makes me a starlet.'

'I don't care who you are, get out of –'

'Twinkle twinkle,' Beth said, waving the letter right under his nose. As she guessed, he had no time actually to read the letter. 'They say I've got a smile rather like Lisa's,' Beth said and gave the floor manager a ghastly little smile, all syrup and front teeth. He backed away.

'I suppose I could find myself sitting here,' Beth said sweetly. She minced to the ring of armchairs surrounding the speakers' tables and sat down in one right next to the plushiest armchair, the star's chair, Lisa's special chair. 'Thirsty work, being a telly star!' she said brightly. She reached for the special glass, a handsome smoked goblet, ready-filled with water, facing Lisa's chair: and drained it.

The floor manager exploded. He grabbed Beth's arm, shouted, 'Get this brat out of here!' to the ASM and pulled furiously at Beth. She said, 'All right, all right, I'm going!' and let herself be pulled upright. Then she said, 'Look! – I'll even tidy up after me!' She seized the big carafe holding fresh water. 'Refill Lisa's glass!' she explained. She was playing for time. 'Leave things *alone*, get *out* of here!' shouted the ASM.

As she spoke, what Beth wanted to happen happened. The director's voice squawked urgently. The ASM heard it over the speakers, the floor manager in his earphones. Both went off at the double.

Beth refilled Lisa Treadgold's glass.

She did it very deliberately, as if to say to the world, 'This is me, Beth. I am a helpful little girl. See! – I am about to refill this glass with cool, clear water!' Everyone around her was in a fury of last-minute actions; Beth was calm. Her handbag was neatly placed on the glass-topped table; her hands were neatly pouring clear liquid into the glass.

The floor manager came back. He said, 'Right. Yeah, got it, number five camera . . . OK' Then he turned on Beth and this time, made no mistake. He frogmarched her off the stage, twisting one of her arms between her shoulder blades. 'Get the hell *out*,' he grated, and almost threw her into the arms of a man in a T-shirt who said, 'What's this, then? Not *another* one? All right, leave her to me. I'll bounce her.' And suddenly Beth was outside the theatre, in the crowded street.

Being Beth, she had very little trouble in getting inside again and back to her seat. Now her parents were there and the auditorium was completely full Mac said, 'Where did you get to?'

'Oh, just looking around,' Beth said.

'But you went on the *stage*!'

'That's right. Oh, look! There's David Hambleby! Wow, celebrities everywhere! And who's that girl! Ooh, it's Tricia Wilding, isn't she *short*, I always thought of her as *tall*!'

She was still bubbling with girlish excitement when the house lights dimmed and the Roller Dixieland Band played, 'Rolling Along'. And she still clutched her little handbag.

The handbag was an ounce or two lighter now.

DEATH CASSETTE

Timothy's letter, dated the next day

Dear Mr Fisk,

Do you remember telling me off about using exclamation marks? Perhaps you don't, because you weren't yourself when you wrote that letter. Hardly anyone was himself or herself then. Only Beth and a few others. A very few.

Anyhow, you could be in for a storm of exclamation marks now! Because it was a historic occasion, wasn't it? I mean last night, of course. It was historic because the world had either to end or to be saved.

I wish you'd been there. It was unbelievable. Seeing it on TV isn't the same thing. However many times they repeat that programme, however many times people run it on their videos, nothing could match *being there*.

I was there. So this letter is a historic document. This is what happened.

First there was an MC who went on too long . . . you know the sort of thing, 'That great and wonderful woman, Lisa Treadgold, who has brought new HOPE . . . new DIRECTION . . . into the life of a once great nation!!! A woman who, single-handed, guided only by the burning light of her own determination, her own personal vision, has rekindled the dying flame of . . .'

But you've seen and heard all that for yourself on TV. You'll replay it again and again, I suppose, like everyone else. The whole audience grinning and yelling, 'ROLLING along, singing a song, SIDE BY SIDE!'; then the curtains opening; and there they all were, the celebrities – the woman Minister, the Leader of the Opposition, the Bishop, Sir Tobyn Knight in his spotted bow tie, that American film star with the diamonds – but you saw them all. And you saw the gap in the middle, the place to be filled by the celebrity of celebrities, Lisa Treadgold.

Didn't they stage-manage it well? I liked the way they backlit Lisa's chair – the chair itself was dark but there was that halo of light behind it, getting brighter and brighter for the first five minutes while the celebrities waffled about the Inner Meaning of D.D.D. or whatever it was they were saying. I wasn't listening to them. I don't suppose anyone was. And then the light behind Lisa's empty chair spread upwards until it made a great spearhead of golden radiance – and the full studio orchestra went into

'Rolling Along' – and there she was! At last! Lisa Treadgold!

No wonder the audience went mad after a build-up like that. All singing their heads off . . . 'ROLLING along!' And when she made her entrance, there was literally a standing ovation. I've only read about standing ovations before, never seen one. Well, now I've been part of one. The standing ovation made the audience into sitting ducks. A woman behind me was actually crying when Lisa raised her arms. 'It's like a blessing!' she moaned. 'A heavenly blessing!'

Anyhow, Lisa went into her speech and you must admit it was clever stuff, especially the bits about 'I've said so much about the three Ds . . . But tonight, I feel I must add three more: D for my Delight in this wonderful, this incredible welcome; D for Determination – my determination to help bring about still greater changes in your lives; and, finally, D for Destiny. Your Destiny – and mine.'

I wonder how many people knew the bitter joke behind the words? Beth, Banjo . . . but how many more? *I* didn't know. I was like the rest – carried away. She looked so beautiful and gallant standing there. I just thought how great she looked and what smashing arms and shoulders she has. Or had.

She took her chair, with the other panellists clapping and smiling (but Sir Tobyn kept his frown simmering nicely). The chat started. You've seen it all several times on your video, no doubt – but you haven't seen the final bit, the bit that really mattered! I have. I was there, right up in front. So read on!

The important thing to look for is, the speakers getting thirsty. That film star was the first. I think she was fed up with Lisa getting all the attention and looking so beautiful, etc., and wanted to draw attention to herself. So she moved her head about and fiddled with her glass. She began taking sips of water to make her diamond ring flash. Soon most of the speakers were taking sips of water. You'll see this starting to happen when Lisa was talking about the need for the Punishment to Fit the Crime and smiling away like anything to show that harsh words don't mean a nasty person.

If you look very carefully, you can see Lisa's eyes flicking sideways now and then. She must have been thinking, 'Ah, so it's about time for me to be thirsty, like the humans. Soon I'll take a sip of water.'

It was also at this time that she first said, 'You remember me.'

The exact words are, 'You remember me . . . you remember me saying, in Manchester,' etc. I was waiting for her to say the words, so they didn't affect me as they did the rest of the audience. I felt a sort of thick, heavy feeling in my mind, nothing more. I shook it off. But as you can see from your video, the audience was hit hard. People sort of swayed in their seats. Lots of them started nodding their heads as if to say, 'We are good little boys and girls.'

I looked sideways at Beth. She was on the edge of her seat, saying the same word again and again. I had to bend down to hear her. The word was '*Drink! Drink! Drink!*'

Now follow your video. It goes like this.

Woman Minister: 'What – with all respect – you refuse to recognize, Miss Treadgold, is the importance of *environment* in the creation of antisocial behaviour. I mean, your delinquent youth – your football hooligan, your mugger – it's too late to punish these people *after* the crime, it's more a matter of prevention . . . I mean, you can't raise sound plants in sickly soil,' etc., etc.

At this point, look at Lisa. She's not bothering to pretend to listen. She's scanning the audience, judging how far under they are. Her eyes are dark and glittering. I suppose this could be because she has to widen her iris to take in the dimly lit audience. But don't they glitter!

Look at her lips. They are smiling, of course, but also forming words. She is saying, 'You remember me! . . . You remember me!' Say the words yourself and you can see how they fit in with her lip movements.

The woman Minister now gets on to Mercy – we must be merciful to offenders, not always think in terms of punishment. The Bishop nods agreement and cuts in. He says, 'The quality of mercy is not strained, Miss Treadgold, it falleth as the gentle rain from

Heaven.' A part of the audience doesn't like this. There are grumbles and interruptions.

Someone in the audience shouts, 'What about the victims?'

Lisa says, 'Perhaps we ought to ask the opinion of the audience, don't you think? The young people, too!' (Here, she looks directly at Beth but of course you can't tell this from the video. *I* can tell you that Beth flinched back when Lisa's eyes stabbed into her. But then she sort of spat and went on muttering, 'Drink! Drink!')

Lisa says, '"The quality of mercy is not strained", the Bishop tells us. The words are Shakespeare's of course. "The quality of Mercy" . . .'

She pauses here as if expecting a reply from the audience. She gets it. Everyone you see on the screen applauds like mad. *Everyone*. If you listen carefully, you can hear voices shouting, 'Mercy!' – 'Kindness is the answer!' – things like that.

Now Lisa makes a damping-down movement with her hands. The audience at once falls silent. The Bishop is smiling, obviously delighted that the audience is on the side of mercy. Lisa says, 'But then . . . but then, there are some people who think that the quality of mercy has become more than a little strained! Strained to breaking point! What about the three Ds – Decency, Discipline, Dedication? Who'll vote for them? Particularly Discipline!'

Again she gets her reply from the audience. Once

again, everyone applauds like mad. Everyone agrees. *Everyone*. And you can hear voices shout, 'Flog them!', 'Hang them!', 'Bring back the birch!'

Look carefully at your video recording. The faces of the audience are drunk with ecstasy: like those revival meetings where people scream 'I believe! I believe!' and throw money and jewellery at the stage.

Now Lisa is sort of *basking*, head back, arms outspread. She is being bathed in adoration. But look at her lips! All the time they are moving. She is still repeating, 'You remember me!'

But the most important thing to look at is the Bishop's face. You can slow down the video and see his expressions change. First, he's pleased with himself because everyone has agreed with him. Second, Lisa says the opposite thing; everyone now agrees this *opposite* thing – and the Bishop is shocked. You can see his face lengthen and his mouth open with disappointment and surprise. He looks hard at Lisa, no doubt wondering what went wrong, what's happening.

Watch his mouth.

You can see his lips beginning to move. He is imitating Lisa's lips. He is repeating her words – 'You remember me!'

And now he begins to smile! He puts his hands on the edge of the table, straightens his back, nods his head. Now he's saying other things, loudly. We can't hear him over the general noise. He pats the table with his right hand in time with his words. Can you work them out by reading his lips?

I think I can. I'm pretty sure he's chanting, 'Bring back the birch! Bring back the birch!'

The audience, very cheerful, won't stop applauding. Lisa takes the opportunity to reach behind her and pick up her glass.

She sips from it. She makes that smoothing-down gesture with her hand to ask for quiet. The audience won't stop. She takes another sip and repeats the calm-down gesture. The noise begins to die down.

She takes a third sip.

And raises her arm in a sort of Nazi salute, and *commands* the audience to be quiet. Instantly there is silence.

She opens her lips to speak.

(At this point, Beth was clutching my shoulder. She was half-standing in her seat. Her nails were digging into me. She was hissing like a snake. '*She's done it, she's drunk it!*' she kept saying. Her eyes were glaring, mad.

(And I began to understand what could be happening.)

Skip the next minute or so of your video recording and get to the bit where Lisa Came Out With It. Where she actually *said* it.

She's asked the audience for their support – asked

them if they'd follow her, asked them if they believed not only in D.D.D. but also in *action* – and they've shouted 'Yes! Yes! Yes!' They were almost Sieg-heiling her. 'You want a better *Britain*?'

'YES! YES! YES!'

'You want a better *world*?'

'YES! YES! YES!'

Now comes the part I'll watch again and again . . .

Lisa has her arms raised to embrace the audience. Slowly, she lets them drop to her side. To gain time, she takes her fourth sip from her glass. She goes to the front of the stage. The audience falls silent. Obviously this is to be the big moment. The camera closes in on Lisa's face until it fills the screen.

She speaks.

'*So that's what you want*,' she says, her voice low and soft, her mouth curved in that little smile. '*A better Britain. A better world* . . .'

Nobody makes a sound. The cameras pick out faces in the audience: faces suddenly young, like the faces of children when they cluster round the birthday cake to see the candles blown out.

'*I promise you a new world*,' Lisa says, solemn and lovely. '*Completely new! A world full of wonderful promise – for me! A world of pleasure and delights – for my race! A world full of riches -for me and your conquerors!*'

And everyone applauds! The people are *clapping*, *cheering*!

But not for too long; Lisa has more to say, they must hear every golden word.

(That was when Beth pulled at my arm. 'Look!' She pointed at the big repeater TV screens on either side of the stage, big as the old cinema screens. They were filled with Lisa's face. 'Look at her eyes!'

(I looked. Lisa's left eye was jittering, very slightly. Jittering is the only word I can think of. I don't think you can pick up the effect on your small screen, the movement of the pupil is too small and quick. The right eye was all right.

(Lisa opened her mouth to speak and again Beth said, 'Look!' She was clutching my hand in both of hers. I saw what she meant. Lisa's mouth was leaking something from the left-hand corner. It was as if her mouth had overflowed very slightly, as if she were dribbling.

('You see!' Beth said, her face wild. 'It could be working!'

('*What* could be working?' I said.

(She was too excited to answer.)

Now Lisa speaks almost her last words.

'You are the first!' she says. 'My pioneers! You and a few million more like you, slaves chained to your TV sets!'

Her smile is as sweet as ever. And the smiles of the audience are the same as before – beaming, childlike, warm. (My parents were smiling, Mac was, I was. Was I? I suppose so, but most of my mind was my own, not Lisa's.)

'*Chained to your TV sets; chained to me!*' Lisa says. '*And your chains are real. You will feel their weight; feel them goad and grind your weakling flesh, just as my mind, our minds, will clamp themselves on yours . . .* We will feed on you!'

The audience cheers and applauds, wildly.

Lisa pauses. She is still smiling, still as beautiful as ever – still like a goddess telling the faithful they have been good, she is satisfied with them. But now you can see the shine of dribble at the corner of her mouth – I can see it on my little TV screen quite plainly so you must be able to. And look at the way her left arm moves when she reaches for her glass. You can see it better in slow motion. It moves in jerks.

'*From this moment, your world is ours!*' she says, in that sweet, clear, sensible voice. She picks up a glass tumbler and holds it high, so that it glitters under all those lights. '*We are strong. You are weak. We command. You obey. Your world is ours to crush . . .*'

She crushes the glass effortlessly in her human-looking hand. The pieces fly, sparkling. The audience nods, smiles, applauds.

'*Ours to crush and devour!*' Lisa says. She invites the cameras to close in on the palm of her hand, with some crushed glass in it. She puts her hand to her mouth and swallows the glass. Then gives a wide, radiant smile to acknowledge the cheering.

But the smile goes wrong!

If you push the Pause button and hold on that smile, you will see that it never again changes. Her face is locked into the smile, as if it were candlewax poured into a mask of iron. A tortured, fixed, staring grin.

Her fingers are the next to go. It starts quite slowly. I did not notice it on the night when I was there, but it's easy to spot on video.

Her fingers begin to have a life of their own. They crawl, slither, creep, then scuttle like crabs over her neck and face. They find her mouth and scrabble over it, discovering the wetness leaking from one corner They scratch and scrabble at it, each finger a twisting, hurrying, writhing snake.

And that is when Banjo jumps up on the stage. Poor Banjo . . .

BROKEN BANJO

If you look carefully, you can see Banjo's head coming forward on the extreme right of your screen. His R.O.L. boater spins away – he's thrown it into the audience. He's clutching his banjo, it gets in his way as he scrambles up to Lisa. His face is shining and scarlet, he's yelling at the top of his voice – I can't make out his words on my tape, I think he's shouting obscenities at Lisa.

When he reaches her, he faces the audience and yells, 'Can't you *see*, you stupid apes, she's *finished*!' But there's no response. 'She's only a *machine*!' he shouts. No response.

Then he swings the banjo like an axe and slams it into Lisa's ribs with all his strength, like a man trying to bring a tree down.

Like a felled tree, she falls.

'Wake up!' he shouts into the theatre. 'It's all over! WAKE UP!' The banjo dangles from his big red hand. The drum part of it is caved in and the neck is held to the body only by the strings.

Lisa should be out cold. She is not. She gets up from the floor, still with that staring grin fixed on her face. '*You remember me!*' she says to the other speakers. They smile and nod.

'*Punish him!*' she says.

The film star, the Bishop, Sir Tobyn – all of them move up behind Banjo. The Minister woman has the water carafe in both hands.

She raises the carafe and smashes it down on Banjo's head.

I don't want to watch this sequence again. The blood . . . and the way the speakers move in, so slowly, so polite – and the way they hit him and hit him and hit him.

If they had been in a rage I suppose it would be bearable – but they're not, they're just machines, they smile and smile and hit and hit, taking their time, making sure they don't get in each other's way . . .

And the audience. If you keep your eyes closed and just listen, you can hear the audience's voices. They are buzzing politely, the sound you hear in the interval between acts. An interested, polite hum of conversation.

Above it, you can just hear the wail of Beth's voice, like a distant siren. (She was screaming and sobbing, her head in her hands, hiding her eyes. I remember putting my arms round her but I can't remember feeling any strong emotion, I was half in the Lisa fog, half out of it. My parents did nothing, nor did Mac. They just looked at the stage, observed what was happening – and smiled.)

Lisa is on her feet again. Now her voice is beginning

to break down. She says, '*Punished! You will be punished! There can be no . . . You will all be . . . They are coming, your masters, they are very close . . .*' The fingers of one hand are scuttling over her side, where Banjo hit her – moving like disturbed ants, checking damage, getting ready to repair it. Her arm is horrible, slung across her body with the elbow and wrist out of joint and those fingers like crawling maggots. Her hair no longer seems to fit her head: her left eye has a huge black pupil – the iris mechanism must have gone wrong.

And still the fingers run and knot and scrabble.

I ought not to watch it, I'll destroy the tape some day. But not just yet.

And then the booming noise starts.

BREAKDOWN

Can you hear it, that booming? You have to turn up the sound. At first, it's only a sort of mains hum, a constant bass note. But then it begins to pulse. My father says it is rather like the sound the German bombers made in the Blitz on London.

It is the sound of Them, the invaders from out there.

The noise of their spacecraft.

Did the panel of speakers hear it? I don't know. They are still grouped round Banjo. He moves, feebly. Now they stand and stare straight into the audience, like people in shock.

And the audience changes. Some of them are coming out of the fog. Before, they were all grinning, applauding puppets. Now some of them are people again, with minds of their own. You can see it on your video – the way they turn to each other, begin talking. They seem to be saying, 'What's wrong?' (It was like that with my mother and father. Their heads went together, she took his hand. And Mac was talking to Beth, firing questions at her. She didn't hear. 'Get on with it!' she muttered. '*Die!*')

Before our eyes, Lisa is dying. It is happening just as it happened with Grinny. Or perhaps it is worse: only seconds ago Lisa was so beautiful. Now she is crumbling, breaking up. Her mouth dribbles and speaks gibberish. '*Slaves!*' says her cracking, splitting voice. '*You will serve! . . . We will kill all those who . . . Such fools, it was so easy!*'

Her words are mangled, garbled, choked. Her mouth writhes out of time with her speech.

Then she breaks into Grinnish – that lightning-fast electronic twittering, a torrent of signals, the language she uses to speak to Them. Grinny used that language too. We heard her. Bunny heard her, on that morning she gave Lisa breakfast in bed.

Lisa makes her last effort.

She seems to clutch at the radiance of the hundreds of theatre lights. 'YOU REMEMBER ME!' she shouts.

But now her voice is a squawk, her mouth is a wet, twisting, rubber ring, her left eye is a black hole. She begins to shake as if something inside her is running wild. Again she screams, 'YOU REMEMBER ME!' but you can hardly make out the words. They are just a jangle, an electronic howl through a broken speaker.

The booming becomes so loud that it drowns everything; and the theatre begins to shake.

*

The ceiling plaster above the dress circle comes down first. The video records the screams. You can see the people trying to fight their way through the great cushion of dust that bulges around and over them.

The whole place shakes – the little lamps on the walls, the beams of the big spots on Lisa.

Some people try to scramble over each other in the lines of seats, they're trying to escape. But most are like me, with their hands over their ears, trying to keep the mind-shaking booming noise out. The noise rocks your brain as if it would shake it loose. My father tries to spread himself over Beth and me to protect us. But then two boxes collapse on each other on the other side of the theatre and he says, 'We've got to get out! For God's sake –!'

Then the light comes.

Look at your video, it's all there. Nearly all, anyhow.

You see the light stab down through the roof of the theatre like a rapier blade: a thick, solid rod of violet light, so bright it hurts the eyes.

Down the rod slithers dust, lazy violet clouds of dust, circling like clouds of midges.

The rod of light plunges straight into Lisa's skull.

She is flung to the ground. She begins to knot and writhe and break up . . .

When I was little, we went to town to do shopping in time for Christmas. We shopped till the store closed. We took a last look at my favourite window of the store. It had a fairy grotto, mechanical animals and puppets, and a mother and father and children dressed in their party best. It was magic.

Then a girl – an ordinary girl wearing everyday clothes and special soft slippers – entered the scene and started pulling everything to pieces! She tore the clothes off the dummies until they were naked and bald, and you could see their joints. She busily threw things behind her into a crate, not caring what she did. I began to cry.

A young man came to help. He pulled the mannequin people apart! I began to scream, banging my fists on the window. My parents had to drag me away. 'They're just getting ready another display, darling, something even nicer!' But I couldn't stop crying.

Lisa was like one of those shop-window figures. Except that she moved. She kept moving, she wouldn't stop moving. And her mouth still smiled beneath the glaring eyes.

At the end, there were parts of her, separate parts, that twitched and jumped and snaked about. And an arm with the fingers still wriggling and scuttling. And the violet light digging into the mess, powering it, making it happen. And the people screaming and trying to get out.

But not Beth. My parents were tugging at her. She took no notice. She stayed hunched in her seat, drinking in every moment of Lisa's death throes, biting her lower lip and muttering, 'Go on! Go on!' She was clutching the seat, refusing to be moved.

So we saw the silver rat.

It suddenly jumped out of the mess of twisted clothes covering what was left of Lisa. It was the same machine that worked Grinny: the same hunched, quick, shining rat thing. It was snapping at Lisa's body – snapping, tugging, worrying at it.

It was pulling her to pieces, tearing joints apart, dismembering her.

When it had finished its work it sort of stood up on its hind legs (but of course it was not a rat, it had no hind legs, it was a horrible mechanism). It seemed to look upwards into the beam of light.

Then it flashed and twinkled and moved faster than ever – and *ran up the beam.* It went very fast, as fast as a man could throw a tennis ball. It shot up the beam, out through the roof and into the spaceship.

'Done!' I heard Beth say. 'Dead!'

She turned to me, her eyes on fire with joy, and said, 'We've won.'

SUPERBRAVE

Beth's diary, 1 October

. . . everybody's so ungrateful, I could spit, I saved the WORLD but nobody ever says 'Thank you very much, O you were wonderful, a true heroine, we are so grateful'. All I get is 'Could you put the washing-up away, do it *now* please, not *later*' or 'Beth, your homework was very *slipshod*,' or Timothy makes his stupid jokes about me having spots but I haven't I suppose he thinks he's being amusing I think it's *infantile*.

Of course, everyone was hypnotized & they still don't remember & realize so they cannot remember the awful threat I saved them from. Most great heroines get statues but I don't even have my deeds remembered.

O that night in the theatre!!! I killed her, I did it alone, I am glad I did it tho it was not nice to watch. Timothy keeps asking me how I did it, well if he is that stupid he can go on asking till the cows come home my lips are sealed for all Eternity & anyhow it was partly luck I suppose. I asked Mr Wells what *stopped* a battery making electricity & he said 'O almost anything' so I used almost any liquid I could find so long as it was clear and did not show up. I don't mind telling you, Diary, the Secret Ingredients. It was Liquid Paraffin from the medicine cupboard and surgical spirit & oil of cloves and that junket stuff Rennit I think it is called & lots of other things mostly oily all mixed together. I forget half of them.

I put them in the medicine bottle I kept the acid from School Stinks Lab in a little bottle of its own because it is very dangerous. I still have a black place on my finger where I touched the cork. Wow! Some acid! & I put everything in my grotty little handbag I *hate* young girls carrying handbags but there you are I had to do it & I got on to the stage & I filled Lisa's glass with my Elixir of Death & she drank it. She has not got taste buds, she could not taste the ghastly muck I mixed.

Gosh what would have happened if someone else had drunk it but there you are fortune smiles on the brave I think I was *superbrave* and also very ingenious but a lot of thanks I get.

And she died and I'm glad & I don't care how horrible it all looked, her writing about like that and then the rat thing. Just think how much worse if Lisa had WON and They would come and my parents would be taken away because they are too old poor darling Dad I was only teasing him about being saggy & baggy really he is not and even if he was I would love him still and Mother too. Everyone teases everyone, nobody ever says what they mean, it is a funny thing.

But Timothy said a great thing the day after, he found me crying, I had had the bad dreams I keep getting the dream about Lisa on the stage, he called me Darling Beth, he said I had been Right all along he even hugged me & I know how he hates doing things like that, showing affection or anything, & he was crying too. He did not pretend he was not crying he did not even wipe away his tears he just kept saying 'You *did* it, Beth!' in a choked way & squeezed me which of course made me cry worse than ever because I was so pleased & he said in his American voice, 'That's right, baby, you gotta let it all hang out!'

& then of course we started laughing & crying it was ridiculous.

I am so glad it happened but I wish I could stop having that dream I am writing so much Diary because I am afraid of the dream but doubtless I will grow out of it like Tim says he came into my room last night in the middle of the night he put his hand on my head and I pretended to be sleeping but I was not. He kept his hand there a long time & all the time I felt better & perhaps the dream will go away.

Why should I care anyhow she is dead dead DEAD that is all that matters. Anyhow what is there to be scared of, Timothy is only next door I can hear him typing.

Tonight I will lie in bed imagining that I am being given a medal by the Queen or she is unveiling a statue of me or something stupid like that & everyone is cheering. Think of something cheerful then I will not get the dream.

Letter from Nicholas Fisk to Timothy Carpenter

. . . Is Beth really all right? Are you? I keep re-running my video cassette and thinking of more and more questions to ask you. We will meet soon, but please don't stop writing to tell me more about that night; as you said, it was a Historic Occasion – *the* historic occasion, the salvation of Mankind! The world ought to go down on its knees to that sister of yours.

Already Lisa Treadgold is beginning to slip sideways in my mind. My video cassettes tell me she was there, she existed, she was as beautiful and awful as she seemed. And yet nobody *mentions* her. Have you noticed that? No one says her name! The TV and newspapers are still full of stories about The Night – 'Theatre Disaster, 3 Killed, 27 Seriously Injured', etc., etc. (I'm catching your bad habits!) But of Lisa Treadgold – not a word. I suppose it's like this at the *Gazette* – do Fanny Bishop and Len Sturgeon ever write anything about Lisa? I bet not.

Of the Rollers, there's hardly a trace. I came across one of those Roller boaters the other day. It had blown into a ditch. It still had its R.O.L. band round it. I stood staring at it, thinking how *old* it looked – how ancient, remote, like a snatch of blotched, jerky cine film about trench warfare. Yet it all happened only yesterday. And, yet again, I can write these words – which prove that I can and do remember. But the memory is faded, there's no life in it. What *did* Lisa do to scramble our minds so completely?

One thing is clear enough in my mind. I think I told you that I arranged to give the Rollers one third of my earnings, now and for the future. My Bank Manager tells me that Lisa may be dead – but the arrangement is very much alive! So it's last laugh to Lisa. 'Funny joke, ha ha,' as you and Beth and Mac always say.

Bless you all.

Nicholas Fisk

Nicholas Fisk was born in London in 1923. Before becoming a full-time author, Nicholas served in the Royal Air Force during World War Two, then found work initially as an actor, cartoonist, and jazz musician before becoming an advertising copywriter, illustrator, photographer and writer. He has written more than fifty books, most of which are science fiction for older children. Nicholas's book MONSTER MAKER was made into a TV film for *The Jim Henson Hour* in 1989.

Nicholas's starting point for a story is an IF . . . IF we had a domestic robot, IF we could talk to animals, IF we could move back and forth in time. On such premises he places people – recognisable people living ordinary lives – until the IF explodes.

Nicholas retired as an author in 1998 and still lives in Hertfordshire.